J.B. Aspinall

John Brian Aspinall was born in 1939 and grew up in
Rochdale. After reading History at Oxford he taught English
in comprehensive schools around England, and now lives in
France. His first novel, *Gringo Soup*, is also published by
Sceptre.

J.B. ASPINALL

Sparrow Hall

SCEPTRE

First published in Great Britain in 2003 by Hodder and Stoughton
A division of Hodder Headline

A Sceptre paperback

2 4 6 8 10 9 7 5 3 1

A CIP catalogue record for this title is
available from the British Library

ISBN 0 340 73388 8

Typeset by Palimpsest Book Production Limited,
Polmont, Stirlingshire
Printed and bound in Great Britain by
Mackays of Chatham plc, Chatham, Kent

Hodder and Stoughton
A division of Hodder Headline
338 Euston Road
London NW1 3BH

For Frances

CONTENTS

Prologue

As Quentin loaded the Luger he surveyed the domain.

There were four acres, mostly to the south of the house. First there was a broad verge of grass, then the tarmac drive edged with a balustrade, then steps down to the lily pond, in the midst of which a mermaid embraced a gaping fish that used to spurt water into the basin before the pump broke. More steps descended onto the lawn that ran between herbaceous beds to the yew hedge bordering the back lane. Over to the right, the west, were a rose-walk, an arbour and a summerhouse of glass and wood that resembled a miniature cricket pavilion. The drive curved back on the left, between the house and the walled vegetable garden, to the main gate on the road along the north side of the hall.

The grounds were in poor condition these days. George Ingram was too arthritic to do the work although he was still paid a token wage. It was George's grandson Kevin who used the petrol mower on the lawn and clipped the yew hedge, for tips from Marjorie and Desmond plus whatever his granddad gave him. Apart from this cursory cropping, everything had been let run wild. The flowerbeds were full of willow-herb, bramble, dock and dandelion, fat hen and herb Robert. In the vegetable garden the fruit trees were unpruned and unharvested and the rest of that area was choked with a loutish grass that had seeded and looked like hay. The water in the lily pond was bottle-green and furry and there were bulrushes contending with the lilies.

Seventy-four years old, only eight years younger than the

1

century, Quentin had known Sparrow Hall all his life. At one time there had been trim cultivars along the kitchen-garden wall, grass walkways between the vegetable plots and a little herb garden with boxwood hedges. There had been roses, delphiniums, lupins, carnations, chrysanthemums ... There had been croquet hoops on the longest lawn and a tennis court in the south-east corner. The fish in the mermaid's clutches had sent up a slim and confident jet that fell back to sprinkle and tumble among the lilies and carp. That golden age of Sparrow Hall had been during the tenure of Quentin's father, Rodney Frobisher, a fellow with glossy black hair and a slim moustache who had been slain during the Great War.

Since Quentin was sitting on the balustrade with his back to the house Marjorie, looking out of the french windows of the sitting room, could not see the gun in his hands.

'What's Quentin up to?'

She glanced to see if Jennifer Coram was listening.

Jennifer, the nurse who had lived in Sparrow Hall since the collapse of Marjorie's wits, was a fresh-faced, affable young woman, a cajoler rather than a disciplinarian. Yet Marjorie always behaved as if in great awe of her, remaining silent except when Jennifer spoke to her, in which case she would respond with frantic promptitude and formality as a child might react to a dragon of a teacher. If this was psychological warfare rather than spontaneous idiocy it was a big success: Jennifer had become so cowed that she now absented herself from her patient whenever she could, spending a lot of time chatting with Janet Otterburn and helping her in the kitchen.

When she discovered that Jennifer was not in the room Marjorie added boldly, 'It's such a shame, such a pity about the garden.'

Desmond surprised her by replying. He took a sip of the drink he had assembled – a *pousse-rapière* of Drambuie and fizzy wine that he liked to sandwich between three or four gins as a preface to dinner. Then he glinted his little eyes and snarled his teeth and jutted his grizzly, goatish beard: a show of intense irritation which he often gave if his glance fell on Marjorie.

'You're a pathetic, mindless old hag, Marjorie. You were saying only yesterday how you loved all this picturesque bloody decay. Everything soft and mellow as if it was in a bloody green tea-cosy, you said, or something.'

Marjorie seemed to agree with him, tilting her chin and laughing in that characteristic way she still had. It had been disarming. As usual she did not react to Desmond's abuse, which as usual intensified his detestation.

'Ah, but Quentin . . .' she said.

She stretched out her arm as she spoke and indicated Quentin with the palm of her hand, a theatrical gesture that suited her lean frame and piled white hair. Another recent habit of hers was attributing feelings and attitudes to Quentin. Since Quentin was almost entirely silent these days there was no evidence to either support or discredit her claims.

Desmond belched and tasted his drink. 'Well, I agree with Milton. Let them be left, the weeds and the piss. Bring on the bloody wilderness.'

He turned back to sneering at newsreel of the Falklands campaign. The silly little sod of a television set – with muted colours and dulcet tone – was all Marjorie had permitted to intrude on the tastefulness of Victorian dark oak and green velvet. There had been a time (before her fragile tyranny collapsed with her sanity) when she had rarely allowed the set to be switched on. Her mental illness was extremely irritating to Desmond, but at least it meant that he got to watch as much television as he liked and nobody checked how much he was drinking.

She looked away from him, out of the window at the balding white head and sloping shoulders of Quentin, humped on the balustrade like a cormorant in cold weather. Then she glanced back at Desmond, drifting her gaze between the only two men with whom she had ever had sex.

They did not look like brothers: big, pale, lumbering Quentin – and Desmond, satyr-like, shrivelled, wizened, looking older though five years younger. Yet there was a photograph, somewhere, of a rugger fifteen in which the family resemblance was distinct – though Quentin was loose forward and club captain, sitting with legs akimbo in the middle of the bench, while Desmond lurked behind at the end of a row as befitted a juvenile and elusive wing-threequarter.

If she could keep her mind on it for long enough, the chronology of Marjorie's dealings with these siblings became like a time-chart of Whig and Tory governments she had done when she was a schoolgirl:

1932–33 Desmond
1933–42 Quentin
1942–45 Desmond
1945–50 Quentin
1950–72 Desmond
1972–82 Quentin.

1932–33 Marjorie and Desmond were at medical school together when she was an assertive young woman. In those days he sported a feral prance, an insistent wit and a dapper little dab of a beard on the end of his beard-shaped chin. Seduced and besotted, she lost her yen for a career and proposed to him. Horrified, he dodged behind his brother.

1933–42 Detractors said she was either avenging herself on Desmond or trying to stay close to him at any cost when she married lumpish Quentin in 1934. She subsequently saw little of Desmond, who joined a London consultancy. Quentin bought into a Scarborough firm of architects in 1936, and the couple moved in with Quentin's mother Gwendolyn at Sparrow Hall. Damien was born there in 1939 after Quentin and Marjorie had more or less given up hope of offspring.

1942–45 When Quentin was in the army in 1942 Desmond, as a gynaecologist exempted from military service, paid a summer visit to Sparrow Hall and stayed for the rest of his life. Claiming to be weary of the 'sophistications and contentions of the bloody metropolis', he joined a general practice in Kirkby Moorside where he was a liability for the next thirty years.

1945–50 Though this was ostensibly a period of Quentin's dominance, returning worsened from the war and reclaiming his share of the master bedroom, it was in fact the period in which his stock with Marjorie sank lowest, until he fled to Hong Kong.

1950–72 Desmond's random, cantankerous despotism. At Gwendolyn's death in 1960 Quentin inherited Sparrow Hall but did not return there from Hong Kong until 1965; then behaved like a polite and grateful guest until silence overcame him in the early seventies.

1972–82 Quentin's return to favour in this epoch was the result of his own silence, Marjorie's lunacy and Desmond's bile.

Marjorie had sex with Quentin for the last time in 1946 and with Desmond in 1955. They had been different but equally unsatisfactory lovers: Desmond lewd and brutal and faithless, Quentin sluggish to rouse and querulous in failure. The charting of the vagaries of this technically incestuous triangle gives no notion of much of Marjorie's life: her appalling power-struggle with her mother-in-law; her clumsy and unreciprocated love for Damien; her liking for Sparrow Hall, then loathing of it, then madness.

* * *

Quentin had ceased to consider the garden, although he still seemed to be staring at it. He was remembering the lion-coloured carpet.

This was an Arabian item, hand-woven by underfed children in the middle of the nineteenth century. On a warm beige background there were russets, blues and greens galore in a geometric pattern, enlivened by inconsistencies, that had helped the carpet serve Quentin as both a landscape and an architectural plan. The wobbly blue hexagons, for instance, could as well be water-holes as swimming-pools; and the russet border could as easily represent a mountain range as the outer wall of a fortress.

The carpet had been the stage on which Quentin had directed his fantasies, out of infancy and all through boyhood, to the annoyance of his mother, till Belvedere School was reckoned to have knocked the weirdness out of him. He had always preferred to play on it if he was given a choice: sometimes he was turfed out into the garden, when the weather was deemed too fine for him to skulk indoors, or when somebody had a use for the drawing-room that was incompatible with his presence. Although there were remains of the garden whereas the carpet was gone, he remembered the carpet better than the garden, and the denizens of the fantasy land of the carpet better than the human occupants of the house and grounds.

There had always been lots of folk around – relatives and employees (even when the sociability of Rodney Frobisher was not infesting Sparrow Hall with younger members of the propertied and professional set: picnickers, tennisers, shooters and diners, with their wives, children and retainers) – yet Quentin's childhood loomed in his recollection as a solitary business. Adults seemed to have been as invisible to him as humans were to Kafka's dog. His father, for instance, he could not picture at all unless he had resource to the sepia photograph in army gear, which was still in the bottom drawer of the library desk. His mother Gwendolyn was equally gone from his childhood, superseded by a series of increasingly peevish and querulous avatars culminating in the posh harridan that died in 1960. He could remember playing with one or two children – pilfering redcurrants with his podgy cousin Annabel or trapping wasps in jam-jars with a pale, calm, nameless boy – but no consistent playmates. Desmond had been five years younger and therefore an unsatisfactory companion. Quentin had not been allowed to play with the village children or go to junior school: he had a succession of governesses and private tutors until he was old enough for Belvedere. More vivid than any of the people were the red carp, the screeching peacocks and Bracken, a fat old Labrador.

Yet he remembered Foxy (for instance) most distinctly. Foxy was a milky white marble with a blue island covering about a third of his surface. It was only by remembering Foxy that Quentin was able to conjure up an image of his paternal grandmother: her slow, reproachful look when she was hurt by childish candour or flippancy. Her eyes had been just that veined and milky white, that bleary blue. But the pattern on Foxy was more interesting and decorative than a human eyeball. The blue area was a soft oblong with a promontory sticking from the corner like the brush of a fox. Foxy had been a marble of high standing in the hierarchy of skill and valour. Husky and phlegmatic and dependable. A colonel of snipers and commander of the cigar-box galley that sometimes plied the parquet beyond the carpet's tasselled shore.

There had been about three hundred marbles and they had divided conveniently into uniformed tribes, teams or regiments. The inspiration for the best game was three heavy volumes of *British Battles on Land and Sea* – beginning with Hastings and ending with Omdurman. These books illustrated their somewhat dry accounts by alternating diagrams of the tactical disposition of forces with dramatic drawings (school of Géricault) of the heat of each fray. During the game the imagination had to recall the pictures or supply the equivalent; but the marbles on the marvellous old map of a carpet, formed into infantry ranks or loosely deployed as skirmishers, were much more evocative and glamorous than the black and white rectangles of the plans in *British Battles*.

The red, white and blue marbles usually represented the victorious troops; the blacks, yellows and greens were losers, foreigners and forces of evil. Other codes applied to the personalities (all male) bestowed on individual marbles. Opaque marbles were brave and stupid, thugs or heroes. Translucent marbles were either wise and skilful or cowardly and treacherous. Details of appearance could also affect their personalities as well as give them their names: Tomahawk, Squiggles, Black Spook, Milky Way.

Fortunes in battle were decided by either accident or predestination. Quentin, a god bored by his own omnipotence, sometimes used dice to decide individual encounters. More often he simply collided the marbles: whichever ricocheted out of a coloured area of carpet was deemed slain. This second method allowed him to exercise partiality towards factions and individuals. He behaved very much the way Jehovah does in the Old Testament: capricious, inefficient, downright perverse at times, but his chosen could be confident of long-term advantage.

It seemed to Quentin that these battle layouts on the lion-coloured carpet (or sometimes in the lawns and flowerbeds – though that was not so satisfactory) had possessed a luminous, ordered intelligence that nothing else matched. His actual military experience in the Second World War was a mixture of bilious tedium and shameful nightmare. The Arabian carpet was as preferable to the shattered suburbs of occupied cities as were Midnight and Red Glow-worm to the drunken rapists and sadists that Quentin had been supposed to command.

His career as architect had been less harrowing but otherwise as besmirched as his army experience. There had been blueprints like battle-maps, and the aesthetic that the old carpet had exuded along with its geometry and logic. But buildings had to be bought and sold and used by people – and Quentin was soon promoted from design to administration, at which he had no talent. Millions of marbles all the same size and colour. Once you left the magic carpet everything that was not nauseating was insignificant.

At four o'clock on 3 September 1950, a month before Quentin abruptly left the Hall and family for Hong Kong, he had found Damien playing marbles in the games room. The lion-coloured carpet had been demoted to serve in this room: thirty years older, it was glossy with wear in parts but still magnificent. Damien, ignoring the carpet, had stretched a green cloth over the ping-pong table. He was playing soccer, Portsmouth (the current champions) against Middlesbrough (his own favourites); using a ruler to shove the marbles, a bead as the ball, and an ornate set of rules relating to the recovery of players who missed the ball and hurtled off the pitch. The goalposts were made out of the two halves of the inside of a matchbox.

Finding his son so exercised in solitary fantasy might have been expected to move Quentin to affection as well as nostalgia. Unfortunately he had given up all pretence at fatherhood by this time. He never spoke to the lad or acknowledged his presence except to complain that the racket Damien was causing was injurious to the imaginary maladies that Quentin had brought back from the war. Damien's mouth-organ, for instance, bought him by his wacky aunt Annabel, was pitched on exactly the note that instigated Quentin's queasy globus and the tinnitus in his left ear. And the piping voice of the son seemed to be deliberately aimed at jangling the already taut nerves and speeding the racing pulse of the father.

Quentin said nothing but noticed that Foxy was playing in goal. Foxy in goal! Soccer had not been a game that interested Quentin in the golden age of Sparrow Hall, but it was evident enough to him that if Foxy was to play soccer it would be as a ruthless and accomplished centre-half – maybe a slightly muscle-bound but prolific centre-forward. And Quentin spotted other anomalies. Red Salmon at full back! Giblets on the right wing! Meanwhile Damien, embarrassed by his father's intrusion, had stopped the game and was pretending to take measurements with the ruler, as though the marbles had been laid out as markers for some more practical project.

Over thirty years later Quentin could see that it was all bullshit, and that Damien's interpretation of Foxy and Giblets had been just as valid as his own. He could see now that the personalities he had awarded to his marbles had been as arbitrary and meaningless as everything else on this shit of a planet. The lovely lion-coloured carpet had returned to the stinking chaos that produced it in the first place. Just a few minutes' thought long ago, or the intrusion of some captivating and candid playmate, might have rescued Quentin from his fantasies and saved us all from what follows.

It was a coincidence that the three corpses all fell with their heads towards the windows: the woman with her arm and hand outspread as though waving to the mermaid in the fountain. At the inquest Janet Otterburn and Jennifer Coram testified to hearing the shots and finding the bodies. Two verdicts of unlawful killing and one of suicide were recorded.

The deaths of his father, mother and uncle meant that Damien Frobisher inherited three fortunes on the same day. By this time he was a forty-three-year-old Postal Controller in Walsall and a socialist.

1

Damien's rejection of his political heritage had been a fluctuating process. His psyche was affected by personalities rather than notions: therefore his beliefs did not accumulate like bricks cemented together by logic; they flooded or fell like ocean tides according to whatever lord or lady of the moon had sway.

At school he was no rebel but a shy, hulking lad, lazily gifted and ruefully obedient. He showed a preference for having one buddy rather than being a member of a gang or clique, and an inaptitude for team games. Since one had to have some sport if one was not to be an untouchable wet, he struggled with shot-put and discus, low-status events at which he was mediocre. He was not bullied or unpopular but those whose approval he craved gave him little attention.

When he was in the sixth form the brutal sporting ethos was challenged by one or two masters. 'Pansy' Jackson, French Literature, scathed and scorned what he called 'hefty philistines' and was despised by them in return. The Reverend F. F. Binns, Medieval History, exuded an aura of genteel academia in which anything as inappropriate as sporting macho withered. Yet Damien did not begin to perceive any cracks in the forts of folly until the brief but spectacular apparition of Hambleton.

Hambleton was a cadaverous young teacher of literature who wore long sideburns and a velvet jacket that he called his 'bordello tuxedo'. He had lived in Paris; sometimes he wore a red waistcoat and said, '*Chacun à son* Gautier.' He smoked Sobranie Black Russian cigarettes. While he was not entirely prepossessing – he blinked alarmingly every half-minute and had a speech impediment that made him say 'twack' instead of 'track' (so that he had rather drastic discipline problems in the Lower School) – there were some in the Sixth who were intoxicated by the alternative he presented, not merely to the sporting ethos but to other assumptions that were cramping their adolescence.

He was not much older than they were and quite unlike any other teacher they had met. He used to quit the pulpit-like teacher's desk, from which the other masters lectured and supervised even sixth-formers, in order to sit on a pupil's desk-top with his feet on the seat. He scandalised his students by the explicit language – bordering deliciously on obscenity – with which he expounded, say, 'The Eve of Saint Agnes' or the devotions of Richard Crashaw. But even more spectacular were the political digressions into 'Twotsky' or 'The Social Contwact', which cut great swathes through the literature lessons.

It was no surprise that Hambleton only stayed at Belvedere for a couple of terms. He was a conventional enough school-master to avoid and discourage personal enquiry – so Damien never discovered whether he was sacked or went of his own accord. Nor was the mystery ever solved as to what somebody with such blatantly left-wing views, who had lived in Paris, was doing teaching at Belvedere – though he was questioned fairly directly about this just before he left.

By that time his sixth-form students were all imitating him by sitting on the tops of their desks with their feet on the seat of the desk in front. Literature studies had become subsidiary to the discussion of moral and political matters. A number of students were truanting – scorners of Hambleton, or opportunist skivers who had seen that nothing happened when others stayed away. Some of these absentees had spoiled earlier lessons with their hostility: the atmosphere was pleasanter without them.

Dunhill asked Hambleton the question. Lower down the school Dunhill had been the sort of kid who was always getting his head flushed in the lavatory, at which time Damien, though not himself of high status, would have been ashamed to be seen talking to Dunhill. But now in the Sixth – and especially in Hambleton's class – Dunhill was something of a splinter-group guru: playing chess in his head, reading music-scores as if they were comics and authentically pronouncing the names of Russian novelists and French avant-gardists.

Damien was a bit appalled by the impertinence of the personal question – even to as novel a master as Hambleton – but the latter merely did his blink and treated the enquiry as if it was a debating point, answering in best Socratic fashion with a question of his own: 'Must we pwactise what we pweach? Can our conduct invalidate our opinions? What do you think?'

Somebody said of course we must, of course it does. You wouldn't go to a wife-beater for marriage guidance, or to a fat man for advice about diet.

Dunhill pursed his lips and boggled his eyes in mockery of this naïveté. 'Surely one cannot judge the validity of a hypothesis by the character and conduct of its presenter?' he said. He was perfecting an irritating argumentative style. 'Surely one must judge it by empirical evidence, logic and one's own experience? The application of other criteria is arbitrary and absurd.'

Damien was not so sure. In any case he was disappointed by the teacher's response to Dunhill's question, since he was more interested in Hambleton's motivation than the philosophical issue.

When Hambleton was gone Damien found himself hanging around with Dunhill and a couple of other fellows, Falk and Bevan, whom he had once considered weird and wet. The group of them were known as Hambleton's Harem and were wrongly considered to be a homosexual coterie. They were in fact united by the habit of impersonal argument, which the master had left them, and by a competitive scholarship that had them scouring the school library for new authorities with which to confound the other disciples and new masterpieces to brag about. They spent a lot of spring and summer afternoons out of bounds, walking for miles while waving their arms in disputatious emphasis and smoking Sobranie Black Russian cigarettes.

At Oxford Damien read Modern History and wrote poems, two of which were published in tiny, indigent magazines. He joined the Socialist Club and dipped into Marx and Engels. He was disappointed that his principal history tutor, reportedly a lapsed communist, could not be lured into discussing insurrectionary politics. Without exciting their attention he made the acquaintance of several people who later became influential pundits and politicians – but it was his encounter with the apolitical Ben Stott that was the most significant of Damien's undergraduate career.

Stott had a room on the same staircase as Damien. He was a stocky, ginger-headed, working-class lad from Manchester reading English, who detested the university and spent his time drinking and playing darts in proletarian pubs, when he was not in his room filling cheap exercise books with pastiches of Browning. He subsidised his grant by stealing books from Thornton's and selling them second-hand to Blackwell's – and vice versa. He only went to Hall for breakfast – there was a little café in the covered market did a better lunch, he said, and he never ate at night until he had fish and chips (or pie and chips) on his way home from the pub. He had very few dealings with other undergraduates but made an exception in Damien's case, not because they were fellow poets but because Damien had an LP of Bessie Smith that Stott admired. He made a habit of lurching into Damien's room late at night and requesting a playing of several tracks. He would then fail to listen to the music, instead haranguing Damien about literature or picking an argument with him on some general topic. Damien was a shy and lonely person: except when Ben was so drunk as to be inarticulately belligerent – which was rarely the case – he enjoyed the intrusions. For the most part he found Ben's rhetoric impressive and his studied coarseness entertaining. They showed each other poems and agreed that Damien's were callow, Ben's inscrutable.

Ben said that it was an impertinence for upper-class pillocks like Damien to pretend to be socialists. Politics, he said, was about class struggle, and a middle-class socialist was an oxymoron. The goings-on in the university Socialist Club, as he imagined them, filled him with hilarious disgust.

'I'm no fucking socialist,' he once said. 'I reneged on all that when I betrayed my class and let myself be enticed to this Disneyland shit-hole. But if you want to meet real socialists come down to the Lamb and Flag on Thursday evening.'

Damien went along more for Ben's company than to meet real socialism; but once they were there Ben introduced Damien into a circle of pale and sober-looking young people then went off to play darts. It was rather like the way some working-class men sit their wives among the women then go themselves to stand at the bar and drink with cronies. The young proles with whom Ben played darts – he was a member of the pub's Friday night team – were apolitical, their conversation consisting of banter about the game, lewd jokes and sporting anecdotes.

Damien did not spend a lot of time in public houses, but he could tell that the Lamb and Flag was very different from varsity pubs like the Turl and the King's Arms. There was a more representative cross-section of ages in the Lamb and Flag and quite a few women – though these were mostly elderly. Any girls in the pub were evidently with men, apart from the only female member of the Cowley Road Socialist Militants.

She looked more like somebody's girl-friend than an authentic member of the group. She was togged out in current shop-girl fashion: stiletto heels and nylons, a short woollen skirt and a floppy, fluffy, V-neck sweater. Her hair was dyed with henna and combed back into a beehive style that Kim Novak had popularised and she was wearing quite a lot of eye makeup and lipstick. Her eyes were bland; her lips, plump and regular as the two halves of a small bun, were habitually shut in a pout, which supplemented the pert sexuality of the rest of the ensemble.

Yet she sat among the Cowley Road chapter as an equal. She took a full part in the discussions and received as much serious attention as anybody else. Certainly she got more respect than Damien did. At first the group took a polite if wary interest in him, till his accent and what little he said permitted them to stereotype him. Anything he ventured was then either ignored or gruffly snubbed, as one might discourage a heathen's interruptions to a prayer meeting.

He found that the Cowley Road Socialist Militants did not discuss politics at all as he understood the activity. At school and university dispute was the rule, with some playing devil's advocate if necessary, and nothing going unchallenged except when everybody was too busy parading their own hypotheses to shoot down the others. The Cowley Road Militants did not argue about socialism. It was as if they had come to a complete agreement about aims and principles and were left with the task of working out methods. Or perhaps they had decided, like nihilists, that the overthrow of the old order was the first priority.

Their concerns were practical, narrow and banal: picketing support for a strike at the Morris Cowley factory; arrangements for the distribution of a socialist broadsheet; plans for a base – a cheap room, or even a shed. Damien made a couple of attempts at broadening the discussion: 'Morris

workers are pretty well paid, though, aren't they?' and 'What
do you mean by socialism, anyway?' These sallies were met
only with a queasy silence such as his mother might employ
against the obscenities of Uncle Desmond.

It was clear to Damien that he was unwelcome at the Lamb
and Flag. He was annoyed with Ben for taking him there and
then deserting him. His discomfiture was increased by the fact
that he was treating his bashfulness with Guinness-and-bitter –
the Militants all drank it, referring to it as Black and Tan and
averring that it was the only decent drink to be had in the pub.
Two pints of the concoction had made Damien's head swim
and his stomach churn. He would have left if it had not been
for the girl.

He was beginning to take an acute interest in girls. During
the summer he and his cousin Hilary, Aunt Annabel's plump
and frantic daughter, had engaged in a series of sexual encounters, the first for both of them, accompanied by scares about
pregnancy, moody sunderings and guilty reconciliations. All
the while he had bashfully yearned for a very different sort of
girl: Elaine Moorhouse, the petite, dark and faintly wicked-
looking daughter of the Thornham pub. He had fantasised
over her and masturbated towards her phantom for at least
two years, since he had caught her and a couple of other girls
stealing Frobisher daffodils from the copse below Longacre.

At his peevish protest, Elaine had meekly proffered him
her daffodils. A wide black belt had pinched her waist and
a pleated white skirt had endorsed her hips. The styling of her
dark hair had included a gypsy-like curl on each cheek. She
had tripped across to the other girls, gathered their daffodils
and taken them to the fatuous young lord of Sparrow Hall,
forcing him to lay down his air-rifle to hold all the flowers
in his arms. With her brown eyes solemn and submissive she
had backed away as if leaving the presence of an exotic despot.
Rejoining her chums she had linked arms with them and her

face had relaxed into scornful amusement. The three girls had wheeled like the front row of a scrum and bounced off, yelling and stumbling with mirth, leaving Damien devastated.

Pam, the Militant, had the same disconcerting poise as Elaine Moorhouse. Damien kept catching her eye as he listened to wearisome conversation from which he felt excluded. He wanted to smile at her but did not dare, although the alcohol had made it possible for him to endure her gaze without blushing or looking away. He liked it best when she was talking and he had a full excuse for gazing at her; and since he was more attentive than the others it was natural that she should begin to seem to address herself mostly to him. So he was gradually encouraged in delusion. When she got up to leave at ten o'clock – this was clearly not the sort of gathering that sat it out drinking until time was called – he blurted out, 'Pam, can I see you home?'

The words pealed out in his posh accent across a fortuitous silence. Somebody let out an embarrassed laugh and somebody else gave a snort of disgust. Damien flushed bright red and felt sober at once, realising that his pick-up attempt was as inappropriate to the political meeting as his accent was to the Lamb and Flag. But Pam preserved him from humiliation by treating his request as though it contained no hint of sex.

'That's nice of you,' she said. 'Okay.'

When they got out onto the street Damien was irritated to discover that Gordon was with them: he had been the most hostile towards Damien of all the Militants. Gordon had clad himself in a donkey jacket and was showing every intention of helping squire Pam, who was wearing a belted white gabardine.

Gordon asked, in a tone that effortlessly matched Damien's annoyance, 'What's going on, then? Why's Lord Muck keeping us company?'

'Shush, you, Gordon,' she said serenely. 'He's seeing me up Elderfield Road.'

'I could have done that.'

'I know, but he's offered, and I bet you aren't really sorry.'

She set off under the streetlights, her tall heels clicking. Gordon said to Damien as the two fell into step beside her, 'Went to public school, did you? Did you used to have a fag?'

Damien found Gordon's manner of walking sideways and jutting out his chin to peer up into Damien's face very annoying. All the same he felt that he should try to answer the question with a good grace, because Pam was listening and he wanted to counter the stigma of snob and toff that had been applied to him all evening. But he was baffled for a moment by the second question, thinking it referred to cigarettes.

'I don't quite follow you,' he said.

'Did you used to have a fag? And were you a fag yourself at one time? I understand a lot of buggery goes on in places like that.'

'They have no fagging system at Belvedere. It was abolished before the war.'

'Yes, but I mean, all you boys together.' Gordon walked in silence while he mustered further aggression. Damien was distressed, finding himself prone to lurch and stagger with the unaccustomed freight of alcohol, and thwarted from his timid designs on Pam by Gordon's presence. He took comfort from the fact, assumed from what Pam had said, that Gordon would be leaving them presently.

Gordon asked, 'What sort of house do you live in? I mean, are you very rich? Do you have servants and all that? All you rich twats should be fucking shot, like in the French Revolution.'

Damien couldn't help saying, 'They weren't shot, they were guillotined.'

Gordon left them when they turned from the main road on-to a council estate. Then a silence fell so daunting that Damien half wished for Gordon's contentious presence. He could think of absolutely nothing to say to Pam. His upbringing had made him desperately ill at ease in the company of girls.

He was equally ill at ease in the presence of the working class. When he was younger they had been dismissable: either as employees or as a peasant rabble – teenage yobs who jeered at him in Thornham or who pelted him and his classmates with clods of earth through the bright green palings that circle the grounds of Belvedere. They had been another species, exotic in ignorance and squalor, like the Sioux must have seemed to a wagon-train migrant or like the proles seemed to Winston Smith in *1984*. But now, in addition, his political conscience made him apologetic and appeasing, at a moral disadvantage, as he would have felt if he had been a white South African.

At the same time he was aware of a blissful and dreamy aspect to his predicament as he walked alongside Pam past gardens of stunted privets and derelict prams. Clopping along beside him on her high heels, her white coat collar pulled up to caress her cheeks and her henna beehive made strawberry and filmy as the streetlamps swooped by, she seemed to feel no tension in the silence nor any obligation to break it. Marx and Cophetua shared Damien's consciousness rather as Hitler and Stalin had partitioned Finland. While he was aware that it was patronising and sinister, he could all the same respond to the wistfulness of Flecker:

> And I will change my silk and lace for clogs and corduroy,
> And work with the mill hands of black Riouperoux,
> And walk with you and talk with you like any other boy.

He asked her, 'Have you read Engels's *Anti-Duhring*?'
She just stared at him. It struck him as a ridiculous question to have asked such a girl. With her short coat, high heels

and backcombed hair she looked like a bar-room floozy in a newspaper cartoon.

'Frederick Engels,' he said. 'He helped Karl Marx with *The Communist Manifesto*.'

'I know,' she said drily. 'I did go to school.'

He sank into crushed silence. Relenting, she said, 'It's good of you to see me home.'

'Not at all. It's me that's grateful.'

'No, this is a rough estate. I try to get home before the pubs shut.'

Now that she came to mention it he could see that there was a fair proportion of boarded houses. The streets were deserted as far as could be seen but there was somebody yelling in the distance, while closer at hand an aggressively loud gramophone was propounding rock and roll music.

'The Clanceys live on this corner, so keep your posh voice down.'

He thought she might be teasing him. The Clanceys' door was open. A bare lightbulb lit a hallway of tattered wallpaper and carpetless stairs. Pam lowered her own voice as they passed. 'They're scumbags.'

If he was shocked by her lack of proper socialist sentiment, he was more interested in the fact that she had linked her arm with his, the way working-class girls did with their escorts in imitation of Hollywood films. It enabled him to feel the warmth of her body through the gabardine.

They came to a halt under the next lamp. He turned towards her, half resolved to kiss her. This was prevented when she took her hand from his elbow and pointed beyond him, at the nearest gate.

'Here's where we live,' she said. 'Will you come in?'

He was beset by a prospect of carnal delight in a comfy lounge while her parents were in bed or watching TV in the other room. 'Won't your parents mind?'

'I don't live with my parents. I live with my bloke, Pete.'

'Pete?' he croaked. Yet was there somewhere within him a little whelm of cowardly relief?

'He's secretary of the Militants. Only his chest's bad, he couldn't be at the meeting tonight.'

Damien smiled and nodded, his embarrassment magically dispelled along with his ambitions. 'Gosh, I've just seen what time it is!' He brandished his watch. 'I'll be shut out of college if I don't scoot!'

'Pete'll be disappointed to have missed you. He's the one to talk to about Engels.'

'Some other time, maybe.'

There were other times. Damien was not prepared to accept the raw implications of that evening. He went back on several occasions to the Cowley Road Militants, sometimes taking university acquaintances with him, discussed Marxism in depth with Pete, who proved to be, as advertised, the theorist of the chapter, and learned to talk to Pam without blushing. An invitation to the Militants to attend a university Socialist Club event was not accepted, and the locals and students remained constrained in their occasional encounters, but at least Damien was able to tell himself that he was no public-school, ivory-tower socialist doomed to be for ever remote from the realities of the class struggle. He cited the Militants when debating with fellow undergraduates and was guilty of taking an authoritative stance on the strength of his half-dozen visits to the Lamb and Flag. The fact remained that his most direct and lasting connection with the proletariat was via Ben Stott, class traitor and inverted snob.

Damien did not return to Sparrow Hall after the Easter vacation of his freshman year. He either stayed at Oxford during holidays or went off on backpacking, hitch-hiking expeditions, alone or with male acquaintances. Christmas presented the only difficulty: he eked out one Christmas miserably in digs in Oxford, spending as much time as possible in bars and cinemas to avoid the pitying intrusions of his landlady. The next Christmas he was going to return grudgingly to Sparrow Hall when just before the end of term he fell into a passionate liaison with Glynis, a nurse at the Radcliffe Hospital, who took him home to her parents' farm near Stroud.

When he left Oxford he was still an intellectual and senti-mental socialist: his experiences at the university – discussing the iniquities of the USSR with future editors of *Tribune* and thrilling at the way Barbara Castle laid it on the line at the Oxford Union – had done little to either shake or solidify the notions he had brought from Belvedere. He had a scheme for going to Cuba to give Fidel a hand but in the end he went to Paris where he got a job teaching English and met Dora Schultz. Dora took charge of him for the next seventeen years and smoothed the socialism out of him.

Dora did not seem the sort to dominate anybody. She had a timid smile and soft brown hair. When Damien courted her in Paris she seemed under the sway of her travelling companion and one-time college roomer, Candy Cornwallis, a fat butch person full of noisy agendas. It was Candy's decree that had brought her and Dora to France: she bossed Dora all the time, deciding where they went and what they ate. Damien conjectured that it was going to be difficult to seize Dora from Candy. Then suddenly, amazingly, Dora had arranged everything. Candy was off to Madrid alone, with no hint of resentment or reluctance. Damien could move out of his squalid lodging and take Candy's single bed and share Dora's double room.

The next decade furnished him with plenty more examples of Dora's knack for getting folk to do what she wanted without disturbing her own reputation for compliance. He escorted her home to Wisconsin, where in a large frame house with English Tudor styling he met a bull-necked trio of local football legends who wanted to know what the English slob's intentions were towards their kid sister. Soon he had taken lodgings with Widow Kerrigan, had applied for a work permit and was unmistakably betrothed to Dora, walking with her and talking with her and eating with her family after church on Sunday like any other Wisconsin bourgeois boy. Dora was back in the bedroom of her childhood where Damien was not allowed except once, on his first visit to the house, when he had been led round like a tourist by Dora's mother. It was a shrine of a room: a plump and glossy snow-white bolster and a pink candlewick counterpane. After the wedding Dora constructed a similar bedroom in the flat they rented in Milwaukee.

The wedding was a splendid Schultz family get-together but a disappointment to Dora in that none of Damien's family got there. Marjorie wanted to go but not on her own – she had a morbid fear of aeroplanes – and Desmond refused. Nobody even informed Quentin in Hong Kong.

Dora gave private French lessons and once Damien was equipped with his work permit he sold encyclopaedias while writing poetry and applying for jobs with publishing firms. Although he had given up his plan to help Fidel he still had a notion to visit Cuba, but Dora thought not. She sympathised with his left-wing views but suggested that he exercised discretion in parading them in America, and particularly in the presence of her friends and family. Opinions that seemed cute in Europe, she explained, might in the States be considered crazy and sinister.

Having left America fairly hurriedly after Damien received a communication from the Draft Board – the Vietnam war was in progress – they rented a flat in Camden Town. Damien, who was at the end of several family trees, had come into a

24

legacy from his great-aunt Enid that rendered them financially comfortable. He had a yen to be a full-time writer – was still writing poetry and shyly contemplating a novel – but Dora's more pragmatic views prevailed: he sat the Civil Service exams and became an Assistant Postal Controller. His subsequent professional career took place in London (1964–65), Liverpool (1966–70) and Walsall (1970–82). Dora worked as a secretary while they were in London and did some language teaching in Liverpool but gave up work for ever after Paulette was born in 1968.

Her influence extended beyond his career and politics. When he met her in Paris she announced herself to be agnostic but this proved to be a brief stance suitable for a jaunt to the Old World. In America she resumed Protestantism, which she then imported into England, persuading Damien to accompany her to a church that most approximated to the Lutherans of Wisconsin. By that time her aversion was restricting his viewing of films that she thought contained an undue degree of sex or violence; and one or two books that had been banners of bachelor bravado – Henry Miller, William Burroughs – disappeared from the shelves. She stopped him smoking, sleeping on his back and snoring, using sugar with his coffee and cornflakes. She also influenced him to clean his teeth with dental floss and use an armpit deodorant. She did not manage to stop him reading in the toilet, dog-earing the pages of books, being car-sick on long journeys and occasionally writing a poem. What is more unusual than any of this is that in seventeen years Damien had no impact whatsoever on the character or demeanour of Dora.

She made him resume contact with his parents and uncle, and secretly gloated over the prospect of Damien inheriting Sparrow Hall. She insisted that they visited two or three times a year, herself wallowing in the ancestral odours under the pretence of giving the weird trio access to their grand-daughter. Damien accepted this, though he always went reluctantly, endured his family sheepishly and left with a gush of guilty relief.

Paulette was bullied at her first school so they found an expensive private school in Sutton Coldfield, where they had bought a detached house. After some resistance from Damien she was booked into Sunnymede, the sister school to Belvedere.

Early in 1978 Damien feebly failed to refuse an invitation to be a guest speaker on a weekend residential course, 'Art in the Community', at Wenlock Hall in Shropshire. The Post Office was at this time making mild news by employing avant-gardists to design their stamps, decorate their vans, and so on. Several factors, including embarrassment over the fatuous address expected from him on Sunday and the susceptibility to alcohol that had always amused Ben Stott, got him uncharacteristically drunk on Saturday night.

On Sunday morning he lifted a lurid eyelid to encounter a world made wan by heavy curtains. It was an old-fashioned room in what must once have been the servants' quarters, reminiscent of a Sparrow Hall attic in his childhood though on a grander scale. There was a jug and bowl, willow pattern, on a swart table, two quite elegant but uninhabitable rushwork chairs, an enormous wardrobe, very dark oak, proclaiming with geometrically beaded doors, intestine gloom. There were two narrow beds in the room, on one of which he was uncomfortably perched, the sheet beneath him ridden into ridges, the top sheet and eiderdown tangled upon him in an inhospitable sausage. He was naked but not yet aware of the cold.

On the other bed the bedclothes more decorously and efficiently cocooned their occupant, a woman lying with her back to him so that only the tangle of her brown hair was visible. The mound of her on the bed indicated that she was slender, and the long, soft sighs he could hear if he held his breath indicated that she was asleep. He rubbed his hand across his lips and the drunkard's waking panic, the horror of amnesia, was replaced by a montage of rueful recollections – a series of tableaux emblematic not so much of the Seven Deadly Sins as of the unofficial penances: Disappointment, Humiliation, Chagrin . . .

He giggled, still fairly drunk. Male and female garments were scattered over the varnished floorboards and the coir matting, socks, shoes, tights, sweater, brassière, underpants, knickers, string vest, in a reckless mutual welter like the ingredients of a libidinous soup. On the pot cupboard between the beds there was a packet of cigarettes and a box of matches.

Such untroubled sleep. He stumbled round the bed and sat on the edge so that she was facing him. She was not beautiful – her nose was too long and her lips too hungrily thin – but the relaxation of her features into demure surrender to sleep was disarmingly attractive. He stroked back a hair from her cheek. She opened her eyes, bewildered, then focused on him and returned his smile. He remembered, recognised, the discoloured tooth, the front incisor.

Her disconcerting immediacy prevented him saying anything. She wriggled herself back to the edge of the narrow bed and upflung her left arm to open the bedclothes in invitation.

'Yow, you're cold!' she said, as he perched against her. They put their tongues into each other's mouths.

They copulated competently, after which he said, 'That was better, wasn't it?'

She did not speak but her fingers dug into his biceps, a coded message. Gratitude? Reassurance?

'Sorry about last night,' he said.

'You drink too much,' she said. He heard, remembered, that she had a Yorkshire accent, which reminded him of Elaine Moorhouse and the Thornham village lasses.

'Not usually,' he said, then added unnecessarily, 'I was drunk last night.'

She then appalled him by letting out an intense, intimate little sob and laying her head on his chest. Becoming aware that he was in danger of sobering up, he asked, 'Shall we go to breakfast?'

This got her to lift herself off him, onto one elbow, as she squinted at the wrist-watch that was her only item of apparel. 'Breakfast is over. Twenty to ten.'

'We're late for the session.' Remembering that he was supposed to be addressing the conference that afternoon, he struggled with the oncreep of abject panic but couldn't help adding, 'And they'll be along to clean the room.'

'No, it's a spare room.'

'It's not your room?'

'No.' She smiled, her thin lips curling apart childishly.

Morosely he asked her, 'You come on these courses quite often?'

'Whenever I can.'

'Are you married?'

'Sort of.'

'What does that mean?'

'It means I've a sort of husband and two sort of children. What about you? Are you married?'

'I am. Didn't I tell you last night?'

'You didn't talk about things like that. You talked about Heisenberg and Fidel Castro. And about art and criticism and murdering to dissect.'

'I was drunk.'

'You were splendid. With your flashing eyes and floating hair.'

'I remember us talking. You were . . . pretty insurrection-ary.'

'I'm a lefty weirdo. Famous for it. Feminist. Marxist. Athe-ist. You name it.'

'You were with Derrick Granger.'

'I got you to myself for a few seconds outside the Indian restaurant in Ludlow.'

He smiled uncertainly. 'What happened to Derrick?'

'I quit him there forever in the street outside The Curry House.' She gave a brusque laugh, almost a snort. 'He hardly seemed to notice. Not very flattering.' Then she let out that confiding, surrendering sob again and rested on him: her cheek on his chest and her hair in his nostrils.

He saw that only a glib and facile prologue had been negotiated. He saw a complex and problematic future looming to abash him – the self-grown dirt in clanking armour, a dead princess on a scumwashed shore.

'Are you on the pill?'

'I saw the family as a male device for subjugating . . . I dare say it was just fashionable student stuff then – but now! . . . Now I despise myself for how I betrayed myself, falling for biology and conditioning. My only excuse is how young I was. Terry never tried to adapt to our marriage – but I did! I was besotted with him at first and mindlessly faithful. I craved children and rejoiced in them. I dropped my flashy principles and even scorned them, till I woke up – click! – to find myself lumbered and ditched, a twenty-six-year-old divorcee with two . . . That's how I came to fall into a different trap with Jerry. Terry and Jerry, they sound like frigging cartoon characters. Jerry had none of Terry's selfish macho and he seemed genuinely fond of the kids, and he was a potter with a cottage and workshop where I'd be able to sculpt. It was too enticing to refuse, so having given up my principles and freedom for love of Terry

I gave up my last shreds of romantic ambition for . . . Jerry is as screwed up about his sexual identity as I am about my credibility as a person. Despite which we've hung together for eight years, coming to an understanding, taking turns to baby-sit while I prowl the lecture rooms and lounge bars or he goes off to chess tournaments with his sodomites. We've art in common, and he's a good father, whereas I'm a rotten mother – if somebody has to take up the slack and make the shambles work it's always Jerry.'

Julie's voice was a cool contralto with a Yorkshire accent not much modified by fifteen years in the Midlands. Her speech was spiced with mild proletarian obscenities. In addition to the discoloured front tooth, she was double-jointed and very slightly cross-eyed, like the Tolstoy heroine, which gave her a myopic, trusting look that appealed to chauvinist chivalry. She read Beckett, Kafka, Dostoyevsky, smoked American cigarettes such as Lucky Strike and Camel, cooked Indian and Mexican dishes, which her children claimed to detest. There were a number of operas featuring tragic heroines that she adored – Puccini and Bellini for the most part – but she had no time for Verdi. This penchant for headlong opinions was reflected in other spheres: for cats, Euthymol toothpaste and American Indians; against dogs, veal, Velcro and the sky father.

All these vagaries captivated Damien. He saw Julie in terms of passion, disorder, rebellion, poetry: aspects of his life and psyche that Dora had gently anaesthetised. Yet perhaps what most compelled him – turning a brusque, sexual collision into a momentous amour – was his perception of Julie's unhappiness. It was as if she was languishing among the coils of some spiritual or dialectic dragon, and could count on Damien alone in a universe that favoured dragons. Nobody had implored him so urgently, exploited him so blatantly, made him feel so essential.

She was also a gratifying prize for the lord of Sparrow Hall. Up to then the only women who had consented to love him – Hilary, Glynis, Dora – had been of a class and type suitable for his privileged enclosure. Beyond the pale, out of bounds, had loitered the exotic daughters of the third goddess: Elaine Moorhouse baffling him with daffodils, Pam of the Cowley Road Militants clopping through the tough estate on her stiletto heels. Now the most poignant of these lovely barbarians had chosen him for hero.

Damien pretended to develop an interest in first soccer then cricket, sports about which he knew Dora knew nothing. Julie lived in Brosely just south of Telford, easily reached by the A5. He preferred to do the travelling, though sometimes it would have been easier if she had met him in Walsall or Wolverhampton; the remote lanes of Shropshire were more discreet. They went to Bridgnorth market and Ludlow Castle. They climbed to the Devil Stones, where they reckoned to be able to see four counties, and lunched in pubs and tea rooms in Housman villages like Clungunford and Clunbury. Or they sat in the car in lay-bys that rainy spring and talked. Julie analysed her childhood, recounted the plots of films and books and flexed her doctrines. Damien murmured acknowledgements suitable to the tone of her monologue and answered the questions she threw in to keep him attentive. Sometimes he demurred from what he considered a wild opinion and a spirited dispute followed, appeased by his surrender with a joke and a kiss. Sex took place in the back of the car, or *al fresco* amid underbrush or bracken; once in a barn in a thunderstorm, like a scene from a film.

Disconcerting interludes punctuated this idyll. One Saturday evening in a restaurant near Much Wenlock Julie started to snivel over the devilled whitebait. 'Julie Hatchard's famous, a man-eater,' she said, in a thick voice folded round a sob. 'She's okay for a quick shag but watch her, she's hard to

31

shake off once she's got her claws in you.' She chucked down her fork onto the pile of crisp grey tiddlers. 'And if you stick by her she'll betray you, for she's a disloyal bitch.' She put her head in her hands. The waitress shot Damien a reproachful glance as she brought the roast duckling with *pommes frites* and garden peas.

When he reached home, considerably later than he had intended, Dora had bathed and was in her fluffy dressing-gown, listening to *Country and Western Favourites* (Kenny Rogers was singing 'You Chose A Fine Time To Leave Me, Lucille'), on the dulcet-toned stereo in the sitting-room. She was perched in the big armchair with her feet tucked under her and her hands around a mug of cocoa. With her soft dark hair and delicate complexion she looked young and pretty. She greeted Damien's entry with, 'I maybe flunked math but I can read a mileage gauge.'

He started to deny everything. She hushed him by raising a slow, calm hand. 'Add to which the auto stinks of cigarettes and pussy and cheap cologne.'

He started to confess everything. She clunked the mug onto the glass-top coffee table and rose to her feet.

'It's not a pleasant topic. It isn't of my making and I don't wanna be hassled by it. It'd be sweet if you'd sleep in the guest room.'

After that there was no need for alibis. The following Friday Damien drove Julie along the A5 into Wales, where they stayed at a hotel in the hills near Llangollen. In the bar a crowd of Manchester youngsters, scruffy and ebullient, sang songs of social protest to a guitar accompaniment. Later Damien and Julie wallowed in the surge of a ridiculously deep flock mattress, cajoling each other into several orgasms. In the morning they were only just in time for breakfast of cereal, bacon and eggs, sausage, corn fritter, mushrooms, tomato, fried bread, toast and marmalade and coffee. Then they went on to Aberystwyth where they posed as newly-weds in a sea-front hotel, ordering champagne in their room after dinner. They spent most of Sunday morning dozing entwined, or murmuring preposterous endearments, before they blissfully and wearily headed back towards England via scenic meanders while Julie talked, leaning back and puffing luxuriously at a cigarette, the window wound down and her freckled arm crooked on the sill.

'I went on Vietnam demos, Ban-the-Bomb marches, stuff like that. I left the kids with Terry and went to Paris in May '68, camping in the Bois de Boulogne. It was brilliant, the trees down in the street, the red flags in the Sorbonne, but I couldn't help feeling like a sightseer, not having a lot of French. We went on one demo march, up to Montmartre and back down to the river in the bleeding rain. There was trouble with the fuzz but not in our section of the . . . Then the bloke I was with dumped me and I hitched home. My contribution to the revolution that never happened. For a while after that things still seemed okay for the revolutionary left but it was an illusion. Right-wing governments fell everywhere but they were replaced by capitalist democrats who are not much different. In place of Che and Ho Chi Minh to give us inspiration there's the Gang of Four and Pol Pot to boost capitalist propaganda. People who used to be socialists reel out stuff like, "Communism can't work because it goes against nature." Bollocks. Unless we alter our social and moral mindset the species is doomed and the planet with it.'

Another weekend Damien parked his car by the workshop in Brosely and took the path through the boxwood hedge to the cottage door. Jerry had gone to a chess tournament, staying over Saturday night with some symbiotic crony. Julie had said that it didn't matter whether Jerry was on the premises or not but Damien disagreed.

The cottage looked unremarkable from the outside but the

interior was spectacular. The shabby carpet and furnishings were mostly concealed by a higgledy-piggle of the property of the occupants of the cottage. As well as a ubiquitous toy railway there were shoes and socks, Lego, Meccano, chessmen, a stringed horse chestnut, a football boot, a hairbrush – and blobs of clay and jars of glaze and unfired pots and slivers of metal and squares of glass and worms of solder that had wandered in from the workshop. There was a pot of glue with a solidified drool onto the carpet and two plates that had had cigarettes stubbed out into beetroot stains or the crisped remains of a vindaloo. There was a magazine that looked as if it had been dropped into a bath and a couple of scragged paperback books and several newspapers folded over at ill-attempted crosswords. A black kitten with a short, furry triangle of a tail played dementedly among the mess. A threadbare ginger mog lay on its side with its fat flanks heaving as if it had recently been shot.

The untidiness and grubbiness of everything went beyond neglect. It was as if the items in the room had been selected for their cheap scruffiness then deliberately soiled and flung. It seemed like an anarchist utterance, a calculated antithesis to The Lindens, Coleridge Drive, Sutton Coldfield – where despite having somebody to clean the house from top to bottom once a week Dora was constantly patrolling, polishing and tidying. Even Paulette's toys were subject to rigorous review, so that she had to get accustomed to the replacement of unsightly old favourites.

Julie's workshop, though, was quite different from the cottage. There was a bench with welding and cutting equipment at one end of the room, otherwise almost all the space was occupied by her sculptures. These were composed of glimmering fragments of stained glass set into aluminium frames. Most of them were tall and narrow, having similar dimensions to standing human figures; others were longer than they were tall, like dogs or cattle. Each was mounted on a wooden base on which a number had been carefully stencilled. There were a couple of dozen of them, delicate and intricate, like a tribe of angels or harlequins: classical, tranquil, meticulous, poised, attentive, astonishing.

Her children were denizens of the cottage, not the workshop. Thanks to Dora ('Don't pull Mummy's hair, who loves you so, my sweetie pie!'), Paulette was a civil ten-year-old who treated Daddy as if she admired him. Julie's brats, eleven and thirteen, seemed truculent and cynical. Susan, the elder, a tall lass with her oval face framed by lank hair, had opened the front door and stared at Damien with peremptory brown eyes – then emitted an irritated *tsk* and turned away to climb the stairs to where the Bay City Rollers were chanting, leaving the door wide and the stranger to enter or not as he wished. Later, when Damien tried in vain to fix Tim's Hornby-Dublo engine, which was buzzing spasmodically like a dying wasp, the lad yelled, 'Yow bost that, clumsy tosser! Buy us another!'

Damien was uncomfortable under the scrutiny of Terry's children in Jerry's house, and troubled by the notion that they would be wounded or discountenanced in the presence of their mother's lover. If the situation had been reversed he would not have wished Paulette to be faced so nakedly with the concept of Julie replacing Dora. He was also perturbed by the fact that Julie shared none of his scruples: caressing him without embarrassment and talking about sex with loud candour. He could not help raising the matter with her when they were alone.

'We maybe shouldn't . . . flirt in front of your kids.'

Her green eyes immediately glinted with suspicion. 'Why not?'

'I don't see why we shouldn't display a bit of patience and strategy.'

'Cowardice and hypocrisy, you mean. Have you spoken to Dora yet?'

'She won't talk. I told you.'

'Bollocks. Have you tried to talk to her?'

'I told you, she just says it's upsetting and not her problem.'

'So we'll all fall in with her wishes and carry on as if nothing is amiss. She'll have your home and your weekdays. She'll cede me the weekends and the dripping barns and the . . . on condition that nothing has the bad manners to endanger her frigging decorum.'

He put out a comforting hand towards her but she shoved him away. 'The kids might hear us grunting and be traumatised.'

More testily than he intended, he said, 'I don't see why everything has to be spontaneous and super-dramatic and confrontational and damaging. You said yourself, last week, that you were glad I was considerate.'

'I meant considerate to me! Which includes being shitty to other people on my behalf!'

When Julie overheard Tim's rudeness to Damien she called him an unmannerly little twat and told him that he couldn't go to Dudley Zoo on the Sunday unless he apologised. Damien flinched at this, partly because he had no wish to escalate Tim's resentment, partly because it was the first he had heard of the zoo trip and he suspected Julie of inventing it on the spur of the moment as a sanction. She seemed to alternate her *laissez-faire* with impulsive attempts at disciplining her children by drastic threats she had no intention of implementing. They all went to the zoo despite the fact that Tim did not even apologise when he was abruptly sick in Damien's car. The boy then dissembled his interest in the animals as far as he was able, tainting the day with querulous complaints about the heat that could only be borne if lots of burgers and Coca Cola were consumed.

Julie's references to Susan were full of awe and bitterness, though she gave Damien no specific examples of ill-conduct. She mostly treated her daughter as a warder might treat an unpredictable convict. Yet Susan, though clearly uninterested in zoos, was demurely uncomplaining. When they were having a meal in the cafeteria Julie (out of temper because of Damien's flagrant unease) appalled him by suddenly snarling at her daughter, 'Just order the most expensive item on the menu and leave it as usual, you contrary bitch!' – and Susan merely wrinkled her nose and glanced around as if appealing for witnesses to her mother's unjust folly. But in Susan's narrow face and sullen lips there abided a sense of menace, as if she was composed of a volatile substance that might at any moment send the occasion to smithereens.

As he drove home on Sunday evening rather earlier than usual Damien was able to think. So far he had been inspired by emotions – passion and compassion, nostalgia for hopeful youth and revulsion at the soft-foot creep of destiny – and he had been abetted in this by Julie, who seemed to regard any intelligent reckoning of consequences as betrayal. But a day and a half of domesticity with Julie and Susan and Tim had been sobering.

He tried to be as objective as he used to be – encouraged by Dora – before he woke up next to Julie that morning in Wenlock Hall. Had he been unhappy with Dora these last ten years? Was Julie likely to improve his quota of bliss over the next decade? This weekend his relationship with Julie had been less carnal and romantic, more representative of the companionship that would have to outlast the excitement of discovery. And even on the Sunday, when her mood had been less challenging, it had been an uncomfortable business. He had become more aware of how much she talked and how badly she listened; how tactless she was, feckless, slovenly, egotistical. Her gloom seemed less piquant and her mirth less amusing than on previous weekends.

Was he prepared to give up Dora for Julie? It meant, in effect, giving up the comfort of The Lindens for the Brosely cottage or some equivalent mess. It meant swapping Paulette for Tim and Susan.

Part of him pretended to be undaunted. *For years I've been stifled. Julie has rescued me and given me back my real self and I love her.* But another part of him, Dora's part, less heroically strident than the other but just as plausible, said, *Your real self? Remember who you really are. Julie is Cowley Road Pam. She is Elaine Moorhouse. Even though she is a sculptor who reads Dostoyevsky. She will come to despise the Prince of Sparrow Hall.*

His decision had been taken for him. As he entered The Lindens in Sutton Coldfield he could not hear the strains of the country and western music that Dora had taken to playing constantly, as if to remind him of the brief and fatal conversation it had accompanied a few weeks ago. He realised in retrospect what his absorption had ignored – that Paulette's bedroom window had been unlit, whereas she was normally doing her weekend homework at this time on Sunday, and that Dora's car was neither in the garage nor on the driveway. The house was dark and silent. When he switched on the light in the lounge he saw at once that most of the tapes and books had gone from the shelf unit. She had left him his blues music, the poetry books and the socialist tracts.

'The notion of my coming to your bourgeois shrine even for a night, occupying Dora's place – moving in to fill the gap in your domestic arrangements – strikes me as grotesque.'

'I don't see why. But you say Jerry is leaving?'

'Moving into his lover's flat in Kidderminster.'

'Then if you won't move in with me I shall move in with you.'

'I don't know if I want that either.'

'Only last Saturday you were telling me to speak to Dora. To choose between you.'

'It was wrong of me. I wanted to be sure of you.'

'And now you can't be sure, because the decision was not mine. Now it seems as if I'm crawling to you because Dora ditched me. Is that the problem?'

'No, it's better like this. I don't have to feel so obliged to you.'

'What's the matter with feeling obliged, Julie? It's all part of love.'

'It doesn't do to talk in terms of love.'

'I want to talk in terms of both love and marriage.'

'Please, Damien!'

'I love you and want to marry you. I humbly propose myself as the hero of your story. Marriage will signify that I intend to love you for life.'

'Sue and Tim will back your proposal. They've told me that all their friends' mothers have husbands and that it'd be a good wheeze for me to marry a rich soft touch like you.'

'A soft touch? Is that what I am?'

'You're a perfect, gentle knight, Damien. Perceptive and considerate. Physically and intellectually compatible with me. What I've yearned for and been searching for. It's a miracle that you didn't look at your watch, shrug and slope off like the other one-night stands.'

'So what's the problem?'

'Me. It isn't really me that you're loving and wanting to marry. Next month, next year, whenever I change back to the real me . . .'

'I won't love you?'

'If you do you'll be very unhappy.'

After the preposterous claims of Dora's American lawyers had foundered in the differently vicious English legal system Damien was generous over financial arrangements. He sent birthday and Christmas presents to Paulette with letters enclosed, but gave up thoughts of access in the face of Dora's intransigence and the Atlantic Ocean.

The Lindens was sold and the Brosely cottage refurbished so extensively that Julie felt uncomfortable in it. They moved to Brownhills, north of Walsall, to be nearer Damien's work and give the children a fresh start at a new school: Tim was on the point of expulsion for chronic impertinence, while Susan's report was full of phrases like 'truculent indolence' and 'disturbingly resentful'.

They married in Walsall register office, just the two of them plus a couple of witnesses they picked up on the street, then honeymooned in Venice while Susan and Tim stayed with their father. After that the children accompanied them on holidays, which they learned to take at some resort where there were plenty of pals and pursuits to render Susan and Tim less appalling. Much effort was spent withstanding and trying to modulate Julie's children – Julie with sporadic vigour, Damien with docile perseverance – and this was both a bone of contention and a bond between them.

Otherwise they settled to domesticity: brief, assured sex three or four times a week, then twice a week, in the big double bed with the pastel covers from Habitat. Julie sculpted jagged metal emblems now and Damien was writing a novel, with her encouragement, in the interstices of his postal duties. They worked at cobbling together a social life, though Julie's friends found Damien stuffy whereas Damien's colleagues thought Julie defensive. They never went to Sparrow Hall.

Julie altered, as she had foretold. She was aware of it but helpless, as at the oncreep of a mental malady. She would have been the first to admit that she had a contrary streak, like many of us, that disdained what it had and coveted what it could not reach – but she was horrified by the intensity and scope of her change of mind. Her rescue became a hijacking, her escape a trap. The scruffy cottage at Brosely represented the freedom and poetry of Bohemia compared to the expensive bungalow in Brownhills. Her relationship with Jerry seemed attractively unceremonious and unconstrained. Her promiscuity had embodied a brave concept of sex divorced from property rights and moral strictures – and an assertion of her prerogative to behave as freely and blithely as men.

She felt the same about her children as about herself. She didn't want them to be a rich man's kids incarcerated in bourgeois comfort – she wanted them to be warrior artists, free and strong.

Her attitude to Damien had never been unconditional. Most of her esteem for him arose from his love of her – and now this, too, came into question. *Why me? What does he see in me? Why does he want to be the hero of my story, or me to be the heroine of his?* Marriage and long-term commitment made the questions urgent. Julie had little conceit: the most convincing answer to the question was the most sinister. *I feed his Cophetua complex. I'm his damsel in distress.*

Seeing that Damien would be heartbroken if she left him, she could not just look at her watch, shrug and slope away. This was part of the trap she had landed in. She herself was part of the trap because even when promiscuous she was not fickle. She tried to live with her mistakes once she had made a commitment. Terry Hatchard got seven years of her adult life, Jerry Wilkinson eight, Damien the rest. In the end she both stayed with Damien and broke his heart. Her solution to their plights was a *modus vivendi* that posited freedom and candour, like the relationship she had had with Jerry. Damien had to agree, particularly as the principle was acceptable to him though not the practice. Like any treaty imposed by one party on another it was futile.

'I'm an egotistical bitch, talking about myself all the time and frantic in case I'm not the main agenda. A loony, too

– lying babbling like this in the early hours of the . . . what whatsisname calls the hour of the wolf – watching that frigging inch of light between the curtains and babbling on when any sane person would be asleep including you if it wasn't for me. My other partners wouldn't have stood for it. Terry would have called me a tiresome cow. Jerry had a spare bed organised he could skulk to if I started what he called my midnight maundering. He used to go for a piss and not come back, the twat. But I dare say it's tedious, especially if you've heard it all before. I bet you already know the script so well you could prompt me if I dry up. Are you still awake? You can't complain. It was you came breezing in like Robert Browning – or some medieval thingummy – and took up with the slag of the weekend seminar and cherished me for the very things that made the other lads a bit ginger. Flattered by my need for you. Liking the way, the nicest possible way, you felt superior. What most pisses me off about our relationship is that the things you value me for are not necessarily my best qualities but the things that differentiate me from Dora. Her strength dictating our . . . like that Strindberg stuff, but in reverse. So you should think of all this that's keeping you from your sleep as a pleasant change after . . . as a bit of exhilarating turbulence, eh, after the Dora doldrums? But I bet you do complain, to yourself, these days, more and more. Now the novelty's worn off you can see you've got a bad deal. I'm a mess that shows her knickers and farts in public. I make a litter out of everything I'm supposed to keep in order and a muck-strewn muddle of emotions and relationships. You've given up orderly Dora for this, and the child of your loins for my messed-up kids who are always saying they'd sooner go to Jerry or their shitty daddy if he'd have them. You'd maybe go too, give me up, if it wasn't for Dora. It's Dora's sodding strength that's keeping us together because she's taken your kid and put the Atlantic Ocean and the incompatibility of two legal systems between you and everything you might creep back to. Whereas I shouldn't grumble at all. I should be grateful. You've put yourself to considerable trouble and expense to rescue me from my sordid desert. You've married me and made an honest woman of me. I've fulfilled those pathetic ambitions that scrambled my brains and betrayed my political principles and took my youth from me. I've a family. I've a man I can trust to love me and try to look after me. It wouldn't have been a good idea for us to have more children and my hysterectomy has solved the contraceptive problem. I've got security, eh? Thirty-seven years old. I've found you and I've no excuse not to love you forever. You're steady and reasonable and strong. You've none of the bully's weaknesses – the need to save face, the need for power. You're a rare item in a social system that's just about guaranteed to turn men into shitheads, and you're surely my last chance of finding anybody that's remotely likely to endure my shambles. I've had a stroke of luck and found you and that's that. The happy ending. Shit. I hate the way you lie there and let me get away with all this. You even give sensible answers if I ask you questions to check if you're listening! I hate your strength and steadiness and patience and reasonableness and the sickening compassion that creeps into your voice. I hate the way whenever sex is disappointing, like it was tonight, you take the blame, even if it's my fault. Even if I'm bitchy and sneering like tonight you don't retaliate. You're so insufferably generous. So calm. When I let Tony shag me at the Christmas piss-up you were generous and calm about that too, though it was absolutely no business of yours. I hate all that. I hate marriage and love and the pretence we're soul-mates like Cathy and Heathcliff when we don't even like each other. You're what we used to call a snob when I was a kid. You pretend we've got literature and socialism in common but you don't really think, not deep down, that I know anything about literature, not having been to Oxford and all that. And you're not a socialist – can't be any sort of socialist – except when you're feeling a bit nostalgic for the rot you used to talk when you were a student. Even the lefty principles you pretend are smeared with that same sodding . . . You see it all in terms of co-operation and the application of reason. I see it in terms of busting heads. I hate . . . Most of all I hate the happy ending. That was it, was it, my life, brought to a successful conclusion? Zoom, gone. Now I can look forward to us living together happily ever after until one of us is a peevish invalid and the other a resentful nurse. We'll have grandchildren by then and take long, expensive vacations and everybody will call us the old folks. Ugh! I want to be an artist – I mean a great and famous artist, not a housewife farting about as a hobby. I want to hitch my way round the world. I want to be an infamous paramour. I want to be an engine driver and a brain surgeon. I want to be a political revolutionary. I don't mean somebody who puts a Labour Party frigging election poster in the window every so often. Are you still awake?'

Susan murmured, 'If we're this rich, can I have a motorbike?'

Julie pleaded, 'Don't, Sue! Damien's upset.'

Not long ago she would have snarled at her daughter, calling her an insensitive bitch. The new diplomacy was the result of Julie having recently abandoned her family and spent August in Almería with Darren Strange, a property developer she picked up in a Walsall pub. She found it difficult to maintain an unapologetic stance with Susan, who seemed more betrayed and outraged by the jaunt than did Damien, though she normally showed no need whatsoever for her mother and was a self-proclaimed moral anarchist.

Susan turned her insolent, seal-brown gaze directly on Julie. She was seventeen now and bigger than her mother. Her face had filled out, too, with plump cheeks bracketing her sulky lips. Since she became a Goth she had dyed her hair jet black and backcombed it till it fell about her head like a mane. She would only wear black clothes – which had been handy for the funeral – painted her lips and eyelids purple and was experimenting with ways of making her complexion more corpse-like.

'I thought he couldn't stand his family and wouldn't have anything to do with them.'

'Exactly. Now that they're dead in shocking circumstances how do you think he feels?'

Julie was clad for the funeral in a poncho that looked as if it had been made out of a grey parachute. Her hairstyle was masculine short back and sides and she was wearing flippantly large black plastic ear-rings. Her face was brown from the Mediterranean sun.

They were both talking *sotto voce* so that Damien wouldn't hear them. He looked less bulky than usual in the dark suit that seemed to separate him from Julie and Susan as if he was their lawyer or probation officer. His pale brown hair had thinned and the glasses he wore had complicated lenses, which made his eyes look little and furtive as he stared out of the french windows of the sitting room at the balustrade, the lily pond and the mermaid fountain.

'I never had any sort of relationship with my father,' he said.

He was calculating that he and Quentin had cohabited Sparrow Hall for only five years of his childhood. His memory was of a chill, remote presence that he was constantly being told not to disturb. Whenever they had met in recent years Quentin had never initiated conversation, only responding when directly questioned, then laying the conversation to rest with some banality, uttered in an eerie, bloodless voice like Nosferatu in sunlight or the hollow men on the beach of the tumid river. It seemed weird that suddenly this phantom, so late in his career, should have found flesh and sinew sufficient for the slaughter of himself and two other human beings. It was difficult to relate this abrupt splurge of blood and bullets to that wan reticence, just as it was impossible to envisage that accusing abstraction called Father ever having engendered Damien by any human process. Damien had more difficulty than most of us in contemplating the notion of his parents having sex.

Behind him, Susan said grumpily, 'Tim will be supping cocoa now and watching *Tiswas*.'

'Funerals aren't for kids,' said Julie. 'Anyway, he's got a cold.'

'Has he bollocks.'

'You needn't have come, Sue. I told you that. It's not as though it's our family.'

'No, but you wouldn't let me stop at home, would you?'

'Not on your own after last time, no way.'

'Meaning what?' Susan's baleful glare, together with her makeup, made her look very wicked. 'You're a fine one to fucking talk!'

Julie gazed levelly at her daughter. 'You could have gone with Tim and stayed with your father for a few days,' she said quietly.

'Bloody Terry!' Susan narrowed her eyes into slits of detestation. 'He's always saying us Goths are sick and Becky don't allow smoking in the house. I'd sooner go to a funeral than stay there. Did you ever see such a bunch of stuck-up zombies?'

During the weeks awaiting the inquest somebody had removed the rug and suite covers that had been stained by tragedy, and the smashed television where a bullet had lodged after passing through Desmond Frobisher. Somebody else – Janet Otterburn? – had fitted fresh suite covers of dark green velvet to match the curtains, but the varnished pine floorboards were still bare.

Julie opened a cabinet, discovered half a dozen bottles of gin, and closed it again. 'Becky's not so bad.'

'I'm not talking about Becky. I'm talking about that lot at the funeral.'

Julie permitted herself an unfunereal grin. 'Some of them weren't best suited when there was no food on offer, eh, Damien?'

Damien did not respond. He was deciding that if he had an Oedipus complex it was directed at Desmond, who had always been at Sparrow Hall and who, in contrast to his brother, had skipped and twitched, blustered and pestered with cantankerous life. It was Desmond who had terrorised Damien with his wrath and mirth, beaten the lad at cribbage, draughts, cricket, tennis and scoffed and gloated. It was Desmond who had mortified Damien by appearing with Marjorie – just once – on Founder's Day at Belvedere, and clowning and capering like an obscene little goat on the chantry lawn in full view of half the school while the notices clearly said, 'Keep Off the Grass.' It had been easy enough to imagine Uncle Desmond making the two-backed beast with Marjorie.

Remorse and self-pity, fury and chagrin made it impossible for Damien to think about his mother at all. It did not help to tell himself that, compared with some, his had been a tranquil and privileged childhood. Still looking out of the window, he said, 'I don't want to be a millionaire.'

Julie said, 'Don't worry, when Dora's finished with you, you won't be.'

He turned and was surprised to find that he and Julie were alone. 'I've hated Sparrow Hall and been ashamed of it for years.'

She came over and stood next to him at the windows. She was trying to remember the television series it all reminded her of – a Victorian soap that had included a fiddle-de-dee heroine who went for risky boat trips with a rotter on the park lake. Julie had always responded to the allure of big old houses – country manors with wrought-iron gates, little French châteaux with their steep slate roofs peeping through trees. Wenlock Hall in Shropshire, where she had gone on weekend courses in search of adventure, had always cast its spell on her as she went up the driveway – a sense of anticipation, arrival in a world where the natural laws might be more conducive to gladness. Sparrow Hall was smaller, of course, and dingier, yet seemed to be even more urgently promising and daring her as it deprecated its recent bloody melodrama with autumn morning sunshine. And here the distant hills implored with dark gorse and vivid bracken.

'I'd absolutely no idea about this. It's fantastic! It's like a mansion at the beginning of a romantic novel.'

'At the end of a lamentable history,' Damien said grimly. 'Selling it will be a sod, especially after what's happened. Maybe it will make an old folks' home, or a hotel.'

'It mustn't be sold!' There was petulance in her cry, as if she was already working herself into the role of spoiled manor lady. 'I want to live here.'

'It's out of the question, Julie. Especially after . . .'

'Lots of people have died, in all sorts of agony, in every old house. I don't mean live here with ghosts and cobwebs. I mean turn it into something . . . I'll start a kibbutz here. Practical socialism, half a dozen families, or . . . like we've talked about. It's perfect for it.'

'Perfect?' He stared bemused at the panelling, the dark green velvet hangings, the heavy furniture. 'I thought you said you wanted to see the world.'

Damien's retirement from the Civil Service was fixed for Christmas and they were booked for a four-month world tour in the new year – or had been before she absconded to Spain with Darren Strange. It was the first time either of them had mentioned it since her return.

'I don't want to spend the rest of my frigging life seeing the world. I want this, too. A commune on Trotskyite principles where people are able to free themselves from the profit motive and develop other aspects of their natures – the arts, for instance.'

She lifted her hands and spread her fingers as though she was releasing a bird, a characteristic gesture of hers when she was expounding an exciting notion. Then she scowled at the expression on his face.

He was chilled by the callous impudence of her proposal – her lack of concern at his ghastly bereavement and lack of compunction after her recent enforcement of the *modus vivendi* he loathed.

'Socialism subsidised by a millionaire?' he sneered.

She narrowed her eyes. 'You can make it sound stupid and self-deluding, but at least it'd be a start.'

'A start at what? Socialism is about changing the world. Not about giving up responsibilities and crashing out in a sponsored egalitarian paradise.'

Now her face was sullen, all the enthusiasm gone. She detested his suave, scoffing voice, his Oxbridge fluency. 'What's bothering you? You just said you don't want the money or the Hall. So give them me and bugger off. You don't have to live here. We're finished in any case.'

She turned towards the door and he saw that it was over. She was walking out of his life, his awful velvet room full of ghosts, and this time on terms that would prohibit her return for ever. It was a sundering that he had been rehearsing for weeks while she was in Almería. When he had not been in a panic in case she never returned to him he had been steeling himself, in case she did, to break their contract, satisfy what was left of his pride and bid the bitch adieu. But now that it was happening the circumstances made it unbearable. The script was wrong, not allowing him any of the magnanimous and vindictive lines he had composed. The setting, amid the cosiness and carnage of his history, was grotesque.

He called after her commandingly, 'Don't just walk away and end everything, Julie! If what I say is wrong, argue with me!'

To his relief she came to a standstill then turned slowly and spoke calmly. 'You're better at debating than me. I just thought that there was a chance to do something here, instead of holding a frigging middle-school debating society. Turn Sparrow Hall and all our shitty past into something brave and splendid.'

'Maybe there is,' he said, as though he was examining her scheme even as he spoke. Then, ignominiously, he said, 'Yes, of course there is. I'm . . . not thinking straight, just now . . .

here . . . And you know me, I like to argue a thing through, play the devil's advocate if necessary. I'm sure it's a great idea.'

She shook her head, startled by his prompt and blatant collapse. 'No, you're not. You're surrendering and indulging me, because you're so shit scared of losing me for good.'

For a moment it seemed to both of them that she had said too much. Then, yet again, he abased himself and relinquished retaliation. 'Is that so bad, Julie?'

She looked away from him abruptly, as though she had spotted something on the parquet under the sideboard. She gazed at whatever it was for some time. When she lifted her eyes towards him again they were rimmed with red as if they ached to weep. 'It's terrible.'

'A lot of the work will be done while we're abroad, but the architect will supervise. Upstairs there are to be five self-contained suites along the lines of holiday flats, each with a living room, one or more bedrooms and a bathroom/toilet but no cooking facilities. The ground floor and some of the first floor will contain communal facilities – a kitchen and dining room, an art studio, a lounge, a library and so forth.'

'What are you planning to do with her kids while you're travelling the world?'

'Susan's already in digs in Sheffield – she's at the art school there. We've found a progressive private school that, for a fat fee, is prepared to humour Tim.'

Though he had surprised Damien by asking a pertinent question Ben Stott was not listening to the answer but writing with a biro in a notebook he held propped on his lap. As soon as long hair was fashionable he had shaved the flowing ginger locks and beard that at Oxford had served the dual purpose of seeming *outré* and concealing the ravages of his teenage acne. The rest of his studied ensemble these days was bovver boots, jeans and a brown leather bomber jacket – so that he looked an incongruous companion for a bespectacled nerd in a turtle-neck sweater.

'My handwriting is becoming legible,' he observed. 'I must be pissed.'

It was Saturday lunch-time in the Golden Lion, Southport; most of the warped elmwood stools and wrought-iron tables were occupied by people who had shed their wet waterproofs and were eating salmon and cucumber sandwiches. Ben had his usual seat in the corner next to the bar, with Damien alongside. It meant that Ben could stretch his legs while Damien was cooped behind a table – and that Ben had to reach across to the ashtray on Damien's table with his Gauloises – and that Ben's feet got in the way of customers at the bar.

Ben Stott spent almost every evening in a pub and also drank at lunch-times whenever possible. There was a pattern to his patronage of a pub. For months he would sit alone writing verse and react gruffly to conversational overtures. But eventually the loner poet would be chatting with staff and customers, playing darts and pool and performing in quiz teams. This stage did not last long before his insolent temper gave rise to ugly scenes, or he began to borrow money off fellow drinkers and cash bad cheques behind the bar. He broke his habits for a couple of months when he married Sonia in 1975, then told her that he couldn't write at home – his muse was used to bars. She was an ex-pupil of his and at that time disposed to admire what she didn't understand. It took her a while to realise that he didn't restrict his consumption to 'two or three slowly sipped pints' – and even longer to start wondering whether Bacchus and not Apollo was Ben's true god.

'It's a compromise with Julie's original idea. She doesn't believe that the family unit can co-exist with real socialism, and wanted the upper floors of the Hall dividing into sleeping cubicles for the adults and a dormitory for the children.'

'Do you mind?' said Ben loudly, to somebody who had just trodden on his provocatively out-thrust foot. He had an ornate code of manners that was really a form of antagonism, as manners often are. He would hold a door open ceremoniously, but if the recipients of his courtesy did not respond promptly and appreciatively they got the door slammed in their face at the last moment. When he went to the pub toilet he liked to leave his notebook face down on his seat, turned to a special page that said, 'Fuck off, nosy.'

'She even wanted communal wardrobes – as little personal property as possible – but I thought it sounded too monastic and forbidding at the outset, though we can move towards such developments later if it is the will of the community.'

Ben passed the red notebook to Damien, scowling at him as he did so. It was Ben who had always laid down the terms for their encounters: where they sat, what colours of pens they used, the rules of the game and the topics of incidental conversation. Now Damien was propounding politics, which Ben scorned, with a persistence that was detracting from the customary agenda of drinking, writing poetry and talking about Ben.

After leaving Oxford they had written copiously to each other, mostly poems and critiques. They hadn't a lot in common and didn't like each other much but were differently lonely, and by providing an audience they were necessary to each other. In 1964, when Damien was in Camden and Ben in Lewisham, they met on Tuesday nights in the Nellie Dean on Carlyle Street, Soho, where they resumed the game of writing alternate lines of verse in a notebook with which they had amused themselves once or twice at Oxford. Ben, always on the lookout for grist for his mill, used the hybrids (he called them, typically, Tuesday welds) as a basis for poems of his own. After this, when they were living in different regions of the country, they wrote to each other about four times a year and met about as often: Damien making weekend visits to Ben, who never had a car or enough money to travel, or a wife like Dora to inhibit things. Ben's marriage to Sonia (at which Damien was taciturn best man and Ben and Dora met at last, to their mutual disgust) and the births of Netta and Kimberley did not interfere with these visits, which Ben would announce very solemnly to Sonia, as if they were crucial and arduous poetry seminars rather than self-indulgent piss-ups. He used to borrow money from her housekeeping on the grounds that Damien was a heavy drinker.

'Julie thinks we should draw up an official constitution in detail and present it as not negotiable to those who apply to join the commune. I rather incline to the view that the members of the commune should be consulted about the constitution. It looks as if this, too, will end in a compromise – a manifesto to put before applicants, with a pledge to renegotiate its practicalities in the light of experience and in accordance with the wishes of the community.'

Taking the notebook from the table and inspecting Damien's last contribution, Ben said, not for the first time, 'When are you going to learn to scan by stress and stanza like a serious poet, instead of by line and syllable like Frost and Betjeman?'

Damien acknowledged the criticism with a shrug. 'I want to advertise in *Time Out* and the *Times Literary Supplement* as a cultural community in the widest sense, everything from haiku to heavy metal. Julie thinks we have no hope of success unless everybody is united by socialist convictions – and wants to advertise Sparrow Hall exclusively in the *Socialist Worker* and the *Militant*.'

Ben took a swig of his beer and wiped his chin. He then slowly closed the notebook and put it on the table, dropping the biro, plop, on top of it. Just as slowly he swivelled a patient, weary face towards Damien before saying, 'Artistic community is an oxymoron, so your idea is crap. Julie's plan for a socialist island in a capitalist sea is even stupider. As it seems we must exhaust this topic before we can write poetry or discuss something interesting, I'll deal with your last point first, about the advertising. Wherever you advertise it will attract shitheads. You'll get involved in long telephone conversations with folk who want to sodomise you or ghost-write your biography or sell you a Doberman. Your best plan is to approach people in the street or pick them at random from the telephone directory. At least that way they won't be choosing you.'

Ben took time out from his diatribe to scrutinise a blonde in a short skirt who was perched on a high bar-stool, sneering at her expanse of thigh, then dragging his attention away from her with a chuckle of disgust. He disparaged women, finding some physical or behavioural flaw, rejecting them before they had the option of rejecting him, with a few exceptions: Simonetta Vespucci, Jeanne Moreau. His pantheon of acceptable males was as esoterically and sparsely populated – Crivelli, Thelonious Monk – but their physical appearance was of no importance to him.

'Another thing that needs saying is that it's pathetic how you let women dictate your lifestyle. You have the makings of a poet and should give that absolute priority. Dora imprisoned you in a prosaic, cushy hell and a job for which you had neither liking nor talent. But apparently you learned nothing. This Julie is developing into an even bigger threat to your creative resources.'

He often referred to her as 'this Julie', with a disapproving smirk, though he had never met her, having refused to visit the new Frobisher ménage. ('It is our tradition that *you* visit *me*.')

Damien was glad that he had not broached with Ben the real problem that all this palaver about Sparrow Hall was camouflaging. He had only come to see Ben, at short notice, because Julie was away for the weekend.

'I'm going to let Phil Froggatt shag me,' she had blurted, compelled to be brusque. Her agreement with Damien, based on both logic and principle, made it unnecessary for her to say anything. But she suspected him, justly, of having reservations, wanting not universal love but to be loved alone. Watching his face for evidence of apostasy, she was wounded and offended by what she saw. 'What's the matter? Does his lordship still yearn for the old male monopoly, his property rights, an exclusive concubine?'

He was going to say, 'It isn't a question of rights. I wouldn't want to share a toothbrush with Phil Froggatt, or a condom.' But instead he said, in a tone that had seemed to him abjectly appeasing, 'There's no need to be so brutal, Julie. I agree to all your terms but I need time to adjust. A bit of emotional leeway.'

Her right hand made the bird-releasing gesture, which on this occasion made her look like an attorney who has cracked a hostile witness. 'Typical! That's like a wife-beater saying, "Let me break the habit gradually . . . dwindle it down to a kick or two."'

Ben put a full pint glass of beer on Damien's table next to the almost empty glass that had been standing there untouched for some time. 'I'm skint again, so you'll have to lend me another tenner,' he announced, before resuming both his hectoring tone and the thread of his discourse.

'Your commune is going to be a complete shambles so you might as well settle for deriving entertainment from it. Ensure that all the women are sexually attractive and all the men physically weaker than yourself. On no account admit anybody with serious socialist principles, or their own ideas. Also ban all ethnic minorities and proles, because they will turn out to be lazy, drunken and stroppy.'

Ben paused to quaff about a third of his beer. Towards closing time his rate of consumption increased in proportion to his eloquence.

'What I propose is that I myself join your commune as resident poet and drunkard. I'm better at both those chores than you – and administration and contention won't leave you the time and energy for either. I admit I'm not on the face of it good kibbutz material – my headmaster said recently, I'm proud to say, "He is guaranteed to turn any staff-room into hell" – but you could use my strengths. You're going to need somebody to be obnoxious on your behalf and sort out the shitheads. I'd enjoy doing that.'

4

JULIE 1983-84

Julie did not enjoy her world tour. Most of it was as seen countless times on television more conveniently. What was fresh was distressing, marred by the grisly menace of humanity abusing itself and the planet. In Bombay beggars waved glistening stumps and almost naked little girls fluttered their eyelashes at tourists. In Guatemala a man was beating a tethered, bellowing donkey calmly, pointlessly, with a heavy stick that made a sound like a spade slapping wet earth. In Timbuktu all the heavy work was done by circumcised women with their heads in sacks.

And travelling was a hassle. Ships were lurching jails of swallowed vomit. Aeroplanes were full of geriatric drunks telling their stories in unrelenting detail. Ogres farted and ate live mice beyond the thin partitions between sleeping compartments on transcontinental trains. The car they hired in America was better, but it was difficult to either eat or talk in restaurants because of the interruptions of staff making sure you were having a good time. Beer cans and shit-caked paper littered the Inca Trail to Macchu Picchu, where her shoes gave her blisters and the gradients vertigo.

Travel hindered activities she valued or found necessary. Reading and writing while in any moving vehicle made her feel sick. Sculpture was of course out of the question. She languished guiltily for the children she neglected and resented when they were in her care. She managed three sexual adventures: an hour in a hotel in Hyderabad with a blue-haired Norwegian who claimed to be a rock musician; an abrupt and disconcertingly brutal encounter with a macho in an alley behind a Oaxaca bar; more seriously, a drunken awakening similar to that which had launched her with Damien, except that this time she woke first, next to a fat, snoring American in Sienna when she was supposed to be in Florence.

She had carelessly accepted the itinerary arranged by Damien with Magic Carpet Tours to occupy and entertain her: a complex of transport deadlines and local tour schedules that promoted chastity and sobriety. It also limited her to Damien's company, apart from brief encounters with strangers. Four months is a long time for a second honeymoon between a couple in a state of truce about their obligations and prerogatives. Damien got on Julie's nerves: the bleat of his posh voice, his fussiness, his diffidence, the gumpy, open-necked, short-sleeved shirts he liked to wear. She disliked the way he tried to raise her morale or suffer her disaffection by flinging himself into tourism: underlining great slabs of guidebook text with a fine-point felt-tip, listening avidly to the spiel of guides, taking photographs with the expensive camera he had bought for Julie. What she disliked most was that he was doing it for her sake, against all his own inclinations.

If Damien had hopes that the 'Four Continents Tour' would either drive Julie's new project from her mind or exhaust her enough to postpone it, he was disappointed. Even while their plane was circling to land at Heathrow she was composing the advertisements that were to produce candidates for the Sparrow Hall Commune.

Julie had vetoed Ben Stott's offer to join the commune. From Damien's reports of Ben she had formed an impression of an arrogant male chauvinist and an intellectual snob. This was not the basis for her rejection, or the reason she advanced to Damien, but it certainly helped her to have no compunction. 'The idea is, we agreed, didn't we, to have a social and cultural mix? Two bloody Oxford poets banjos that principle at the outset.' She went on to point out that she had a number of friends and acquaintances who were disqualified on the same grounds. Damien, as usual, did not resist Julie's verdict. He was not sure that he himself wanted Ben at Sparrow Hall, either as a member of the commune or as an observer of the role Damien was going to play. Furthermore, Damien suspected that when Ben had volunteered himself (and family) for the commune he had been tipsily facetious.

LIVE IN HARMONY WITH YOURSELF AND OTHERS AT
THE SPARROW HALL COMMUNE

Share your resources, skills and needs on socialist principles amid the
beauty of the North Yorks Moors. Families, couples and
individuals welcome. Mature and serious applicants only.
Telephone 0715 537 or write PO Box 10, Pickering, York YO6 6TE.

In an ancestral home in the village of Thornham in the North
Yorkshire Moors a rather special social experiment is proposed. Accommodation will be provided; individuals or families will contribute to the
communal economy according to their means. If you are sympathetic to such
a project and feel you have something to offer, telephone 0715 537 or write
PO Box 10, Pickering, York YO6 6TE for application forms
and/or further information.

One or other advert appeared in a wide range of periodicals, national newspapers and evening papers of conurbations. A shortlist of ten was to be drawn up from returned application forms. The selection process would then move on to interviews – Damien and Julie travelling the country for the purpose – in order to reduce the ten applicants or applicant groups to fit the five suites in the Hall. Suitable applicants would be invited to visit the Hall, view the facilities and discuss final arrangements.

A lot of the pre-planning was obviated – the question of selection made as irrelevant as the rejection of Ben and Sonia Stott came to seem a bit hasty – by the utterly disappointing response. Repetition and variation of the advertisements over a period of two months brought only eight enquiries and four completed application forms.

In 1983 socialism was in retreat: Margaret Thatcher retained power triumphantly in the June election. All the same, the lack of interest in Julie's project was surprising. Where were all the socialists, the hippies, the peaceniks of the sixties and early seventies? Had they all been put off by the stern tone of the adverts, which Julie had intended to discourage scroungers and layabouts? Or were they all now dubbing mixers, business consultants, tax collectors living in semi-detacheds, reverting to their youth now and then at concerts and festivals?

Four couples. Three married. Two with children.

'We bought this boarding-house with Bobby's army pay-off, didn't we, Bobby? Our dream nook, our Dunroamin. We've always liked Scarborough. But it's proved to be a nightmare. We've had bad luck and people have let us down, but we've also had to come to terms with the fact that we're not tradespeople. Too proud and too trusting.'

It was hard to imagine a more unlikely member of a socialist commune than Delia Pocock: a middle-class housewife in her sixties with a blue rinse, a knitted twin-set and a string of pearls. She had schooled out most of her northern accent in favour of something more prestigious. And it was already clear, even before any tea had been poured from the china teapot or a single arrowroot biscuit consumed, that her appearance was in keeping with her outlook and personality.

'Bobby has been trying hard to find work, the poor old sweetie, and I've even looked at the "situations vacant" on my own account, but we're of an age when anything appropriate . . . when it's hard to find anything at all. Mercifully, we have Bobby's army pension, and in a few years several investments will mature. What we need in the meantime is somewhere pleasant but inexpensive to live.'

These were the Pococks' private quarters in the boarding-house, where the punters had not been permitted to tread. Bob and Delia were sharing the floral sofa with a vast marmalade Persian cat. Julie and Damien were sunk into big matching armchairs. They had begun with an attempt to use prepared questions, but many of these seemed discordant and even impertinent.

'Since you're in our vicinity we've taken the liberty of visiting Thornham and having a look at Sparrow Hall – "taking a shufti", as Bobby says – from the outside without making ourselves known to you, a couple of weeks back, just prior to the sale of our car. We were surprised at the modest size of the Hall – hardly a stately home, is it? – but otherwise fell entirely in love, didn't we, Bobby?, both with your property and the quaint village.'

'I wouldn't mind doing a spot of shooting there if that could be fixed up,' Bob Pocock said suddenly. He pointed his forefinger between the velvet drapes, through the net curtains and across the greenery of Columbus Ravine to a similar terrace of tall boarding-houses with similar curtains, then waggled his thumb to simulate the hammer mechanism of a pistol. The notion of joining a commune had clearly not originated with him, a silver-tashed ex-army man with a more effortlessly pukka accent than his wife's. He was taking the loss of the boarding-house dream better than Delia, since he had never been much use there, having no practical skills apart from artillery deployment.

'And we're keen walkers, aren't we, Bobby? And having been in the boarding-house business for fifteen years – at the genteel end of the market – we are used to getting along pleasantly with a variety of people and have no reservations about our ability to adapt to your little community.'

Julie had been trying to catch Damien's eye for some time, but he was keeping his spectacles trained on Delia.

'But I must say from the outset that we wouldn't want to share our belongings and eat in a canteen like communists. We're very keen on our bit of independence and privacy, aren't we, Bobby? And it isn't as though we have any skills or resources to offer to a community. We would want a straightforward rental arrangement – but of course we can't afford to pay a lot of rent.'

Julie said brusquely, 'We have to be on our way. It's been a pleasure meeting you and very helpful. We'll be in touch.'

'What we would like is a self-sufficient suite in as secluded a part of the building as possible. We certainly would not wish to be near children – we have never had any ourselves because we decided, a long time ago, that we simply do not like them. Isn't that so, Bobby?'

The view through the next applicants' window was of council houses, privet hedges, a small boy mending a punctured bicycle tyre on a muddy lawn. Damien was drinking tea again but out of a blue and white mug. Julie had opted for coffee.

On the basis of their application form Chris and Catherine Hunter had seemed a more plausible proposition than the Pococks. They also proved, in the flesh, to be much more of a conversational double-act than the Scarborough pair, though it was Catherine who was bearing the brunt of the diplomacy.

'Like it says on our applications,' Catherine was answering Julie's redundant question with only a microscopic trace of impatience, 'Chris is now an ex-miner, on a disability pension. I haven't worked since I was having Clive.' She nodded through the window at the little boy in the garden.

Meanwhile Chris Hunter, a weedy-looking little chap, had adopted a compensatory and somewhat nerve-racking stance: arms folded and craggy face tilted aggressively as he subjected the Frobishers to fierce scrutiny. He spoke in a loud, crass, slow, unapologetic brogue, like somebody caricaturing a Yorkshireman. 'I'm a bit worried in case this Hall of yours is too lah-de-dah for my taste. You may as well know for a kick-off as Chris Hunter weren't born with a silver spoon in his gob.'

Julie laughed. 'I bloody wasn't, either.' She pointed at Damien. 'But he was!'

Her attempt at camaraderie fell flat when Chris relaxed neither his facial expression nor the ponderous, censorial tread of his voice. 'Aye, well, I weren't joking. I warn you straight, dear, if you don't like plain speaking you won't like what you hear from me, for I speak my mind.'

Julie laughed again as if he had said something witty, then returned to Catherine. 'But now you say you've got a job in Pickering?'

Catherine gave a wan, smug grin. She was a comely if faintly porcine blonde in her mid-thirties, about ten years younger than her husband. 'At the infant school.'

'Because you want to live more in the country?'

'For Chris's lungs. And we want to get into a better area before Clive starts secondary school. The schools round South Elmsall are all rough.'

Chris said, 'She wants our lad brought up a posh little smart-arse. What sort of folk are we going to rub up against in this commune, anyroad? Toffs like his lordship?' He jerked an unceremonious finger in the direction of Damien, who was reminded of Gordon, the Cowley Road Militant.

Julie said, 'We hope to have people from various walks of life.'

'That's not got a right lot to do with socialism, then,

has it? For as I've always understood socialism, it's a class struggle. The working man against the bosses. Like when the miners did Heath in '74. We'll do the same to Thatcher, an' all.'

'Chris's bark is worse than his bite,' Catherine apologised fondly.

Julie said gently, 'We don't intend the commune to be dominated by doctrinaire theories. We want it to be about practical co-operation and sharing. We do think, though, that anybody who doesn't have basic socialist principles – or egalitarian principles, whatever you like to call them – will be unsuitable for Sparrow Hall and unhappy there.'

Chris Hunter snorted. 'Don't talk to me about basic principles, dear. I've been a card-carrying member of the Labour Party all my working life as well as a militant trade-unionist. I don't hold with all that abolition of property and everything, though. That's communism. I'm a good Methodist.'

Catherine said, 'That's something that's been bothering me. Just how much sharing are we expected to do? It just isn't feasible, for example, for me to share our Mini with anybody. I shall need it to go to work and back.'

The remorseless thuds of Chris's voice drowned the last phrase of his wife's utterance. 'Co-operation is my middle name but I'm not sharing what I've worked for and earned, you can stuff that. If you abolish rightful property the only folk you'll get in your so-called commune will be scumbags who've never earned owt and don't plan to start.'

Julie said, less gently, 'Nobody will be asked to contribute unreasonably. Once the community is established everything will proceed by consent, with a democratic system of discussion and decision-taking. But I'd expect anybody who joined such a community to be in favour of some sort of communal resource and responsibility.'

'You won't flummox me with your posh words, dear. I may

not have had a lot of schooling but I'm a self-educated man and proud of it.'

'Another thing that's bothering me,' Catherine interposed, 'is cooking. I may as well tell you now I'm a rotten cook.'

She was drowned out again by her husband. 'I've read more books than you'd imagine, good educational stuff. *The Ragged-Trousered Philanthropists*, that's a good book, down to earth. And there's a lot of sense in the Bible, too, if you know where to look for it.'

It was difficult to get Tommy Johnson and Selina Wright to say anything. Their application form had been marginally less reticent. He was twenty-two and she was twenty-three. They rented a maisonette on Ballard's Lane in Finchley. He had been a promising footballer until a knee injury had aborted his career, and he was now a garage mechanic. She was a nurse in a hospital casualty unit. The only reason advanced for their interest in the commune was 'want to get out of London'.

Since they had only heard the cockney voice of Selina on the phone Julie and Damien were surprised to discover, when they reached the cramped flat in the dingy terrace opposite the Moss Hall Tavern, that Tommy and Selina were black, second-generation Jamaicans. They were each dressed in jeans and T-shirts, and equipped with short-cropped hair and a gold stud earring, but otherwise were quite different in aspect. Selina had languid, sculpted features and her long limbs seemed to be held together by high-quality elastic. Tommy was squat and shifty, with darting eyes and hunched shoulders as if he was expecting a giant blow to fall on him at any moment.

Positive discrimination kept Julie patient. Tommy could not be prevailed on to say anything other than, 'Sel can do the rapping, she's the brainbox.' When Julie ignored this to the extent of asking him a direct question he appealed wordlessly to Selina, who intervened and answered for him.

Julie asked Selina, 'Why do you want to live in a commune?'

Selina sat frowning until eventually Julie added, 'Do you know what a commune is?'

'Course I do. I'm not stupid.'

'Are you a socialist?'

Selina parted her lips and did a slow circuit of them with the pink tip of her tongue. Her eyes were fathomless pools. 'Do I have to be a socialist to live in your commune?'

'No. I'm just curious about your political views.'

'I don't have any.'

'How about Tommy?'

Tommy looked at Selina, who smiled for the first time, a radiant relaxation of the tension. 'You're joking!' she said.

'So why do you want to join us?'

'I said on the form.'

'To get out of London? Why do you want to do that?'

'Personal reasons.'

'Too personal to explain?' Julie's voice was friendly and bright, like a social worker.

Selina was wary again. She frowned, smiled without showing her teeth, then said, 'My family don't like Tommy. It's getting heavy, y'know . . .'

Damien suddenly said to Tommy, 'Do you know that Tommy Johnson is the name of a famous blues singer and guitarist?'

Tommy looked at Selina but she didn't help him with this one. Julie groaned within and tried to catch Damien's eye to get him to desist.

'Do you like the blues?' Damien asked Tommy.

Tommy looked cornered, cleared his throat twice then said carefully, 'Yeah . . .'

'I'm a great admirer of Afro-American music and particularly of the early country blues. Have you heard of Charley Patton?'

Tommy tucked his head further into the protection of his shoulders, narrowed his eyes and sucked his teeth.

Julie said, suddenly brisk, 'For a community like ours to work the members have to be prepared to offer their individual skills – or resources – for the benefit of everybody, in exchange for their own particular needs being catered for by the community. Have you thought what particular skills you and Tommy might be able to offer to the rest of us?'

Selina was silent for a long time before saying, 'Tommy can fix the lawn-mower. I can do first aid and fry banana sandwiches.'

Julie looked in vain for the light of humour in Selina's eyes before continuing resolutely, 'I ought to warn you that one or two aspects of Sparrow Hall may come as an unpleasant . . . Our commune will, hopefully, be based on political convictions, which you don't have – so you may well not feel comfortable there. Add to this the fact that Thornham will seem very quiet and remote after Finchley. The only entertainment is a pub that is mostly full of old fogies. Most crucial of all, Ryedale is a rural area where it will be very difficult for you to find a job.'

'Sounds cool,' Selina said.

Jack Norris threw back his head and laughed. Not many people can carry out that sort of manoeuvre without being thoroughly irritating, but Jack had long blond hair, a full beard and an easy, dashing manner that gave his gestures grace. The tilt of his beard revealed the strong throat that emerged from the open-necked denim shirt.

Julie said, 'You've no idea how much better you're making us feel. We were on the point of chucking the whole project.'

'We're having a kiln put in at the Hall,' Damien said to Toni. 'A Benson Craftmaster B, as you advised.'

'That's really super of you!' Toni cried, in her high, clear, expensive voice, as she distributed the dregs of the Moulin-à-Vent among the four tumblers. She wore ethnic togs, had prematurely grey hair, and bore a striking resemblance to the country and western singer, Emmylou Harris.

The fact that Toni was a studio potter had nearly disqualified the Norrises on the same grounds as the Stotts. And there were other respects in which the Norrises were not dissimilar from the Frobishers: being roughly the same age and having two teenage children. Their cottage in West Sussex, furnished with bean-bags and coir matting, was almost as scruffy and bohemian as that which Julie had shared with Jerry.

But Jack Norris was very different from Damien. Jack was the self-educated man that Chris Hunter claimed to be. Born in a Black Country slum, Jack had been a foundry worker, an electrician, a plumber, a merchant seaman, a film stunt-man, a private detective, a prison warder, a social worker, a freelance journalist, acquiring culture and strong socialist views along the way. He was enthusiastic and articulate about Sparrow Hall: it combined the excitement of yet another new venture with an acceptable political purpose, which he had not found in his several brief careers. He also wanted the Hall for Toni, whom he had encouraged to return to pottery now that her twin boys were grown.

'Another bottle, lambie?' he said to her. She obediently tripped out of the room as he turned his bright blue gaze back on Julie. 'I honestly can't see what's bothering you. The whole point of Sparrow Hall is the challenge, isn't it? The challenge to ancestral inertia, personal stereotyping, the drab norm. From what you tell me we've a fascinating crew on board! The two young Finchley blacks, for instance, sound decorative and intriguing enigmas.'

Julie grimaced. 'My theory is Tommy's done some ghastly crime and they want to disappear.'

70

Jack tutted and shook his head chidingly. 'If I didn't know you better by now, Julie, I'd say there was a smidgen of racism lurking there. Those two both hold skilled, responsible jobs. They're not tearaways. And they'll bring us a bit of youth and verve.'

'The twins are playing soccer this morning,' Toni announced, as she reappeared with the wine. It was the second time she had given this information. Just as redundantly, she added, 'As you know, they go to university in October, Gabriel to Warwick and Daniel to Exeter, which is why we feel free to face this new adventure.'

Jack threw back his head and laughed. This time Julie noticed a thin gold chain round his bronzed neck. 'The scamps will be at Sparrow Hall for the holidays, though. When they're not scaling Alps and wrestling crocodiles.'

Toni beamed at him. 'Jack's been a super dad for those boys. They were at a difficult age when we married, but he's straightened them out.'

Julie had been unaware that the twins were not Jack's children. 'You're divorced from your first husband?'

'Widowed.' Toni drooped her eyelashes in commemoration of the bereavement. Jack put a supportive hand on the nape of her neck.

Julie drank from her orange plastic tumbler. Her burning cheeks told her that she looked flushed, as soon happened when she drank alcohol. Her ugly mood of the morning had largely been dispersed by Jack. All the same, she now shook her head crossly. 'Say what you like but all the other applicants are impossible. They don't have the remotest commitment to any degree of socialism, or any intention of trying to make it work.'

'It isn't all that difficult to get folk to pull together,' said Jack. 'It needs a good example and a dash of psychology, that's all. The old soldier will toe the line and play the game. The miner sounds like the salt of the earth – the no-nonsense voice of traditional working-class dissent. If Sparrow Hall is to be worth anything it must have a place for the likes of him. Their wives sound like decent, politically cautious, well-meaning biddies who'll give us a bit of unity and stability.'

'I've tried to tell all of them how unsuitable . . . lay it on the line, but it doesn't seem to register,' said Julie. She was a bit distracted from what she was saying by the insistent, discreet, sympathetic pressure of Jack's blue gaze. He had what she usually referred to disparagingly as 'come-to-bed eyes'. 'All they seem focused on is free lodgings and whatever other perks might be going.'

Jack spread his arms in an expansive gesture. 'You've already decided you can afford to subsidise any lame ducks. But I'm confident you won't have to do that. We'll pay our whack, and I'm sure the others will. None of them sound like confidence tricksters or wastrels.'

Julie shook her head again, but less emphatically. She was just greedy for more of Jack's optimism. 'It won't be what I had in mind, though. I wanted a commune based on proper principles. "From each according to capacity, to each according to need . . ."'

Jack took her hand from the tabletop and squeezed it with gentle reassurance. 'That's what we all want, but what's the point if it's given to us? It's what we have to strive towards, create out of the material we're given. If we begin with a bunch of like-minded, card-carrying communist bohemians, what's the point and what is there left to achieve? Let's thank our lucky stars that these new chums are refreshingly different from each other and us, and challengingly unused to any sort of communal life.'

Toni said, 'And you've got the advantage of having Jack on your side – and he's skippered rockier boats than this.'

Jack retained his hold on Julie's hand while he and Toni kissed extensively, chewing at each other's lips.

The last applicants did not complete an application form. Julie returned from a trip to Hintons in Pickering to find an ancient Ford Transit blocking access to the garage at the back of Sparrow Hall. Its grey paint was oxidised and bubbling with rust; it had bald tyres and an illegible number-plate. The back doors of the vehicle hung wonkily ajar to disclose an immense black hairy dog sprawled in the interior with snout and one paw dangling over the sill.

Lifting its head at the approach of Julie's Golf, it scrabbled out of the van and lunged towards her, baying in *basso profundo*. She hastily closed her window then sat intimidated by the fangs and slobbering tongue a few inches from her face.

Her ordeal lasted only a few seconds before the dog abruptly shut its mouth, swivelled its head to peer over its shoulder then slunk off, in so far as such a monster could slink, to reoccupy the back of the van. Julie saw Damien and another man crossing the yard towards her.

It was a fellow in his early thirties, clad in a donkey jacket, jeans and a black woolly hat such as are worn by muggers and urban guerrillas. When Julie was out of the car and the three were at close quarters she saw that he had hairy ears and nostrils and a shaggy stubble round a mouth that reminded her of the snout of the dog. Greasy brown locks dangled from under the woolly cap and his complexion was ingrained with the grime that results from a long campaign rather than the whim of a day or so.

'You must not mind Michael,' he said to Julie, in an Irish voice that was gentler than the rest of his aspect.

'This is Colin – Mr Spillsbury,' Damien said blandly. 'Mr Spillsbury, this is my wife, Julie. She will answer better than I can any questions about the commune.'

'That won't be necessary, sir. You've told me all I need to know for the present. I'll phone, like I said just now, in a couple of days or thereabouts.'

He strolled to his van, causing Michael to retreat hastily into the interior, closed the back doors and fastened the handles together with a piece of wire produced from the pocket of his jacket.

'I'd think it'll do very nicely,' he said over his shoulder, then went round and climbed into the cab of the van. The battery strove, the engine turned over, the ignition failed six or seven times till the battery was almost dead, then suddenly sparked and caught. Dense yellow smoke billowed out of the exhaust. The van lurched backwards narrowly past Julie's car then swung away through the gateway into the lane.

Damien said, 'He has a wife and five children. I got the impression that they are travelling people. What's the word?'

'Tinkers.'

'No. Something beginning with D. They're weary of travelling and want to settle, he says.'

'Five kids?'

'Young children. The oldest is nine.'

'Christ. So what did you say?'

'I didn't say anything. I showed him round the Hall.'

She stared at her husband then almost writhed with irritation. There was something of a hippopotamus about him, it occurred to her, as he stood solid and stupid in the sunlit yard. Something of a mole, too, with his paw-like hands and his little eyes squinting through spectacles.

'Didn't you tell him to piss off?'

'On what grounds?'

'Are you joking?'

'No. What's the matter? Don't our socialist principles extend down to his level of society?'

Julie opened her mouth, then closed it again, gobsmacked

74

by his shaft, which had hit the mark. But as he helped her take the shopping out of the boot she said, 'Didn't it even occur to you to tell him that the Hall is full?'

'The Hall is not full, Julie,' said Damien, then departed with the larger box of groceries towards the house.

This last remark, or the tone of it, had even more effect on Julie. There was that insufferable note of compassion in his voice, which seemed to her to imply a financial, educational and even moral advantage. He had learned to guard against employing the tone, so that now it only occurred when he had something particularly serious to forgive or bad news to give her. So apprehension seized her as she followed him into the kitchen and put her box of provisions onto the table next to his.

'The Hall is full,' she insisted. 'Or it will be. Selina was categorical on the phone last night. And the deadline has passed for the Hunters changing their minds.'

'The Hall is not full. Do you want a drink?'

There he went again, with his gentle, fussy, irritating concern.

'Damien, what the frigging hell are you talking about?'

'Jack Norris rang. They're moving to Devon.'

'It's absolute bollocks that Toni is bothered about your bloody family holocaust because when I told them about it, early in our first chat, she never turned a hair, she thought it "added character and intrigue". It's just a frigging excuse that the sort of wankers make who string you along and bugger you about when they haven't the remotest intention of . . . The sort of shitheads who ring you up and tell you not on any account to sell your car to anybody else, they're on their way this minute with the money in cash in their hands – and it's the last you hear of them. Mind you, it's not surprising I let myself be conned by Jack Norris because I've been a sucker for blandishments all my life. I hated my mother because she wouldn't call me brilliant or beautiful or praise my deeds beyond their deserving. Whereas my father was partial and unconditional, telling me what I wanted to hear, and I adored him. I've always believed bullshitters. Flatterers and optimists and tender pretenders and romantic spoofs have always found it a pushover to get control of my heart and my knickers and my wallet. If I showed you my full catalogue of seducers and betrayers you'd see that most of them had nothing like Jack Norris's charisma. He even seems to have imposed on you, though I dare say you suspected all along, or even secretly nursed a squalid hope as you listened to his spiel and watched me staring into his glisteny blue eyes. Julie swallowing another line, letting her emotional mess interfere with her judgement. Easy to see through my communist manifesto and my babble about creating a politically acceptable island in a sea of capitalist crap and laying the ghosts of Sparrow Hall. That was bullshit too, you've been telling yourself, because what I really wanted was to stock the Hall with a handy supply of lefty studs to shag me and bullshit me whenever I got bored with my rich husband and rescuing hero. Because you know I'm sometimes driven by lust and loneliness you assume that any other motives are sham – silly Julie, transparent scrubber, pretending to be a rational intellectual. Even men that claim to be reconstructed find it very hard to accept that a woman can have genuine political principles, whereas a man can whore around and be an emotional disaster area without anybody thinking less of his work or his opinions. You've disbelieved in my sincerity from the start and thought my project hateful and ridiculous and sneered at it – oh, so discreetly! – while waiting for something like this to happen to put a stop to the bullshit and call my bluff. Now you can pretend to be as disappointed as I am but are secretly delighted because you think you don't have to go through with this expensive and embarrassing farce. You'll sell the Hall just as it is, with the five new suites upstairs, ready for somebody to turn it into one of those hotels that advertise in *Country Life* or the *Dalesman*. It's a pity about the sodding custom-built pottery studio with the Benson sodding Craftmaster B – Julie was looking forward to having a dabble in there with the help and guidance of her chum Toni but she'll get over it and we can go abroad, maybe to the South of France, as you secretly yearn to do, to the extent that you've let the idea slip out a couple of times. You reckon you'll feel securer about me if you have me to yourself, isolated among strangers who don't speak my lingo, like on your bloody world tour. But the bad news for all your plans is that Julie isn't ready yet to admit that everybody including you has been right about her all along. This ill-assorted bunch of self-seeking misfits may not be anybody's ideal commune but they've volunteered to live together in Sparrow Hall and I'm going to see that they do that successfully, if I have to kill them in the process. Even if socialism doesn't manage to enter into the equation, getting that circus to share the same premises and co-operate over facilities will be something to fully occupy me and no mean achievement if I pull it off. Julie the slag, the bit of stuff you picked up on a weekend beano, is going to take your gift of Sparrow Hall, this useless relic and family curse and home of grisly ghosts, and turn it into the home of a viable community.'

'Susan, are those nibbles ready?'

'I'm just putting the sticks on the little sausages.'

'Forget it. They can use their sodding fingers.'

Susan's querulous brown eyes left the salver of edibles on which she was working and turned to observe her mother. Julie was in a simple little black dress, tights, high-heeled shoes. Her hair was gathered at the crown of her head and fell behind in ringlets, a Grecian fashion that should have completed a youthful and glamorous ensemble if her tense scowl had not made her look more like Medea than Aphrodite.

Susan was in navy-blue velvet trousers and a silk blouse. Her hair was neat and glossy, just long enough to cover her ears. As if she had finally discovered how to rebel effectively against her mother she had given up her Gothic image, then given up art school in favour of a catering course at Scarborough Tech, living in digs during the week but coming home at weekends. Now she was engaged to the president of Ryedale Young Farmers and disapproved of the lefty use to which her mother and stepfather were putting the Hall, but her catering expertise was proving invaluable on this occasion. Janet Otterburn had been hired for the day and between them, under Julie's intermittent supervision, Janet and Susan had prepared the entire inaugural dinner.

The inauguration of the Sparrow Hall commune was a week later than intended because the Spillsburys had fallen foul of the police in Darlington. Their Ford Transit had been impounded and they had no means of towing the small caravan in which the seven of them lived. Colin's plan had been to sell the caravan and bring the family and their few belongings to Thornham in the Transit. Eventually Damien went to tow them in the Ford Granada and Colin Spillsbury was prevailed on to leave his disgusting van in custody and postpone selling the almost equally decrepit caravan. The Darlington police felt that honour was satisfied if the Transit was not actually on the road, and the caravan was parked in the Hall grounds for the time being. As for the rest of the commune, the Johnsons (Tommy and Selina were now wed) had only appeared the week before, but the Hunters had been there a month and the Pococks had actually been in residence since October.

Julie had a clear idea of how she intended this evening to proceed. She had discussed it with everybody beforehand – if only to ensure that they were on the premises – and had given out a typed leaflet, copies of which she had also posted here and there in the Hall:

SPARROW HALL COMMUNITY
INAUGURAL DINNER 25/2/84

Now that everybody has moved in we take great pleasure in inviting you all to the inaugural dinner which will take place on the above date. There will be drinks and an aperitif snack available from 7.30 in the Television Lounge and we hope to begin eating in the Dining Hall at 8 o'clock.

It is intended as a pleasant, informal occasion (please don't dress up for it!), though we hope to be able to discuss one or two basic arrangements and fix a date for our first Residents' Meeting.

As it will be the first chance for several of you to get to know each other, and for us to welcome you as a group to Sparrow Hall, we very much hope that everybody will be able to attend. If there are any difficulties (e.g. a baby-sitter needed for young children) please see Julie or Damien before Saturday.

The last sentence was the first official recognition of the infant Spillsbury problem. The youngest child was a babe in arms, the eldest a nine-year-old, silent, skinny lass, but the other three were preposterously filthy and hyperactive boys, aged respectively three, four and six, who in the two days since they had arrived at the Hall had swarmed and ravaged like a Tartar horde. All three were lank-haired and gremlin-visaged, snub-nosed, lipless, gap-toothed and more or less identical except in size and articulacy, the eldest being capable of letting out volleys of bloodcurdling obscenities while the youngest was unintelligible. They had slid down the banisters and tumbled down the stairs, put mud all over the ground-floor parquet and a rusty old bicycle onto the sofa in the television lounge, stolen food from the kitchen and cracked three squares of glass in the scullery window. Outdoors they had tried to set the winter grass alight, terrorised cats and stamped on frogs, pelted the neighbour's hens with rotten apples and detached a portion of the balustrade and chucked it into the lily pond. In the midst of these activities they waged ceaseless, ruthless war on each other: Brendan the eldest tormenting his brothers; Patrick bullying Brian and complaining about Brendan to his mother and sister (but never to his father), who would slap or kick Brendan if the mood took them, so that both Patrick and Brendan were wailing some of the time but Brian wailed most of it, and did not even have the consolation of retaliation by proxy since nobody could be bothered to decipher his testimonies.

Julie had already received complaints about the behaviour of the lads from both the Hunters and the Pococks but was averse to tackling Colin Spillsbury about it, having noticed the extreme wariness with which his wife, children and dog all comported themselves when he was present. She started to broach the matter with Mary Spillsbury, but such hapless horror came into Mary's foolish red face that Julie hastily retreated. In any case she did not want to abet any closing of ranks by other residents against the Spillsburys. She already felt guilty (as well as triumphant) about the stand she had taken over Michael: not only forbidding him the house but insisting he be kept chained next to the comfortable kennel she had provided at the garden end, if he was not being 'exercised or otherwise supervised'. Colin Spillsbury had bared his mossy teeth in a snarl of piratical wrath but had said nothing. Michael had so far howled throughout the night and terrified pedestrians in the lane beyond the hedge with the insane thunder of his barking and the clanking of his chain.

Julie was keen that the three little gremlins should not attend the dinner, but should be fed sausages and chips on the trestle table in the lounge then either be allowed to watch TV or put to bed. Her wish that Mary Spillsbury should be able to attend, either with or without the baby, just as she wished, was given further determination when Mary herself would only say, 'You must ask Colin.'

The idea of a baby-sitter had therefore presented itself, and Julie's first thought had been to manoeuvre Tim into the role, since he was outraged by her insistence that he attend the meal and was going to be at best a morose and curmudgeonly presence. Tim was now in the fifth form of the comprehensive in Pickering. He had spent twelve months in a private school trying to avoid ridicule by schooling out his Midlands accent, then another twelve months shedding his new posh voice and struggling to become proficient in Yorkshire dialect. This, added to the humdrum problems of adolescence (acne, social gaffes, gruesome incubi) and fortified by a growing awareness that he was a child from a broken home and entitled to a chip on his shoulder, had rendered Tim particularly truculent towards his mother at this epoch. Julie was aware that her new suggestion would be as bitterly resented as the meal itself, but was not deterred by this so much as by the consideration that Tim's problems with his own image would render him incapable of baby-sitting the Spillsbury gremlins. He would be too surly to entertain them, too proud to control them, and almost entirely irresponsible.

Susan would have been ideal: provenly strong-minded, with a long history of controlling her brother when it suited her, she had already shown herself to be the equal of the three infants on a couple of occasions. But Susan refused to have anything to do with the 'little shits', adding that she would not in fact be staying for the meal, since her fiancé Paul Drummond was calling to bear her off dining and dancing. Julie did not even protest: she still felt fairly confident of being able to bully or bribe Tim but Susan was another matter.

This defection by her daughter scuppered Julie's third plan, which had been to transfer Janet Otterburn to baby-sitting duties once the food was ready to serve. Now Janet and Julie would have to serve and clear and wash up, with whatever help they could scrounge from the gathering. Julie was even tempted to regret the scorn with which she had dismissed Damien's suggestion that they hire caterers. But Janet came up with a solution to the baby-sitting issue by recommending Sally, teenage daughter of Elaine Dobson (*née* Moorhouse, now landlady of the Apple Tree) and a baby-sitter of known experience and reliability.

Julie picked up the tray of biscuits and the tray of olives. Susan followed with the cheese cubes, silverskin onions and cocktail sausages more or less on sticks. There were already crisps and various drinks in the French style on the trestle table that had been erected in what used to be the sitting room and was now the television lounge.

The Hunters were first there, being believers in promptitude, but being also teetotal were nursing little tumblers of orange juice and looking impatient for the beginning of the proper meal. The Pococks arrived at the same time as the nibbles and congratulated themselves on this fact in a loud and jocular manner intended to break the ice. Bob awarded himself a gin and tonic while Delia had a more prudent mini-schooner of sweet sherry. Despite Julie's plea (which she herself had ignored) not to 'dress up', both Bob and Chris were togged out in suits and ties, their wives in outfits suitable for christenings. But Tommy and Selina Johnson turned up in their habitual T-shirts and jeans, their only concession to the occasion being that Tommy was for some reason wearing a black woollen hat which looked exactly like the one Colin Spillsbury had worn when Julie first met him. Colin made his appearance bare-headed for the first time in Julie's short acquaintance with him, his greasy locks caught into a pony-tail by means of an elastic band. Otherwise his clothes and grimy complexion were as usual. His wife was as usual wearing a shapeless green frock that seemed to let large areas of blotched and flabby limb escape, and, also as usual, was carrying a baby that looked like a maggot made of soiled white wool, such as might be used to impersonate a baby on stage.

Though Julie and Damien greeted them unctuously it was clear that nobody else wanted to talk to the Spillsburys, which did not seem to either surprise or discountenance Colin, who equipped himself with a glass of whisky and buttonholed Damien about a plan to keep a couple of pigs in the vegetable garden. Colin Spillsbury was the only applicant to have arrived at the Hall with a positive agenda of proposals. Meanwhile Mary's fat, frantic face turned towards Julie, who found her a glass of white wine and a chair but could not bring herself to stay and make conversation.

Bob Pocock talked to Chris Hunter and Delia to Catherine. These two couples had begun by disliking each other, the Hunters thinking the Pococks thick and snooty while the Pococks deemed Catherine pretentious and Chris bombastic and common, but since the arrival of the other members of the community they had formed a horrified alliance. Now Bob and Chris had discovered a mutual interest in the Yorkshire cricket team – an alternative to the minefield of politics where they were both aware of the unacceptability of the other's views. At first Pocock was able to exploit his greater age to dominate the discussion: 'Hedley Verity was the last great left-arm finger-spinner in the Yorkshire tradition. They've never had his like since the war. Wardle was a wrist-flipping clown.'

The gremlins were chasing each other round the sofa and under the trestle table while emitting an ear-splitting din, which their parents did not seem to notice. 'I have never seen such filthy children,' Delia said to Catherine. 'And the language they use is horrific.'

Catherine said, 'We've brought our old stove and washing-machine and Chris is installing them upstairs. There isn't really room, but we don't fancy sharing facilities with that lot.'

Delia said, 'We feel very strongly that it is up to Damien and Julie to properly equip the flats.'

'Those outhouses are full of stuff needs selling for scrap,' Colin was saying to Damien. 'Clear the space for poultry and make a few bob at the same time. I'll see to it.'

Julie dipped into the conversation *en passant*, like a practised society hostess. 'All proposals and initiatives should be aired at the Residents' Meeting,' she intoned sweetly. 'Tonight is just for friendly fun.'

Nine-year-old Clive Hunter was pretty sure he was not going to find it much fun. His dad had provisioned him with crisps and a can of Coke then breezily told him to 'play with the other kids'. Catherine had immediately said, 'I'm sure Clive won't want anything to do with them,' but had not proposed any alternative. Clive sided with his mother's opinion, but didn't get a lot of choice. The gremlins welcomed, disgusted and intimidated him. They then plagued him like wolves stalking a lame elk. Soon they were throwing peanuts at him and shouting things like, 'Fucking fattypig! Fat fuckpig!' which astounded as well as mortified him because he had rarely been teased in South Elmsall, being not nearly as fat as Blobby Smethurst.

Tommy Johnson was clearly determined not to talk to anybody. He was rocking to and fro as if in time to invisible earphones, stuffing nuts and crisps into his mouth and washing them down with a can of Red Stripe, which he had selected because Damien had seemed to expect it of him. Selina left him and took her sherry over to Mary Spillsbury.

'Is it a boy or a girl?'

Mary looked warily at the young black girl and there was a degree of hauteur in her tone as she said, 'A girl.'

'What's her name?'

'Emeline.'

'Cool. Why did you call her that?'

'It's the name of her saint because her birthday is the twenty-seventh of October. All our children bear the names of their saints.'

'Can I hold her?'

Mary looked rudely reluctant, then relented and proffered the woolly maggot.

Selina wrinkled her nose and backed off. 'Pooh! No, perhaps not!'

Bob was saying, 'I'm strongly in favour of the good old tradition that you have to be born in the county to play cricket for Yorkshire. The rest of the country could benefit from a bit more of that sort of pride.'

Bob and Chris were discovering that their negotiated topic was not without its snares and cul-de-sacs. Chris, remembering Catherine's pleas to him at the outset of the evening, had managed to hold his tongue during a speech from Bob strongly in favour of the good old tradition of amateur 'gentleman' captains. But at this last utterance of Bob's he could no longer contain himself, and launched out with, 'Happen, but I'd call it racist prejudice, not pride. There's thousands of Pakis as was born in Yorkshire can't get a sniff of decent club cricket, never mind the county team.'

'Another thing you should do is buy a decent-sized van. You can't do anything at all, in the way of trade or so forth, without a fucking van.'

Colin's domestic and informal speech was heavily peppered with expletives but he had the ability to suppress most of these according to his audience. His mind was not really on what he was saying: he had been watching Selina talk to Mary, and had almost interfered when it seemed that Selina was about to take hold of the child. Now he said to Damien, 'I didn't know there'd be niggers here.'

Damien was appalled. After a moment of equally appalling hesitation he said gently, 'Better if you don't use that word.'

'What word?'

'The word you just used.'

'What are you on about?'

'"Nigger" is an insult.' Damien's tone was appeasing, even wheedling. 'These are nice people. I'm sure you don't want to insult them.'

Colin showed his mossy teeth then hid them again. He had high hopes of Damien and decided to let him have his way. 'What do you call them, then? Blacks?'

'I think they prefer that.'

'Well, I didn't know there'd be fucking blacks about, did I?'

Meanwhile Theresa Spillsbury, hitherto invisible, had rescued Clive Hunter by beating up all her brothers, kicking and flailing at them till they were snarling and snivelling in their bolt-hole under the trestle table. Then she led Clive out of the room into the reception hall.

'I'm double-jointed,' she said, in a faint Irish voice, a whisper. 'Like a witch. See.' She held out her hands with the fingers interlaced and slowly and contortedly rotated both thumbs simultaneously in a clockwise direction. 'I bet you can't do that.'

He shook his head without attempting it. In any case his hands were occupied with Coke and crisps. She was a weird lass, thin and bony with lank brown hair that didn't cover her teapot ears. She was interesting, though, and had done him a favour, so he said, 'No, that's clever.'

'It's nothing,' she said. 'I can walk on my hands. Watch.'

She dropped her hands with total confidence onto the

parquet and floated her thin legs into the air so that her sack-like dress enshrouded her torso, revealing grubby white knickers that were almost the same colour as her grubby thighs and belly. Clive was paralysed with embarrassment. After a few demonstration paces she did a nonchalant, slow cartwheel back into a standing position. 'I'm going to join a circus when I grow up.'

'Great.'

'You can come with me if you like.'

Abashed by the leaping trust, the brave generosity of this statement, he said, 'I don't think I'd be a lot of use in a circus.'

'You'd be a grand ringmaster. Or a clown. Shall I show you some more of my tricks?'

'No,' he said politely. 'That'll be enough for now.'

Susan came out of the kitchen, untying her apron, clopped past Clive and Theresa and into the television lounge. 'Everything okay?' she called out, and everybody stopped talking at once to murmur appreciation. Even the gremlins were hushed for a moment or two. Susan would have made an effortlessly competent schoolteacher. She put her apron into Julie's hands. 'Have a good time, Mum,' she said, with a *soupçon* of malice.

'Before you go will you find out where Tim is skulking and tell the twat to get down here this minute?'

'I can't do that. Paul has just driven his passion-wagon into the ancestral yard.'

Damien said to Julie, 'Do you want me to go and find Tim?'

'No way. If you go off to find Tim, pretty soon somebody will have to find you.'

Delia said quietly to Catherine, 'The dark girl looks lovely, very poised and athletic. They're so good at running and dancing and things like that. But I just don't like the look of the boy.'

Catherine said, 'He's very rude and arrogant, like a lot of them unfortunately seem to be. Me and Chris are not prejudiced – Chris is a life-long Labour internationalist and we both have a strong Methodist missionary tradition in our families. Chris has tried to talk to him twice and been cut dead.'

'Doesn't he look just like all those muggers and rapists you see on TV? He gives me the creeps.'

'What gives me the creeps is that huge black dog of the tinkers that lives at the bottom of the garden.'

Diplomacy between Chris and Bob had finally broken down over the vexed topic of Geoffrey Boycott. Chris, who needed no alcohol to fuel his bluster, had taken to prodding Bob in the chest. 'Don't talk wet! All that crap about sportsmanship is stuff the toffs put out as they sit on their fat arses in committee rooms. What pillocks like them can never forgive Geoff Boycott – or Fred Trueman before him – is not trying to kow-tow and talk proper, and being better at cricket than all your public-school chinless wonders.'

Julie pretended to talk to Tommy but her cursory efforts deserved no better than the minimal response they got. She wanted the baby-sitter to arrive so that she could proceed with the dining arrangements. At the same time she was aware that several matters needed her attention. She didn't like it that the men were all talking to men and the women to women, she could hear the increasing rancour between Bob and Chris, and she needed to keep an ear tuned to the harangue that Colin was still giving Damien in case her husband agreed to anything undesirable. Yet she was immobilised not so much by indecision as to where next to focus her hostess faculties as by panic now that she could see her community together in one room and savour their blatant incompatibility. She was grateful when her immediate role was defined by the entry of the baby-sitter, Sally Dobson, a meek and dreamy lass.

She'll be a pushover for those bloody gremlins, Julie worried, not knowing that in a couple of minutes Colin Spillsbury was suddenly going to crack at the racket he seemed so far not to have noticed and send all his children supperless to bed with their mother to mind them.

As Julie moved away from Tommy Selina rejoined him. 'Okay, sugar?' She reached out to remove the woolly hat, but desisted when he clamped a hand onto it and scowled at her. Instead she lightly stroked her fingertips down his cheek. She was confident enough of Tommy not to take his ill-humour personally. They had been sweethearts since they were at school together.

She had wanted to get him out of London, away from the bars and raves and bad company that lured the recklessness of a twenty-two-year-old whose life's triumphs and disasters seemed behind him. Now she felt guilty. For her he had lopped his rasta locks, given up dope and worked in her uncle's garage. Now he was here at her insistence, sundered from his black buddies, his dens and diversions.

'There's a lot of booze here, eh?' she said. 'We'll get pissed.'

He took a sip of Red Stripe but did not return her grin. 'This is a shit of a place, Sel.' He turned his head in glowering scrutiny of the room and its occupants. 'The other side of the fucking moon.'

5

SPARROW HALL 1984–85

FIRST GENERAL MEETING OF THE
SPARROW HALL COMMUNITY, 18/3/84

Agenda: (i) election of officers (ii) acceptance of Sparrow Hall Constitution (see below) (iii) any other business.

SPARROW HALL COMMUNITY CONSTITUTION 18/3/84

1. FINANCE

(i) The owners of the Hall have opened a bank account with a deposit of £20,000. This account is to be known as the 'community fund'.

(ii) Each adult person or family unit will pay into the community fund either ten per cent of their net annual income (after tax) or £5,000 per annum, whichever sum is smaller.

(iii) The Community Fund will supply provisions for breakfast, an evening meal and snacks during the course of the day if required.

(iv) The money remaining in the community fund can be used to finance proposals that are agreed by the community.

(v) All charges such as rates, water, electricity and structural repairs will be borne by the owners without resource to the community fund.

2. PROPERTY

(i) Residents will keep their private belongings in their suites on the upper floors. All the contents of the ground floor and

library are common property and must be left available for everyone or only temporarily removed by agreement with the 'chores monitor' (see below).

(ii) Residents can park private transport in the Hall grounds at their own risk. Volkswagen Golf MLD 283T is insured for any qualified and licensed driver and at the disposal of the community.

3. DIVISION OF LABOUR

(i) Residents will be responsible for the upkeep, decoration and cleaning of their own apartments.

(ii) The following permanent officers should be annually elected by the community:

   (a) a chairperson to call General Meetings and supervise proper democratic procedures.

   (b) a secretary to keep records of all meetings and decisions.

   (c) a treasurer to supervise the community fund, collect contributions and disburse payments.

   (d) a cook/caterer to provide and prepare food as outlined in 1 (iii) above, on weekdays only.

   (e) a 'technical monitor' to take responsibility for electrical equipment, plumbing faults, vehicle maintenance, &c.

   (f) a 'chores monitor' to devise and draw up rotas and take responsibility for incidental chores (see below).

(iii) There are incidental chores that need to be done by everybody on a rota basis:

   (a) maintaining the kitchen in good condition and helping the cook.

   (b) cooking at weekends.

   (c) tidying and cleaning the communal part of the Hall as necessary.

4. DECISION-MAKING

(i) There will be a General Meeting at least once a month,

formally conducted and documented.
(ii) All adults (over 16) will have a vote, except that each family unit will be restricted to 2 votes.
(iii) Except in the election of officers (when a simple majority will do) a two-thirds majority of the adult community (i.e. 7 votes out of 10) is needed to implement any proposal.
(iv) Proxy voting is not permitted; 7 is therefore the minimum number of members to constitute a quorum at a General Meeting.

Eight members of the adult community were present, the absentees being Tommy, Mary, Susan and Tim. Julie apologised for the absence of Susan and Tim, pointing out that they had been deliberately given no vote in 4 (ii) of the constitution, so as not to give the Frobisher family more votes than the rest, but it was possible that one or both of them would attend future meetings, and be entitled to vote, if one or both of their parents was absent. Selina did not comment about where Tommy was or why he was absent. Colin said that Mary 'had other things to do'.

Delia raised the question of smoking in the communal area of the Hall, including the library where the meeting was being held. Julie said that there were a number of rules for living together which the community might like to consider in due course but that the next item should be the election of officers. She explained that only five officers were to be elected. She had already found out that no resident wished to cook permanently for the commune, so had agreed employment terms with Janet Otterburn, on a four-hour-day, twenty-hour-week basis, starting the following Monday, 26/3/84, provided that this was agreed by the general meeting now in session. Chris interrupted to suggest that since that left five officers to appoint, and since there were five couples or family groups resident in the Hall, it would be fairest if each group provided one officer, rather than any group taking two posts and gaining 'an unjust dominance'. There was a delay while the point he was making was further explained to members, then further delay for discussion, because Julie and Damien felt that no such rules should be laid down before the officers had been appointed and the machinery for decision-making approved. But after a few minutes Julie suddenly withdrew her objection and said that what Chris was suggesting was fair enough.

(i) Election of officers

Julie proposed Bob for chairperson, on the grounds that his army career had made him used to responsibility. Bob thanked her for her compliment, was elected unopposed and took his place at the head of the table. Chris then suggested Catherine for secretary, because she knew shorthand. She protested that her shorthand course had only been a hobby, but was persuaded not to refuse and elected unopposed. Colin then proposed himself as treasurer. Chris argued that it was out of order to propose oneself, but Damien pointed out that there were no rules as yet and that it was helpful if people volunteered rather than waiting to be proposed. He went on to propose Julie for treasurer, which caused further uncertainty about procedure. Damien suggested that the two candidates for the post should step outside the library while the vote was taken, but Chris dismissed that as 'flummery', saying that he preferred the candidates to see the vote 'open and above board', and that he was sure none present were ashamed of their opinions. Damien withdrew his suggestion and Julie was elected by five votes to nil, the chairman abstaining as he said was proper except in the case of deadlock. It was decided after discussion that the chairman should vote like anybody else, whereupon the vote was taken again and Julie was elected by six votes to nil. Colin then proposed himself as technical monitor. The treasurer proposed Tommy. Colin argued that nobody who was not actually at the meeting could be proposed, and Selina said that Tommy was very unlikely to accept the appointment. The treasurer then proposed Chris, but Chris pointed out that by the rule he himself had suggested he was not eligible because his wife was already an officer. Colin was elected unopposed. That left Selina, the last eligible candidate, to accept the last available post, of chores monitor, which she did reluctantly.

(ii) Acceptance of the Constitution

Delia again raised the issue of smoking but both the treasurer and chairman felt that the making of rules should wait until the constitution had been accepted. Delia then said that she and the chairman were unhappy about the financial arrangements for the provision of meals. They thought that the owners should install cooking units in all the suites, such as she understood that Chris and the secretary were installing at their own expense, so that all couples and family groups would have a choice as to whether or not they used the communal facilities. The treasurer said that the financial arrangements had been agreed by everybody before the establishment of the community, adding that what the Hunters did in their own suite at their own expense was their own business but cooking and eating together were 'necessary for the validity of the community' and the owners of the Hall had certainly no intention of equipping all the suites with cooking facilities. Damien suggested that with Janet Otterburn cooking an evening meal for everyone and taking over the provision of materials for breakfast, &c., some of the problems that had arisen 'in the present *ad hoc* and ill-defined situation' would hopefully disappear. Delia was not satisfied by this and formally proposed that cooking facilities for the individual suites should be provided out of the community fund. Her motion was seconded by the chairman and the ensuing vote split 4–3 in her favour, the technical monitor abstaining and the chores monitor siding with Damien and the treasurer. The motion was therefore defeated, which gave rise to Chris questioning the seven votes rule, which he said was 'a scheme to prevent anybody getting a new idea accepted or otherwise challenging the existing constitution'. The treasurer defended the rule as 'a safeguard against ill-considered and divisive measures being adopted', but Chris proposed that a simple majority of those present should be enough to adopt a proposal. This was also defeated, the voting splitting exactly as for the previous motion. Damien then suggested the compromise that six votes should be enough to pass a proposal at any meeting where there were fewer than eight people. This was accepted by seven votes to zero, the technical monitor abstaining. The last mentioned admitted that he had been paying little attention to recent proceedings and did not understand the intricacies of the system. He then launched his own attack on the voting system, on the grounds that seven human beings should be more heavily represented than two, therefore he and his wife should have more voting power than, for example, the chores monitor and her husband. Meeting with no support for this idea, he changed his approach by stating that his wife had other things to do than attend meetings, was too stupid to understand what was going on and would vote as he told her, so that he should have two votes at all times. After some discussion as to what was meant by a 'proxy vote' he received unexpected support from Delia, who said that after the absurd rejection of her own proposal she had no interest in attending future meetings, would be very happy to entrust her vote to her husband, and did not see why she should not be allowed to do so. Chris, on the other hand, declared that he hoped that nobody had the idea that because his wife necessarily had to be at meetings as secretary they were going to be spared his presence and contributions. He went on to say that in his opinion anybody who let somebody else represent them when they were entitled to speak for themselves did not deserve a vote. The technical monitor was instructed to put his motion, which was seconded by the chairman and defeated by five votes to three. The treasurer then observed that the meeting was running out of time and proposed 'that the constitution be conditionally adopted, with any further proposals for amendment left for future meetings'. This proposal was also defeated by five votes to three. The treasurer pointed out forcibly that the main terms of the constitution had been seen and agreed by everybody when they were applying to join the community, and that unless it was accepted as a basis for progress no votes either for or against anything were valid, no financial arrangements could stand, nobody except the owners had any entitlement to accommodation and the community would have to be disbanded. Chris wanted to know why, in that case, were they wasting their time in a pretence of consultation? Damien explained that while it was possible to change the constitution – with a two-thirds majority, which had been the point of the previous debates and votes – it was not possible to reject it without refusing the entire concept of Sparrow Hall. People were, of course, entitled to do this, 'but should in fairness make arrangements to leave the premises as soon as possible'. The treasurer put the proposal again and hands slowly rose until seven were in favour. Chris abstained and said that he wanted his protest registered against 'an utterly undemocratic carrying on'.

(iii) Other business

(a) Delia raised the matter of smoking, proposing a ban throughout the communal area of the Hall. This was passed by seven votes to one. The technical monitor immediately left the meeting.

(b) The treasurer proposed that a list of rules should be drawn up, relating to conduct in the Hall and the use of facilities, to be considered and voted on at the next meeting. Delia and the chairman volunteered to provide this list.

(c) The secretary said that rules and constitutions were all very well, but what was to be done with residents who continued to refuse to co-operate and showed no consideration for others? Damien explained, with the chairman's permission, that so long as no criminal offence was involved it was a matter for the community to deal with and was provided for in the constitution. Offending individuals or groups could be expelled from the community and the Hall if seven people voted in favour of that action at a General Meeting (or six if there were less than eight present at the meeting).

(d) Other matters referred back to arrangements outlined in the constitution. Chris thought that those who chose not to have the evening meal should receive some financial adjustment to their rent, but did not call for a vote since it was clear that the proposal would not receive six votes on this occasion. The treasurer requested that those who were not going to have the evening meal, either on a regular basis or on any particular occasion, should inform the cook in good time.

(e) Several people were worried about the weekend cooking chore. Damien thought that any problems could be sorted out individuals swapping chores (and hopelessly poor cooks could always provide takeaway food), but the treasurer held that this would make the task of the chores monitor very difficult unless she was consulted well in advance. It was proposed by the chairman that couples or family groups should feature on the chores rota, rather than individuals. This was passed unanimously.

(f) The next meeting was fixed for Sunday, 8 April, at 3.30 p.m.

Damien went to see how Julie was doing, as he needed to do every so often. What he saw as the ghastly débâcle of her commune project was filling him with concern for her morale.

She was running her school in the pottery where the wheel and kiln had so far never been used. The room was set out like a nursery school with games, puzzles, paints, play-dough, musical instruments, a table full of books, a sandpit and a tub of Lego.

Julie was trying to read a story to Brian, who was on her lap. Brian hated human contact almost as much as he hated having to listen to stuff. He was wriggling like live bait and had thrust most of a forefinger up a nostril. When she saw Damien Julie gave up the story and handed Brian a drum and drumstick. He at once began to beat the drum compulsively, which interfered with their conversation but kept him from direr mischief.

'You've not much help,' Damien said reprovingly. There was only Mary there, whom he knew Julie regarded as little use ('She can just about do the four-piece jigsaws'). Yet only that morning Julie had told him that she didn't need help from him. He assumed it was from pride, because she knew he was sceptical of her projects and enthusiasms. He had been happy enough to accept it, having work of his own that he wanted to do – then he had become anxious about how she was coping.

'I can manage if I'm not interrupted all the time,' she now snapped, then relented and said, 'It's nice of you to worry but I really don't need help.'

Mary was bottle-feeding Emeline while nervously watching Brendan mess with play-dough. He had a great dollop of it and was throttling it between his fists in a manner that was suggestive and sinister. Suddenly he detached a portion and whanged it at Patrick, narrowly missing his head.

Julie called out sweetly, 'Don't chuck the play-dough around, Bren, or you won't have enough left to play with.'

Julie's initial idea had been that the community took responsibility for the education of its young children, on child-centred Steiner principles, letting the kids learn by play and discovery at their own speed with no compulsion or punishment. She held the opinion that schools, certainly in a child's early years, did more harm than good. But her Steiner principles, like her Marxism, languished for lack of adherents. The Hunters, who claimed to be socialists, were the biggest stumbling-block. Catherine was the sort of teacher that Julie's doctrine traduced – and there was no way they would submit Clive to sharing his education with Theresa and the gremlins. Left with the Spillsburys, Julie had consoled herself that they were the very kids who would get least from ordinary school and benefit most from her system.

Damien asked her, 'Where's Selina?'

The Pococks had demurred – they frankly detested children – but Selina had offered to help, despite having been advised by Susan to have nothing to do with Julie's crackpot notions.

'Selina isn't helping. Colin doesn't want a nigger helping to educate his kids.'

Damien was shocked – partly because, not for the first time, he noticed that Julie spoke up in Mary's presence as if the latter was deaf or unconscious. But Mary was occupied in whingeing at Brendan, trying in vain to get him to pick up the play-dough.

Theresa and Patrick were painting with poster colours on huge sheets of white paper. Theresa was not a talented child but she loved whatever she did so long as she was not being threatened or scorned, so was easily Julie's most rewarding pupil.

'Is that what Colin said?' Damien called over Brian's drumming, which the child was now augmenting with a system of contrapuntal shrieks.

'It's what Mary says he said. Maybe it's her idea.'

'You can't accept it.'

'Selina can. She's withdrawn her offer to help.'

'She can't.'

'Of course she can. Piss off, Damien. I'm busy.'

Patrick had been having fun spooning paint on to his brush and flicking it at the paper, action-painter style. He now discovered that it was even more diverting to flick it at Theresa's paper. She uttered a wounded cry, dropped her own brush and gazed aghast at her besmirched oeuvre. Then she lunged at Patrick, seized him by the hair before he could escape round the table and bunched her fist.

Julie called out sharply, 'Tessa, we don't use violence!'

Theresa did her the compliment of hesitating before slamming her fist into Patrick's face. The four-year-old was felled by the blow and lay kicking and bellowing with his nose bleeding. Mary waddled over shouting obscenities, the now-complaining baby clutched under one arm, and aimed several swipes at Theresa who dodged them by ducking and weaving like a boxer on the ropes. Brendan laughed at the entertainment as he perfected a new, more lethal missile by sticking bits of Lego into play-dough until it resembled the head of a medieval mace. The one mitigation of the bedlam was the sudden silence of Brian's drum. He had discovered a weakness at the edge of the stretched skin and was gouging at it with the drumstick.

Damien said, 'Look, let me help. I'll take a couple of them for a nature ramble.'

He felt that he was making a generous offer, since she had told him horror stories of rambles with two or more of the Spillsburys – of the amount of destruction they could wreak on local flora and fauna and telephone kiosks even when unblinkingly supervised.

Julie shrugged. 'Thanks, but it's all over in any case. Tessa and Bren start at Bilberton next week.'

Michael had been forced to witness events from a remote distance, if at all. The chain that was his tether at the bottom of the garden was just over two metres long and he abbreviated it by winding it round the tree to which it was attached, so that sometimes he could no longer reach the shelter of his kennel. Theresa untangled him whenever she came to see him but he would soon become tangled again, being a restless spirit in an impulsive frame.

From start to finish he did not have an easy life and his stay at Sparrow Hall was not the worst of it. The kennel Julie had provided for him was a distinct plus: he was used to sleeping either inside the Ford Transit or underneath the caravan, and the kennel was not only warmer, being a more enclosed space, but was lined with a fleecy old bathroom rug. His diet was also much improved: instead of subsisting in the famished margins of the Spillsbury family he now received the leavings of a dozen well-fed adults, as well as special titbits that Theresa scrounged or stole from kitchen and scullery. Thirdly, he saw very little of Colin, who had 'taught the dog respect' so thoroughly that Michael's tail slunk between his thighs at the very sight or sound of his master in the distance.

Yet Michael was ill at ease in strange surroundings where

he had no option but to stay. Lack of habitual human contact left a void. He missed the gremlins, who hailed him as they passed or threw the odd brick at him but whom he was unable to seek out and romp with and be tormented by as he was used to do. He even missed his outings with the drastic Colin, who had apparently lost interest in dogs. Most of all he missed Theresa, though she fed him and he saw more of her than of anybody else. He was accustomed to following her everywhere and fawning on her, when he was not either visiting terror on any two-legged or four-legged creature he encountered or himself being terrorised by Colin.

Therefore he grieved. At night he was a whimpering insomniac watching the moon or lighted windows from his kennel doorway, occasionally lifting his nose from his paws to let out a low howl so heartbreaking that it made him feel even worse. Throughout the day he prowled, like a tundra wolf in a zoo enclosure or a madman in a padded cell: six paces north, swing of the snout, swivel of the haunches, six paces south . . . He interspersed this compulsive and hypnotic routine with gnawing and pawing at the chain as he lay in the grass; or bouncing and barking insanely, jerking and straining at the rattling, throttling limit of his tether, whenever Binky and Braithwaite, Julie's cats, came near, or any pedestrians winced past along the sunken lane that ran beyond the boundary hedge of the Hall.

He hated all foreign traffic and made no exception in the case of Clive Hunter when he blundered into range. Clive knew well enough of Michael's existence and for a fortnight had been careful to avoid him. But Clive was becoming obsessed by the gremlins and the blight on his existence which they constituted: they pursued him with cries of 'Fatty fuckpig!' and bombarded him with any objects in their vicinity, to the extent that he was reluctant to leave the family suite and venture into the rest of the Hall. It did not matter during the week, since he went with his mother in her Mini to her Pickering school and the Hunters prepared and ate breakfasts and evening meals in their own quarters. But there were times at weekends when his mother or father would oust him from the apartment, sending him on some errand or simply telling him to 'get some fresh air'. It was on one such occasion that he gingerly stepped into the Hall grounds and hearing a gremlin or so let out a whoop or a yowl beyond the orchard wall, went sidling across the lawn, like a prairie schooner running blindly from Comanches, and fetched up in Michael's domain before he even remembered the existence of the dog.

Michael bounded towards the lad, his virulent bass incorporating a note of serious purpose as he realised that Clive might be within the range of the tether. Clive stood paralysed, but immediately – so that it was almost simultaneous with his previous actions – the dog dropped his ears, licked his snout, writhed his hindquarters and lashed his tail in a frenzy of sycophantic greeting.

Theresa had been watching out for Clive ever since the evening of the inauguration dinner. Now she was happy to rescue him again. She fondled the jowls of the dog, who rolled onto his back and writhed with ecstasy. 'Come over this side,' she called, in her frail and husky voice. 'Michael will do you no harm.'

The perfervid dog scrabbled to his feet and swarmed at her, butting his snout into her groin. She leaned over and scratched his matted back as hard as she could, digging her nails in under the hair. She knew well that Michael considered this the most delicious experience in the universe. The dog now stood stock still in a trance of bliss.

Clive made a slow, crabwise approach. 'Michael's a daft name for a dog,' he said. 'Why not call him Mick?'

'Because his name is Michael. Scratch behind his ears.'

He obeyed warily. Michael turned his head slowly and looked at Clive as if to say, *I will tear your throat out tomorrow but permit this liberty today.*

'Your name's Clive,' Theresa said. 'Do you know what mine is?'

'No, I don't,' he lied.

'Theresa. Shall I tell you a secret that I know?'

He took his hand off Michael, who reared and put his paws onto Theresa's shoulders, slobbering into her face and streaking her with saliva. 'You can if you like.'

'It's that I love you and always shall. We'll marry when we're grown-up.' She pushed off the dog, who gave a gratified woof and took her thin forearm gently in his jaws, then she started to scratch his back again, which quelled him utterly.

Clive had hardly thought of her at all, though he knew what his parents said about the Spillsburys and agreed with every word of it. He saw that she was wearing the same brown dress that hung from her bony frame like a sack. Her big ears peeped from her sullen brown hair.

'You can catch rabies off dogs,' he said, 'then you go mad and run round biting people. Everybody you bite goes mad like you.'

She turned her face from the dog to narrow her eyes and peer at Clive complicitly. 'Do you like it here?' she asked sombrely.

'It's okay, mostly.' It was none of her business.

'I don't like it. There's spooks. Some folk were shot here not long back.'

'No, that's crap.' Clive had heard stories at school but his parents had told him that they were untrue.

'It is not crap. Michael howls here. He never did that nowhere before.' Then her face cleared and she smiled at him, revealing the same gapped, tombstone teeth that all her brothers carried. 'I've been on the watch for you. Where do you hide yourself?'

'I stop in our flat. I do homework and watch TV and make models.' He was backing off as he spoke, making his escape, hardly aware what he was saying. 'I'm building a *Star Wars* Intergalactic Delta Cruiser.'

'Can I come and help you build that?'

He seemed to consider this. 'My mum wouldn't let you. I have to go.'

'I hate Colin Spillsbury,' Julie said, after taking a long drag of her cigarette and blowing a plume of smoke into the afternoon. It was the first time she had admitted it in such uncompromising terms.

Damien asked her, 'Has this been growing on you, or was it hate at first sight?'

They were descending the rough cart track towards the river and the ridings on a brilliant spring day. Hawthorn and bramble had almost made a tunnel of the shrunken track, with shafts and ponds of sunlight here and there.

Julie insisted that they took a walk together each day – a circuit of the back lanes that ringed Thornham in medieval style, or a long ellipse through the village, down to the river and up the ridings back to Sparrow Hall. It was the best chance for her to talk to Damien except at night in bed when he was invariably passive and laconic, sometimes falling asleep in the middle of what was effectively a soliloquy. He had started writing a book about the pre-war blues that were his passion – a historical novel, semi-documentary, relating a trip by a group of blues musicians from Lula in Mississippi to the Paramount recording studios in Grafton, Wisconsin. Julie had encouraged Damien's earlier efforts at novels but thought this one a ridiculous undertaking, since

Damien knew little about music (was practically tone deaf) and had even less first-hand information about how Mississippi blacks talked and thought. She diagnosed that the project was a refuge from both his family and the Sparrow Hall community, but did not want to let him disappear into it entirely, the way his father had disappeared into his own unhealthy interior.

Since she hadn't answered his question, Damien added, 'I dare say it was the inaugural dinner that first sparked your antipathy.'

She grimaced. Colin had certainly unveiled himself to her and everybody else at the dinner, removing any shred of hope that his rough exterior might be misleading. After sending his wife and kids to bed he had gruffly rejected Julie's plea on their behalf. He had smoked roll-ups throughout the meal, eaten so brutishly as to remove the appetite of those adjacent, delivered a drunken rigmarole full of expletives until he had driven almost everybody to bed, then himself departed unceremoniously with an almost full bottle of brandy in his fist. She said, 'No. I hated him before that, because his wife and kids and dog are all terrified of him.'

'There's a rabbit!' said Damien, but Julie did not look. There were also skylarks, thrushes, sparrows, chaffinches, starlings, robins, crows; but she was walking with her hennaed head bowed, her eyes brooding on the earth immediately before her, which was how she usually did the circuit, oblivious to the scenery, with something else on her mind.

Damien asked her, 'Are you scared of him?'

She sneered. 'You mean you're not?'

He laughed, not resenting her attack. 'I'm scared of him all right. He's just the sort of thing to terrify a rich, privileged brat like me. But I didn't think you were scared of anybody.'

'It would help if you could do your share of dealing with

him. But you're a pushover for him, even when you don't forget or chicken out.'

At first Julie had not liked to admit that Colin intimidated her, but she had known it. She had felt it when she had won the chaining of the dog as much as when she had lost at the inauguration dinner. Now she saw no shame in it, since it was not cowardice but as logical a response to Colin Spillsbury as it was to his dog, Michael. It prompted her to confront Colin on issues she might otherwise have let pass, as a teacher might pick on a pupil regarded as a threat to discipline. She had complained to him about smoking in the house since the general-meeting resolution, and about his drunken tantrums disturbing the sleep of other residents; stopped him playing Irish fiddlers *altoforte* on the drawing-room stereo and retrieved the stereo after he relocated it in the Spillsbury apartment. She had insisted on retaining the keys to the Golf, which he thought should be the prerogative of the technical monitor, and objected to him using the vehicle to gather scrap metal for the collection he was building in the vegetable garden. She had forbidden him to remove or alter anything in the Hall or grounds and refused him money for poultry-runs, poultry, a van or trailer, a cement-mixer, a hydraulic jack, instructing him to put proper proposals to a general meeting. She had got him to promise to let Theresa exercise the dog – which for some reason he had forbidden. Most harrowing of all, she had obtained, by the careful timing as well as force of her demand, a social-security chit from him so that she could calculate the Spillsbury contribution to the community fund. Getting any money would be another matter. His attitude to her was of scornful phlegm, as if he was dealing with a fool who must not be antagonised. Julie understood that Colin's raw menace, compared to Michael's, was tempered by self-interest; but neither this, nor custom, nor the relative success of her transactions could stop her feeling tense and timid when she approached the fellow, or from waking in the night or morning with the immediate unpleasant awareness that she needed to see him about something.

They emerged from the tunnel, crossed a sunlit meadow, causing sheep to trundle away, and came to the bank of a quiet river bordered by ash and sycamore. At this point there was an island in the river where Damien remembered watching village children play when he was a child, building a bonfire and using a tractor tyre as a raft.

Julie lit one cigarette from another. Susan, who was living at home now that her course was finished, objected to smoking in the Frobisher suite and there were rules governing the rest of the Hall.

'What I most hate about him, of course, is that he's wrecking the commune, him and his shitty tribe. The Hunters and Pococks won't have breakfast in the kitchen or come to evening meals – and those of us that do can understand their objection. His kids are demolishing the place and I can't even complain about that because I don't want them beaten up.'

They helped each other over the stile and started to climb the riding towards the path through the copse. Julie went on, 'It's ironic that he took Jack Norris's place, the bloke I was counting on to make the commune work. Now I feel that if Colin frigging Spillsbury wasn't there I wouldn't have any need for Jack Norris, we'd all get on just fine.'

'We can get rid of him easily enough,' Damien said.

'You're joking.'

'Of course we can. Seven votes is the most it takes. The Hunters and Pococks will vote him out like a shot. All that's stopping them proposing it is that they don't think we would support it. They think we're do-gooders who feel responsible for the Spillsburys. Once we propose it, that's six votes for a kick-off, plus Selina always votes with us and in any case must be sick of those kids calling her a nigger.'

'You're joking. This is rich, coming from you. You're the one who showed him round in the first place, and took the moral high ground when I objected to the scumbag.'

They both had to stop talking, as the gradient became sharp, until they reached the stile into the copse. After she had paused there to get her breath and puff at her fag, Julie continued, 'And the bloody trouble is, you were right. The problem is we *are* do-gooders who feel responsible for the shits. If we throw them out all our socialist pretensions will collapse like a buggered balloon.'

The daffodils were persevering in Long Acre Copse, the descendants of the daffodils that Elaine Moorhouse and her attendant maidens had been forced to surrender at gunpoint to the young lord of the manor. Damien said, 'It's lovely here. Don't you have even a tiny, treacherous wish that we didn't have to worry about Colin and the commune, about the purpose of life and our responsibilities, and could just stand here and admire the daffodils?'

In actual fact he did not want to stand and admire the daffodils, but to get back to the Hall and return to work on the chapter where Louise Johnson climbs over the long front seat of the Buick to leave Charley Patton for Son House. His speech had been metaphorical and referred more to Julie than himself.

At first Julie looked irritated by what she regarded as existentialist bullshit, then her gaze softened as she looked at her husband, so that his heart leaped and he forgot his book.

She said, 'Foolish frigging daffodils. I'd be bored to death in five minutes.'

Selina was asleep on her back, her lips pursed and a frown furrowing her brow. The stern expression, together with her boyish crop and the sculpted effect of her dark head on the white pillow, made her look like an androgynous, disapproving angel. Tommy leaned up on an elbow to admire her.

He blessed his luck, effortlessly re-creating the elation he had felt eight years earlier, when they had both been in the fourth form at secondary school and she had consented to go out with him. The sense of privilege that her favours had conferred on him had survived all his own fame as a future football star at West Ham. While he had sometimes had other sexual encounters, he had been unswervingly loyal to her as a long-term preference.

He put his hand onto her breast under the duvet and she woke immediately to stare askance at him, the whites of her eyes creamy with sleep.

'Gerroff,' she said, but without urgency. She squinted at the little watch on the inside of her wrist. 'What time is it?'

'Dunno, but them kids have gone to school.' He pinched her faintly interested nipple very gently between his thumb and forefinger and grinned. 'We don't need to get up just yet, though.'

She pushed his hand away and gave him a critical look. 'What's got into you? This last week you've been like the cat that got the cream.'

Susan noticed it too, as she dished up plates of egg and bacon in the kitchen. 'It's smiling again!' she cried, as though aghast.

Tommy moved up facetiously close to Susan, whom he found attractive. 'It's you. You make me happy.'

'Eek! Give him his ear-muffs, Sel.' Quite often in the past Tommy had carried his ghetto-blaster to breakfast and worn earphones, talking to nobody.

Susan served Tommy and Selina egg and bacon but ignored Colin, though he appeared at the same time. On weekday mornings there were two breakfast shifts. Julie and Mary prepared breakfast for themselves, Damien and those who had to catch the school bus, but Susan, Tommy and Selina lurked in bed until the bus had gone. Sometimes Julie cooked breakfast for everybody but more often she retreated upstairs when Tim was gone and Mary moved into the battered lounge with Brian and Emeline to watch TV. Susan, who got on well with Selina and Tommy but with nobody else, usually cooked something for herself and the Johnsons. When Colin came he made toast and finished the tea his wife had brewed. Damien usually lingered in the dining room drinking coffee and reading the *Guardian*.

The kitchen table was a mess of spilled milk and cornflakes, chewed crusts, blobs of jam, so Susan and the Johnsons took their plates and cutlery into the dining room.

'Shit, what a mess,' Susan said. 'Who's on kitchen rota?'

'We are,' Selina said dolefully.

'No sweat,' said Tommy. He grinned again at the astounded Susan. 'I'll fix it, man.'

This made Selina scrutinise him worriedly, and before she left for work she had another try at interrogating him. 'What's going on, Tommy? It's driving me frantic.'

'What, because I'm cheerful?'

'Too right. You've been miserable as sin since we left Finchley. Now suddenly this.'

'Pulled myself together, innai? Like you been telling me to.'

She was disentangling her bicycle from his. They kept their bikes in the little hallway of their apartment, so the kids wouldn't let the tyres down, steal the pumps and ready the vehicles for their dad's scrap farm that was gradually engulfing the vegetable garden. The bikes had been a brainwave after Tommy's motorcycle was sold and were now indispensable. Even if you could book the Golf you couldn't count on Colin getting it back in time for when you wanted it.

'Are you going for that job?' she asked him.

'Which is that?'

'The garage in Helmsley, you know which bleeding job.'

'Yeah. Kiss us goodbye.'

'What for?' They never kissed goodbye. He scoffed at such endearments.

'Just for the badness.' He tried to bob his tongue into her mouth. 'Keep away from them horny piss-heads, eh?'

'At Westmoor at lunch-time? Leave it out!' She gave him a last, long, hard look. 'Don't forget about the job.'

'Lend us a fiver.'

'I'm broke.'

When she was gone he packed one or two items into his saddlebag and tucked his little wallet of darts into the back pocket of his jeans. Then he donned his black woolly hat, although Selina always told him not to wear it when he was looking for a job. And when he reached Kirkby Moorside he turned off the main road into the town centre and propped his bike outside the Waggon and Horses. Selina had also forbidden him to drink before presenting himself for employment, but he didn't want the job anyway.

The Waggon and Horses was where he spent his lunch-times and evenings while his wife was more lucratively employed at the Half Moon in Westmoor – and where he spent his dole money and as much of Selina's earnings as he could scrounge off her. It was the closest thing he could find to the pool rooms and bars of Finchley. There was a pool table and a dartboard where his skills could usually keep him in play and earn him beer.

'Now, Tommy!' said the landlord, and poured a pint of Tetley's bitter without waiting for the order. Tommy engaged neither the barman nor the other two or three customers in conversation, though he had been a talkative lad when drinking with his black mates in Finchley. Nor did he even glance towards the fruit machine, since games of chance were a vice he had abjured. He went to the dartboard and had been practising for almost an hour, going round and round the board in doubles, making his drink last till it was flat and warm, when Gary walked in: a tall, slender, blond, laconic, dry young fellow.

Tommy did not offer to buy Gary a drink. Gary reciprocated by buying himself one without offering one to Tommy, then watched Tommy practising while he took his own wallet of darts from his pocket and carefully unfolded the flights and fitted them into the stems. 'Is it fixed up for Sunday?' he asked at length.

'Yeah, but just one thing, I got my kit outside on the bike. You keep it and bring it to the ground on Sunday, eh? I don't want the wife to know I'm playing.'

Gary raised an eyebrow, took a swig of his pint, wiped the froth from his lips and raised the other eyebrow. 'Don't want her to know you're playing football? That's a new one.'

ELEVENTH GENERAL MEETING OF THE SPARROW HALL COMMUNITY 9/9/84

Agenda: (i) minutes of last meeting (ii) matters arising from minutes (iii) Treasurer's report (iv) resignation of Janet Otterburn (v) any other business.

Seven adult voters were present. Absent (without apology) were Colin, Mary and Tommy. Bob thanked those present for their attendance, which made it possible for him to declare a 'quorum' for the first time in four meetings.

(i) Minutes of last meeting
These were unanimously accepted. Catherine was complimented by both Delia and Bob that her report had less 'jargon' and was easier to understand than earlier ones.

(ii) Matters arising from the minutes

Selina had complained in April that people were not doing chores, or doing them badly. She now said that there had been some improvement after her complaint but that at present things were if anything worse. As a result of this, combined with the misuse of facilities, some areas of the Hall, i.e. the kitchen, lounge, laundry room and toilets, were in a run-down and 'depressing' condition.

Delia raised the possibility of taking firm action against the Spillsburys. Selina said that the Spillsburys were not her worst problem. Mary needed reminding from time to time, but then either she or Theresa did the chores without complaining, which was more than could be said for some other members. Chris declared that since he and Catherine made use of none of the food or facilities he did not see why they should be included in kitchen duties of any sort, whatever it said in the constitution. Delia supported this view and added that it would make much more sense if people cleared up after themselves – then they might be more careful about how much mess they made.

Julie intervened to say that any discussion of duties, especially those connected with meals, should await the item later on the agenda about the resignation of Janet Otterburn. This was agreed.

(iii) Treasurer's report

Julie reported that the community fund showed a consider-able deficit. Salaries, provisions, repairs and other expenses had so far come to over £10,000, whereas contributions were less than £8,000, including £5,000 from the Frobishers. She said that she would provide a full audit for the Annual General Meeting in March, and suggested that further discussion might be included under the next item on the agenda. It was agreed to move on to the next item.

(iv) Resignation of Janet Otterburn

Julie said that Janet had given in her notice to take effect from the end of the month. While some early problems had been overcome once the Spillsbury children were banned from the kitchen, Janet felt that her efforts were very little appreciated by the community, and the work and responsibility greatly outweighed the rewards.

Julie proposed that Janet should not be replaced, but that each family should be responsible for its own provisions and cooking, with a second kitchen installed on the second floor and modest cooking facilities in each suite. There should be no cooking or kitchen duties, those who used communal facilities being responsible for leaving them ready for further use. A new cleaning and maintenance rota should be drawn up. Each family should pay £20 a week rent towards the community fund, which would be used to pay for repairs and replacements and finance any projects or requests for aid approved at a General Meeting. If the community fund ever rose above the £20,000 starting level the surplus should at the end of the year be divided among the members. The constitution should be redrawn in the light of these proposals if they were accepted.

All the proposals were passed unanimously.

(v) Any other business

(a) Julie expressed her bitterness at being forced to go back on a number of principles that were precious to her, and complained about a general lack of support and failure to keep to undertakings. Chris asked Catherine to put on record his strong rejection of Julie's *'insinuations'*. Far from it being the case that he and others had gone back on their word, the truth of the matter was that conditions at the Hall had turned out to be very different from what had been promised. This was supported by Catherine, Delia and Bob.

Damien intervened by saying that most of the dissatisfaction with the Hall and subsequent reluctance to co-operate in a community arose either directly or indirectly from the presence of the Spillsburys and their behaviour. He proposed that the Spillsburys be asked to leave the Hall, and that the community fund should pay for the renovation of the Spillsbury caravan and the purchase of a suitable towing vehicle. Julie said that such a motion was against her principles but that in view of the shambles that the Spillsburys were making of the community she was prepared to abstain from voting. Bob commented that in effect an abstention counted as a vote against the motion, since the constitution demanded six votes in favour. The result of the vote was five to one, with Julie abstaining and Selina against. Selina was asked for an explanation, particularly as she and Tommy had come in for a lot of racist abuse from the Spillsbury children. She said that she wasn't too bothered what kids got up to and that it was 'shitty' to put the Spillsburys out, especially with summer over and winter on the way. Supporting this, Julie proposed that in spring the Spillsburys be given both an ultimatum about payment of rent and behaviour, and an inducement to leave along the lines of Damien's suggestion. Chris counter-proposed that both the ultimatum and the offer should be made immediately and expulsion enforced in spring if the offer was refused and there was no improvement. Selina protested against this on the grounds that it was wrong to take such decisions about people who were not present to defend themselves or vote. Julie's proposal with Chris's amendment was passed by six votes to one. Julie volunteered to draw up and present the ultimatum. It was not felt necessary for her ultimatum to be approved at another meeting before she presented it to Colin Spillsbury.

(b) Delia raised the question of the Golf, which she said seemed to have become the private property of Colin Spillsbury. Damien said that Julie had striven to keep control of the keys, but if others would not make firm bookings for the car on a rota basis it was difficult to deny Colin the use of it. Bob said there was no point booking the car if it wasn't returned for you to use it when you wanted it. Julie proposed that there should be a charge of £1 per hour for use of the car, the money to go to the community fund. This was passed unanimously.

(c) In answer to a question from Delia, Julie said that Susan was to be married in February in Westmoor parish church, the reception to be at Westmoor Grange. Susan was entirely responsible for arrangements and invitations and it was an internal family matter not suitable for discussion at a community general meeting.

(d) The next meeting was fixed for 3 p.m. on Sunday, 25 November 1984.

'For five minutes he were brilliant. He ran length of pitch, beat everybody in t' Wrelton team twice and laid on an open goal for Doug Waines, who missed it, the tosser.'

The Apple Tree was quiet as usual on a weekday at nine thirty; it did not offer bar meals and tended to fill up after ten o'clock.

'Next minute he were sat on t' floor screaming – the darkie, I mean, not Doug – and we had to get him to Scarborough Casualty.'

Kevin and Dean were playing darts. Kevin was a bucolic, red-faced lad in overalls, Dean a leather-clad rocker with long black hair.

'So that's why he's been hobbling around in that contraption?' Elaine asked them, her voice carrying easily across the snug orange room from the bar. Elaine Dobson was a matronly figure now, a bit prim-looking for a landlady, but with those cool, brown, mischievous eyes that had once confounded Damien.

'He played for England schoolboys once over, but he's been told if he plays more football he'll end up a cripple for life.'

'That's why he's been coming in here these last months. But now he can ride his bike again he goes down Kirkby.'

'Good riddance, now we can get ont' bloody dartboard.'

Bob came in. He liked the high stool in the corner of the bar where he could lean against the wall. He spent about an hour in the pub each night, between half nine and half ten.

'Now, Bob! How's things at Kremlin?'

'Don't ask. It's a madhouse. Usual and a panatela, Elaine love, please, and will you have a drink yourself?'

Elaine shook her head, as always. The darts players had turned their attention to their game and the only other customers in the pub took up the conversation.

Ken and Dobbo, forty-year-olds, were playing dominoes. Ken was fat, his belly swagging out a T-shirt inscribed *Gross Moral Turpitude*. Dobbo was thin, bald and dressed in a pale denim suit; homosexual in aspect, though he was married with three children. Nobody could remember why he was called Dobbo. His real name was Arthur Lumb.

'Have t'cops questioned him yet?'

'What are you on about?'

'The darkie,' said Dobbo. 'Happen t'cops are frightened to arrest him, with all this race-relations bullshit.'

Ken held up his glass to the light and frowned at it as if he thought the beer was cloudy. It was a move he used to tease Elaine. 'Just because he's a coon doesn't mean he's bound to be a burglar, you pillock.'

'It stands to reason, though. There's been a break-in a month round here since last spring. There were never owt like it before that youth moved in.'

'Don't talk wet. He's had a gammy leg. How's he supposed to have been roamint' countryside and clambering into places?'

'What do I want?' Dean asked, in the ensuing silence. He had a dramatic darts stance, like a circus knife-thrower.

'Double eighteen.'

'Thirty-five, get a three.'

'Eights left.'

'Bust.'

'Nine left.'

'Double two . . . Game shot!' Kevin raised an arm in the air and spun to face the room like a goal-scorer at football.

'Jammy cunt.' Dean then put his hand over his mouth and glanced towards the bar. Elaine had been known to complain if the language got too colourful.

'How about that other one of your lot? The Irish twat,' Ken called towards Bob. 'Has he been back in here since that night?'

It was Elaine who answered, grimly: 'No, nor will he, if he's any sense.'

'Is he still driving that Golf of her ladyship's?'

'No, he's got a van now.'

'And Christ knows where he's found the shekels for it,' Bob couldn't help interposing.

'Happen he's the phantom burglar,' said Ken. 'You've a bright bunch yonder at t'Kremlin, Bob.'

'It's no laughing matter.' It was Bob himself had christened the Hall 'The Kremlin'. He had rather regretted it since.

'How's his lord and ladyship, Bob?' Ken's habitually derisive manner seemed to intensify whenever he spoke to Bob.

'God knows. She's been away somewhere. You never see him, he's supposed to be writing something. Delia and I keep out of their way.'

'You do right,' said Ken, 'for she's a jumped-up, toffee-nosed bitch, and Damien's in t'land of the daft. It runs in the family. Both his mother and his father were a jack short of a prial. You wouldn't breed from pigs with that sort of pedigree.'

Elaine said, 'You want to watch what you say about people, Ken Filbert.'

'Sup up,' Dean said to Kevin. 'It's your round.'

'I'm not stopping. I'm off to Westmoor.'

'Ooh, aye?' Dean grinned, showing several very bad teeth.

'To see Neil Babcock.'

'Ooh, aye? Give over! We know who thoo are going to see.'

'Don't be pathetic.'

'Is she still barmaid at the Half Moon?' Dobbo asked Ken. For some reason he only ever spoke to Ken.

'Sensational Selina? She is that!' Ken glanced mischievously at Elaine to make sure she was listening. 'That's what we could do with round here. A bit of exotic glamour.'

'That's your taste, is it?' Elaine sniffed.

'Not just mine. She's got that pub packed out. It's like a cabaret turn, the way she serves beer and collects the empties. She moves like a leopard. With them long legs and that sexy bum and them big dark eyes.'

'Her skirts up to her waist,' said Dobbo, not so approvingly.

'And hundreds of teeth when she grins,' said Bob sourly. 'Might I have a packet of salted peanuts, Elaine my love?'

During the summer holidays, on a campsite in France, Clive had at last explained to his parents why he hated Sparrow Hall. Chris and Catherine had noticed that he was reluctant to leave their apartment, and that he had no friends apart from at school in Pickering, but had not appreciated the extent to which the taunts of the Spillsbury gremlins had weighed on his spirit and made him a recluse. Chris, who invested a lot of time in Clive and liked to think of himself as a good pal for the lad, was particularly aghast that Clive had not confided in him earlier.

At the end of August when they got back from holiday Chris had broached the matter with Colin Spillsbury. Colin's usual response to complaint was either evasion or brusque apology: he did not like to run foul of authority or find himself in direct conflict with respectable citizens. But when Chris was not prepared to be fobbed off Colin ran out of his meagre ration of civility and an ugly little scene ensued, avoiding violence partly because Chris's small stature precluded him from defying threats and accepting challenges and partly because Damien intervened, at which Colin at once adopted the stance of a provoked pacifist. Chris left the encounter daunted and frustrated, yet it produced the gratifying result that the gremlins at once stopped all harassment of Clive.

As the next step towards the restoration of their son's morale Catherine negotiated for him to exchange home visits with a schoolfriend. Clive had previously resisted this, not even consenting to visit friends in Pickering for fear that the visit would have to be reciprocated. He had been filled with horror at the prospect of anyone from his school – or even any stranger, any of the village kids that his parents sometimes suggested he befriend – witnessing the taunts of the gremlins, the atrocious, unjust insults, and thinking of him for ever, whatever they said or did not say, as Fucking Fattypig or Fatty Fuckpig. It was two months after the last insult before he ceased to feel panic when encountering the glowering silence of the gremlins and consented to a visit from Nigel Butterworth.

Catherine was not entirely happy at Clive's choice, because Nigel was one of the naughtiest boys at the school, but now that they had got Clive to concur it was unthinkable to censor his selection. Nigel's parents, who ran the fish and chip shop in Pickering, were pleased to think their lad might come under the influence of quiet, brainy Clive, the son of a teacher. They delivered Nigel to the Hall on a November Saturday morning at ten thirty, giving plenty of time to play with Clive's Lego before lunch.

By which time Nigel had had his fill of constructive indoor games. As he was eating his lunch in the little dining nook that Chris had carpentered his gaze went out of the window and down the garden to where Michael was patrolling his tether. 'What's that?'

Chris answered. 'A big, nasty dog. It's best keep well away from it.'

'It's tied up, though, isn't it?'

'What are you lads going to do this afternoon?' Chris had wanted to take them fishing, but Catherine thought it better to leave them to each other.

'I'd like to go outside and explore,' Nigel said promptly.

Clive was a bit apprehensive about Theresa. He had not forgotten what she had said six months ago during their disconcerting interview brokered by Michael, and he knew that she had not forgotten either, though they had hardly spoken since. What he had first thought interesting in her he now diagnosed as weirdness, and her undeniable services to him were an embarrassment on account of her despicable social standing. Most of all her announcement that she loved him, her blithe and impudent claim on him for ever, had rendered her insufferable. So whenever they had met he had nodded at her queasily, looking at his watch and shrugging, or saying, 'Can't stop!' if she tried to begin a conversation. As it happened there had never been anything to prevent an immediate getaway. After a while she had stopped trying to talk to him and contented herself with greeting him in passing or waving from a distance. It was sufficient for her, because it had to be, to stand in his way and greet him, with her clear eyes and smoky voice, reminding him, by her stance, her look, her smile, that he knew her secret, and that she had not forgotten, never would, as long as she lived. The need to further renounce her by not acknowledging her greeting became as strong in him as had been the need to avoid further conversation. But he could only sometimes manage to ignore her. Something often compelled him to nod at her and even give her a brusque grin. He was hoping, as he went into the garden with Nigel, that if Theresa was anywhere around today she would have the discretion not to trouble him when he had company – because he could foresee that Nigel's presence would remove his option of a prompt escape.

She was nowhere in sight. Brendan Spillsbury, however, the eldest gremlin, was on the terrace, kicking a plastic ball against the balustrade. Nigel skipped across and booted the ball high and far so that it landed in the green scum of the lily pond.

Brendan's jaw dropped. He said, 'Fucking bastard cunt!'

'Piss off, kid,' said Nigel jovially, pushing Brendan in the face so that he tumbled back down the shallow steps from the terrace.

Brendan, rising and retreating, hurled gravel at Nigel. Nigel leaped and caught him, slapping him round the head. Brendan, wailing, ran to a distance, searched in vain for missiles, then bellowed, 'Fatty Fuckpig! Fucking Fattypig!'

Nigel, a lean and saturnine child, looked at Clive and laughed. 'Is it you he's calling that?'

'Not me,' Clive croaked, his nightmare come true. 'I never touched him.'

'Little shit-bag,' said Nigel. 'Does he live here?'

'He's one of the Spillsburys. They're all like that. I don't bother with them. That's their dog.'

Nigel was already moving down the garden and Michael had risen from his kennel to confront him. Nigel judged it nicely so that he halted just provokingly beyond the range of Michael's tether, then sneered at the snarling, baying, choking dog.

'Look at them fangs!' he said appreciatively. He took up a fallen branch, quite a heavy one, and pitched it onto Michael, so that the dog yelped with pain and alarm, practically somersaulted backwards, ran round the tree and advanced again, doubly furious but further restricted by a shortened tether.

Nigel was looking round for more weaponry when Michael's aspect changed abruptly. He flattened his ears, licked his snout, whimpered and writhed with delight – signs that Clive knew only too well.

Theresa went past them and knelt to comfort the dog, who lifted an allegedly damaged paw for her inspection. She was wearing a sweater and jeans that Julie had bought for her, but they hung from her spindly form as lank and soiled as her hair. She turned her face silently towards the boys when she had the dog in her arms.

Nigel asked, 'Who's Skinny Lizzy with the teapot ears?'

'It's Theresa,' said Clive, mortified. 'Another of the Spillsburys.'

Theresa flinched as Michael put his tongue in her ear but kept her eyes fixed on Clive.

Nigel sniggered. 'Does she let the dog fuck her?'

Clive was shocked by this, but instead of protesting he laughed and said loudly, so that she was sure to hear him, 'She stinks. And she's got mucky knickers.' He wanted to shout, *She says she loves me and she's going to wed me!* but he dared not shout that and be rid of it, for fear that it would make him ridiculous to Nigel. Instead he shouted triumphantly, 'She wants to work in a circus but she never will. They don't have ugly scruffs like her.'

Friday 14 December 1984 is selected as a typical sample of life at Sparrow Hall that autumn and winter.

The Frobishers saw little of each other that day, as had become usual. Susan, who had grown impatient of convention and moved in with her fiancé on the farm he managed for his parents, was with Paul in Paris, having persuaded him that the farm was a healthy enough enterprise to do without its manager for a week. Tim left the house at eight fifteen on the Bilberton Junior School bus, which dropped the senior pupils at the bottom of Thornham Common to await the Pickering bus. He got back home for tea, then, after dedicating half an hour to dirtying and distressing his new motorcycle boots, set off back to Pickering on his ancient Ducati where he hung around with a gang of youthful motorcycle connoisseurs, went to a disco with some of them and arrived home fairly discreetly after midnight. Julie cooked breakfast for herself, Tim and Damien (egg and bacon), lunch for herself and Damien (tuna salad) and dinner for the three of them (corned-beef hash and veg). She washed up after breakfast and lunch, Damien after dinner. She had given up the practice of taking a walk with Damien, using that time to make pottery in the studio. Much of the rest of the day she spent in preparing herself for a weekend film-study seminar (*La Règle du Jeu*) at Wyedale Hall: bathing, anointing herself, clipping her toenails, driving to Helmsley for a hair appointment. She had a rendezvous at Wyedale with Gavin Meadows, an unimportant old flame who was now a lecturer at the art school at Malton – among his attractions was his access to a source of fascinating narcotic substances. After dinner she left immediately in the Granada. Damien walked alone, as each day now, regardless of the weather, having asked Julie, as he did each day, whether she would like to accompany him and accepted her refusal with inscrutable aplomb. She assumed that while walking he occupied his mind with his literary affairs, which she had given up trying to control, and which he worked on for the rest of the day, either in the library or the Frobisher apartment on the second floor. His book had reached a crucial point at which he needed to describe the amazing music that his subjects produced in Grafton, Wisconsin, in contrast to their drunken, desultory lives. He therefore spent the evening listening to tapes he had made from vinyl LPs of the scratchy, blurred old Paramount recordings.

The Johnsons didn't see much of each other either, after they had breakfasted at ten – on toast and coffee, since they didn't have Susan to cook bacon and egg for them. Friday was a busy day for Selina at the Half Moon, where she had become essential to the widowed landlady and worked six lunchtimes and six evenings a week. At one time she had insisted on having Friday as well as Tuesday night off, booking the Golf and getting Tommy to squire her to clubs and cinemas in Scarborough or York, but now that she was two months pregnant she preferred to work on Friday and spend Tuesday evening vegetating in front of the TV. When she set off to work that lunch-time Tommy left, also on his bicycle, in the opposite direction: down the common to the Waggon and Horses in Kirkby, where he was the pool and darts star. When the pub shut he cycled seven miles to Pickering to check the job centre there: since Selina had become pregnant he had been seeking employment a bit more purposefully, but so far without success. Returning to Kirkby he mooched around the marketplace until the chip shop opened, arriving back home at six o'clock with pie and chips that were still hot enough to eat out of the paper and save washing up. Selina financed him to do this once or twice a week. Some evenings after Selina had gone back to work he would settle to watch a video he had hired in Kirkby, but on the Friday in question he had a darts match in Beadlam and had to be back at the Waggon and Horses in Kirkby by seven thirty.

The Hunters saw much more of each other than was the case with either the Frobishers or the Johnsons. They had fruit juice, cereal, bacon, sausage and tomatoes together in their dining nook. Chris then drove Catherine and Clive to school, since he had need of the Mini. He had advertised himself discreetly via Thornham Post Office and the Methodist Church in Kirkby as a general odd-job man/gardener/electrician/plumber/decorator and was now receiving commissions, ironically in view of the fact that there was work at the Hall, which he would have done more competently than the technical monitor and/or more cheaply than imported labour. He cooked himself a lunch of two jacket potatoes stuffed with cheese and onion in the calor-gas oven he had installed in the apartment. As he ate he gloomily watched the news of the miners' strike on TV. In the afternoon he did some work for the Spanish class he attended at Scarborough Tech (preparatory to a camping holiday next summer) and prepared mutton hot-pot for tea. At half past three he set out to collect his wife and son from school. Catherine had had a tiresome day as usual, with most of her charges being obtuse, several mutinous and one sick. Clive, though, expressed satisfaction at the day's events, which included a personal triumph of five team points for spelling (including *reign* and *neighbour*) and a spectacular incident when Lee Nuttall, a strange, highly strung child, climbed below the teacher's desk proclaiming that he was a dog, growled and snarled terribly when Mrs Halmshaw approached him, bit the wrist of Mr Rees the headmaster when extracted, and was carried away, barking madly. After tea Clive did homework, Catherine watched television and Chris consulted his *Reader's Digest DIY Manual* until the family were reunited for a game of Monopoly at eight o'clock.

The Spillsburys were variously employed that Friday, together and apart. Theresa was kept off school, as was often the case when it was the Spillsburys' turn on the duty rota. She did in fact have a cold, but nobody would normally have kept her at home on account of this, least of all herself, since she preferred the perplexities and humiliations of school to life at home. She snuffled and snotted as she tried to keep Brian out of mischief, shoved Emeline up and down the street in a rusty push-chair, took Michael for the half-hour walk that he and she were allowed on non-school days, mopped or Hoovered the entire ground floor of the Hall, did a load of washing in the launderette and three times more or less effaced the ravages of her family from kitchen and dining room. Her presence thus left Mary a lot of time to watch TV in the lounge, which, much to its detriment, had become claimed as Spillsbury territory. (The children were not allowed in the drawing room, which was intended for reading or listening to music and hardly used by anybody, nor in the games room upstairs, where Chris sometimes played table tennis with Clive and Tommy played snooker against himself.) But it was Mary, not Theresa, who busied herself with dinner. She knew that whatever fuss Colin made if he disliked his food would be nothing compared with his wrath if he could pin negligence on her. So she fried sausages for dinner, along with the pale, podgy chips, cooked in a pan of vile-smelling fat, that were her speciality. For lunch those present made do with bread and jam. Brendan and Patrick were at school where they were furrowing their brows and baring their teeth. Best not say too much about that. Colin was also absent for lunch, since he had as usual risen at eleven, had stewed tea and toast for breakfast, then cooked himself bacon sandwiches to take out for lunch. He spent his day sullenly drinking in pubs, conducting truculent business in rubbish dumps and scrapyards, sitting in his Transit van listening to sentimental Irish music while he spied on the affluent. He did not appear at the Hall for dinner, which sent a chill through his family, for they knew that whenever he did get home he would expect his dinner to be ready to serve to him and acceptable to eat. If it wasn't – and probably even if it was – there would be trouble.

The Pococks were together for most of the day. They ate kippers for breakfast, shepherd's pie for lunch, ham sandwiches for tea and roast lamb for dinner – all prepared with the facilities that had been bought at Comet, installed free by Chris

Hunter and finally financed by the Frobishers. Delia avoided other Hall residents by keeping within her own territory as much as possible. Cooking, washing-up and clearing up took a lot of time: she divided the rest of her day between writing a letter to her sister, watching soaps on afternoon TV and attending to the needs of Nibbles, the marmalade cat. Nibbles was symbolic to Delia of her own plight at Sparrow Hall: because of the mischief of the Spillsbury gremlins and the hostility of Julie's scrofulous tomcat Braithwaite, Delia felt that she could not let her pet out of the apartment. Bob was the hardest-pressed of anybody to occupy himself. He had been the same when they kept the guest-house, though. He had not many skills or interests. In fine weather he went fishing or shooting with Christopher Shore, a gentleman farmer he had befriended at the Apple Tree; or walked alone or with Delia – he had worked out a repertoire of rambles all involving lunch at a country hostelry, Bilberton, Broom Green, Westmoor, Hutton-le-Hole, even as far as the Lion on top of Blakey Moor. But a winter day like this Friday was grim for Bob, who couldn't even go shopping, since shopping day, when the Pococks borrowed the Golf and went to York or Pickering, was Saturday. Bob listened to Radio Four, read the *Daily Telegraph* twice, spoiled his wife's TV programmes for her by being vociferous about what crap they were and waited, in the short term, for his hour of modest bliss in the Apple Tree at the end of the day. In the long term he was waiting for the Pocock investments to mature when (he told himself and Delia) they would arise and leave this cut-price country limbo and cram their lives with entertaining activity.

THIRTEENTH GENERAL MEETING OF THE
SPARROW HALL COMMUNITY 3/2/85

Agenda: (i) minutes of the last meeting (ii) matters arising (iii)
Colin Spillsbury (iv) any other business.

Six were present. Damien presented Julie's apologies, saying
that she was in London but should be back soon. Tommy and
the Spillsburys were also absent.

(i) Minutes of the last meeting
These were read and accepted unanimously as a true
record.

(ii) Matters arising
Bob suggested that these, if any, be held over to 'any other
business', since item (iii) on the agenda might provide crucial
information regarding them. This was unanimously accepted
and he called on Damien, in Julie's absence, to deal with
item (iii).

(iii) Colin Spillsbury
Damien apologised for having been 'evasive or unhelpful'
when questioned by residents in the course of the last few
weeks. A lot of rumour had been flying around, and he and
Julie had felt it best to make a detailed statement, when
sufficient clear facts were available, at a General Meeting.
He once again regretted Julie's absence on private business
and said he had decided it best not to further postpone
explanations until her return.

Colin Spillsbury had opened a Post Office account in the
name of Brian Murphy, in Pickering just before Christmas,
depositing £6,000 in cash. On 4 and 7 January he paid
in cheques for £5,000, seemingly signed by Julie, from the
community fund Natwest current account cheque-book.

He had worked out that Natwest do not issue statements until the end of each month. He had got his hands on the cheque-book, torn three cheques from the back of it and forged the treasurer's signature. On 8 January his nerve failed as he worried that soon Julie was going to notice the missing cheques. He attempted to close his Post Office account and withdraw the entire £16,000, to be told that several days' notice would be required. On 14 January he closed the account and withdrew the money, on the same day trying to cash a cheque for £10,000 directly at Natwest, apparently not aware (which is baffling in view of his procedure with the first two cheques) that crossed cheques cannot be directly cashed. When refused this transaction he climbed at once into his van and disappeared, not even returning to the Hall to collect any clothes or belongings: a shrewd move, since the Kirkby branch of Natwest immediately rang Julie to enquire about the 'suspicious-looking type' who had tried to cash her crossed cheque for £10,000. The missing cheques, then the two transfers of £5,000 into the Post Office account of a Brian Murphy, quickly came to light. Colin's initial £6,000 cash deposit into the Post Office account was suspected by the police to be profits of crime, and the squad assigned to the Ryedale burglaries arrived at the Hall complete with forensic and fingerprint specialists.

Mary Spillsbury was interviewed at some length: the only information the police had so far given Damien was what she told them. Colin Spillsbury is not of tinker stock, though Mary is. Her own husband left her three years ago and only Emeline is Colin's child. Her family had disowned her because of Colin, but she was able to guide the police to her uncle Michael, of high standing in the tribe and held in awe by Mary but so detested by Colin that he had renamed his dog after him. This uncle said that he could come for Mary and the children in June or July.

Damien went on to say that he and Julie were not prepared to make good the £10,000 loss to the community fund, which was now down to less than £5,000. Julie had therefore cancelled the second-floor kitchen project, the tender for which had been accepted from Millbank of Thirsk in November but work on which had not yet begun.

Chris said that the cancellation was a breach of the constitution. The proposal for the second-floor kitchen had been democratically approved in September and 'could only be countermanded by a valid majority at a general meeting'. Damien answered that 'the community could only function democratically within its economic parameters'. Residents could not, for example, even with an 8–2 majority, vote to sell the Hall and share out the proceeds. The permission of the owners of the Hall – that is, Damien and Julie – was 'an implicit requirement for any project, particularly any significant financial outlay'. Chris said that if the 'lord and lady of the manor' could countermand any decision whenever it suited them then it was a waste of everybody's time to sit around pretending to make decisions. It would have been better if what Damien called the 'economic parameters' had been made clear from the first and included in the so-called 'constitution', instead of all the 'hypocritical cant about democracy and communism'. Damien retorted that far from being hypocritical in their hopes of a socialist community the owners had been generous in expenditure of their resources in an effort to bring such a community into being. Their efforts had been undermined by those residents who had never had the remotest socialist intentions, so that now there was in effect no community, but 'a group of separate families living in ridiculously cheap capitalist accommodation under favoured circumstances'. The constitution was nothing but a set of rules that everybody broke whenever they liked, like all the other rules and agreements the community had made. If there was any hypocrisy it was when people flourished the constitution in an argument as though it was something they held sacred. Bob intervened to suggest that it might be pleasanter and more productive to move on to something else.

Delia raised the matter of Mary Spillsbury and her children, proposing that notice be given for them to quit the Hall. She argued that the conduct of the children, who had reduced the ground floor of the Hall to a disaster area and been a constant nuisance, would be even more unacceptable now that Colin was not there, who at least had been able to bring them to order if it suited him. It was the responsibility of Ryedale social services, not the Sparrow Hall residents, to 'provide them with accommodation while awaiting the convenience of their relatives'. Damien said that neither he nor Julie would support the ousting of the Spillsburys until arrangements had been made for them by their family. Delia did not press her point since, as she pointed out, with only six persons present there was no point in voting unless there was complete agreement. Bob suggested that the meeting move on to 'any other business'.

(iv) Any other business
(a) Chris proposed himself ready to take on the duties of technical monitor abandoned by Colin, but said that he would expect to be paid a fair rate for work he did. Damien said that 'even at this last gasp of the socialist concept' he was not prepared to support the notion of a member of the community being paid for activity that should be voluntary and for the general benefit. No vote was taken.
(b) Selina asked that Tommy might use the garage as a car-repair shop. Her father had provided the means to purchase a towing vehicle and other necessary equipment. Chris said that he would not support this until Tommy had had the

courtesy to attend a meeting and put the request in person. No vote was taken. Selina at once left the library and Bob brought the meeting to a close on the grounds that there was no longer a quorum.

The Frobisher–Drummond wedding made a bigger stir at Westmoor than at Thornham. It took place in the thirteenth-century church with the reception at Westmoor Grange, one of the most prestigious and expensive venues in Ryedale. Very few people from Thornham were invited.

Westmoor was Drummond territory and there was no problem about filling the groom's side of the church with Young Farmers, huntsmen, rugger players and their families. There was also a whole tribe (including Paul's parents) of urban Drummonds from Hull: thick-set, blackavised Celts in whom the confidence of wealth was merged with a bluff scorn of pretension.

The bride's side of the church was a less comfortable mix. Susan had left home in November, greatly to Julie's relief, after several months of operatic rows and poisonous silences. She had lived with Paul until the wedding and made all the arrangements herself, maintaining diplomatic relations with her mother and stepfather to the extent of sending them the bills and an invitation (from 'Mr and Mrs Damien Frobisher') to the event. She would not invite her real father, Terry Hatchard, nor Jerry Wilkinson, who had acted as her father for eight years. Nor would she consider any of the residents of the Hall, apart from Selina and Tommy. On the other hand, she was keen to include all the Frobishers that could be found, and was miffed to find them limited to Damien's second cousin Hilary, her husband, athetoid son, egregiously braying mother, Annabel, and two old women (sisters of Marjorie) released for the day from an institution in the care of an attendant. The rest of the places on the bride's side of the church were filled with the various girl-friends (and escorts and infants) that Susan had gathered during her teens in the Midlands, Sheffield and Scarborough.

The meal was a staggeringly expensive buffet; lakes of guacamole, banks of smoked salmon and cohorts of drum-sticks in origami bootees. The guests mounded their plates then gathered in cliques around coffee-tables in the hotel assembly room, which had vast picture windows overlooking a frosted lawn. Red-jacketed waiters like matadors circulated with wines, coffee, champagne . . .

'Heifers need it most. You can get a syringe.'

'He's a real rugger bugger. Salt of the earth. Know what I mean?'

'They brought the wine in a van from France.'

'Do you remember me? Probably not! Ha ha!'

'She's fixed that bastard Scargill, thank Christ!'

'The next time I yawned it was as if an axe had split my head.'

'Daddy doesn't want to have to tell you again.'

'They're related to the Norfolk Howards, Howard of Effingham, the Armada wallah.'

'And she looked under the bed and saw twenty Chinamen.'

'Being so attractive must get you a lot of unwelcome attention.'

'Get a sheet of corrugated iron, that will baffle it.'

'Billikins has done a pukie-wukie.'

'Grunk Funk are crap.'

'I've got a few degrees myself, you know.'

'She can take a joke, can't you, my old dear? She knows I don't mean anything by it.'

'Left at the traffic lights on the bypass and you can't miss it.'

'I nearly died of shame when they took off the bandages.'

Susan supervised, narrow-eyed. So far she was satisfied with events. Damien, for instance, looking portly and distinguished in his hired morning suit, was admirably filling the role of father of the bride. Her relationship with him had always been tolerable, based on dismissive amusement on her part and an unconditional surrender on his, which made him her preferred parent and sometimes got him co-opted as a panic-stricken ally. He had beamed with splendid aplomb and given her hand a reassuring squeeze as he escorted her down the aisle. It gratified her that Paul's parents seemed rather in awe of him, as if he was a social notch above them, though in fact the Frobishers had risen with the Industrial Revolution like the Drummonds.

But Susan scowled as her gaze went beyond Damien and lit on her mother. The blood red two-piece suit that Julie was wearing was wrong, the skirt too short for the mother of the bride. Her piled hair, her nervous laugh and her face flushed pink with alcohol all irritated Susan, who was regarding Julie as a disapproving mother might watch a wayward daughter.

Julie caught Susan's scowl and averted her own gaze. She was often fazed by Susan, whose capacity for a single-minded campaign was quite beyond Julie. Julie had become chronically daunted by the unflinching hostility to herself that had motivated Susan's actions since she was a small child. She was consciously modelling herself on her mother's antithesis. After dropping out of art school she had determined to have nothing to do with culture or the intellect. She was going to be a right-wing wealthy snob; mercenary, calculating, eschewing passion and impulse in favour of prudence and respectability. She was going to devote herself to monogamy and motherhood – two fields in which she rated her mother as particularly deficient. She had already made it brutally clear to Julie that her parental policy would be to avoid everything that she herself had suffered.

She detests everything I do, everything about me. The only thing we have in common is she's getting married stupidly young – even younger than I did – and she's maybe only doing that because I've always advised her against it.

Damien, Julie and Tim, once they had held a constrained little conversation with the Drummond parents, were more isolated in the gathering than Selina (now evidently pregnant) and Tommy, who had already met some of Susan's friends, in sports clubs and Scarborough pubs. Both the Drummonds and Susan's other acquaintances had been told awful things about Julie by Susan, who always made great play of the appalling childhood she had endured and impressively survived. The Frobisher clan were also ill-disposed towards Julie because they had been courted and charmed in the past by Dora, and because they utterly disapproved of the riff-raff that now dwelt in the ancestral hall.

Damien was aware of some of this and furious on Julie's behalf. *These morons are privileged to meet her. She's got more courage, integrity, talent and passion than all of them put together.* He gazed at her and adored her garish suit, her flushed face and nervous laugh. He was going to squeeze her arm, a gesture of support and affection, but stopped himself in time: he knew how she was irritated by his fussing and insulted by his concern.

Tim was drinking too much. He had absolutely refused to attend his sister's wedding, only capitulating at the last moment, as he often did. He detested snobs, sporty types, social functions and anybody who was not seventeen years of age. He turned to his mother and said sourly, 'This isn't exactly what you had in mind when we came to Sparrow Hall.'

She gave him her cool look, an eyebrow raised. He went on, in a belligerent, sarcastic voice, 'Wasn't it all supposed to be about workers of the world unite? There's not a lot of revolutionary Marxists among this bunch of shitheads.'

Julie was too intrigued to resent the attack. The idea of

Tim's head harbouring any political consciousness – much less political terminology – was entirely novel.

'What have you been reading?' she asked him.

He ignored the question. 'But at any rate it's honest here. This lot don't pretend to be anything other than shitheads.' He grimaced and awarded himself a bit more wine. 'There's nothing more despicable than liars and hypocrites.'

Piqued now, Julie said, 'And there's nothing more irritating than a self-righteous young twat.'

Damien said gently, 'The young can afford to be uncompromising.'

Tim snarled. He had recently been paying Damien the compliment of including him as the father figure in his mutiny against the galaxy. 'Patronising bullshit,' he said.

Damien gave a sheepish shrug, not offended. He was less worried by Tim than by the speech he was going to have to make in a couple of minutes. He had prepared a witty effort, based on the fiction of a photo album containing shots of Susan's childhood. Then he had rejected it in favour of something brief, conventional, sentimental and insincere. Now he wasn't quite sure what he was going to say, but was fairly confident that it would diminish the portion of Susan's approval that he had so far gained, because he had never made a formal speech in his life that had not been a stammering shambles.

6

BELL AND COMPASSES, LAZENBY 1985

'His real name is Brian Peacock. He's an Ulsterman from Birmingham with a prison record for petty crime. The police reckon he'll now have changed his name again and be having a holiday till he's boozed away his swag.'

The Bell and Compasses in Lazenby was very different from the Golden Lion in Southport. It was a cosy, dingy pub done out in bottle green and dark oak but remarkable for an acrid smell from the overalls of ICI chemical workers who used it. The evening clientele in the lounge was elderly; snarls and guffaws from the public bar indicated that that was where the serious drinkers congregated.

'The family waited all summer for their uncle Michael. The kids were better behaved when that bastard Colin was gone, which amazed us, since he seemed the only thing in the universe they feared and minded. Mary became a different woman, as they say: scrubbing the mansion from top to bottom and cooking great gruesome vats of stew with dumplings and pale, podgy chips for anybody that fancied it. Even the bloody dog was relatively civil. In the end Julie and I preferred them to the other lodgers and were sorry to see the back of them. We even tried to persuade Mary how much better off they were at Sparrow Hall – with social security organised, accommodation and fuel gratis, etcetera – whereas her status is clearly low among her own folk, but it was unthinkable for her to reject her uncle's once-in-a-lifetime offer of forgiveness and readmission to the tribe.'

'You'd not have tried to talk her round if you'd thought there was any chance of success,' Ben muttered.

It was the fourth time Damien had visited Ben in Lazenby, an old factory village on the south rim of Teesside, so he was pretty well used to the Bell and Compasses, as well as to the black little terraced house where he slept on the sofa in the sleeping-bag he brought. The Stotts had moved there in January 1983, ten minutes' walk from the school where Ben was making his last stand as a pedagogue in a post obtained by a mix of judicious excuse and fake reference. Ben was a charismatic schoolteacher, despotic and memorable; there was a honeymoon period in all of his posts before his headmasters became aware of his shortcomings. These included lunch-time drinking, violence and obscene language in class, criminal negligence and irresponsibility, preposterous hostility to colleagues, drinking with male students and forming unsuitable relationships with female students. Nevertheless, because of anxiety to be rid of him and fear of scandal, he had contrived to move from job to job with some sort of reference in conjunction with his moves from region to region to escape creditors.

'A fortnight ago we got a brusque call to say Michael was on his way. Mary had cleaned out the old caravan and Chris Hunter had mended and decorated it. The Spillsburys put their stuff back in the caravan and lived there, waiting for Michael. Last Saturday he came, a great shambles of a man in muddy overalls with long grey hair and a metal leg. He came in an old Land Rover that looked as if it had been in a multiple collision. The dog, which seemed to harbour some old grudge, leaped at his namesake's throat and had ripped his sleeve before Theresa could intervene, but Michael is not easily fazed. He took up a tuft of grass, wiped the saliva from his torn sleeve, kicked the dog without rancour and hitched up the caravan. He seemed not to want to speak to us at all, treating us like aborigines among whom his kinsfolk had been languishing. But when we asked him where he was taking them he uttered the one word, "Whitehaven," with such Celtic twilight aplomb that he made that dump sound like Paradise.'

'Are you advertising for somebody to fill the place of the Spillsburys?'

If Damien's garrulousness had recently become a feature of their meetings, Ben's tolerance of it this evening was a new development. The poetry notebook was lying neglected – just half a dozen lines in alternate red and blue biro – and Ben was not only doing all the listening but showing no impatience.

Damien was drinking so did not answer at once. Another abnormality was that he was drinking fast enough to keep pace with Ben.

Ben went on, 'I told you three years ago that your concept was a non-starter. You can't just lump together a motley sample of capitalist society and proclaim a socialist commune.'

'We weren't able to choose socialists. We got so little response to our adverts that we had no leeway. Julie wanted to get a project started, any project, rather than mark time and admit defeat. That's how she is. So we needed to fill the Hall and couldn't afford to turn anybody down.'

'Except me and Sonia,' Ben couldn't resist saying. 'But you no longer have that problem – of filling the Hall. All you have to do is get a replacement for the Spillsburys – so you can find somebody compatible.'

The schoolchildren of Lazenby were thick and uncouth, according to Ben, who had neither missionary zeal nor loyalty to the working class. He also disliked the available pubs, since his swagger worked best in bourgeois surroundings. He was planning the great coup that was to free him both from teaching and the need to stay in Lazenby: the fake crack-up due to stress that would provide him with six months' full pay, six months' half pay and a pension for life. Thus the concept of a place at Sparrow Hall for himself and his family was more attractive now than in 1982 when he had first proposed himself. And Sonia would not need a lot of persuading to move from Lazenby.

Damien was responding to Ben's last remark, but without the fluency of his earlier narrative: 'The thing is – what I fear is, now that the Spillsburys are gone Julie won't . . . She's made quite a cause of them since Colin left and the last pretence of a community has been . . . She's constantly tried to counsel Mary and raise her awareness so that she isn't such a pushover, such a drudge and victim for the next male. She's dressed and groomed Theresa and taught her how to throw pots and sculpt in clay. She's made friends with the little boys and given them Tim's Hornby-Dublo layout. According to Tim, she's laid out more time and effort on the Spillsburys than she ever did on her own children. She's even managed to befriend the sodding dog.'

Ben's first impressions of Julie (whom he had never met) had been unfavourable. She was too old for his taste and sounded like the sort of emotional dominatrix he avoided. As Damien had confided in him more compulsively, however, Ben had become intrigued by Julie's promiscuity and short-term lack of discrimination. She sounded like a lass he remembered from his teens in Manchester, who had done nothing more spectacular than behave as the majority of boys behaved, but who had been a legend of awe and derision, the subject of vile jokes and outrageous claims by Ben and his buddies. *Sex mad. A nymphomaniac.*

His interest had been further stimulated when Damien told him, with tactless candour, how Julie had rejected Ben's proposal to join the Sparrow Hall community. He assumed correctly that she had formed an unfavourable impression of him from what Damien had told her – reciprocal to the impression that Ben had gathered of her. There was something piquant in this relationship of antipathy conducted entirely through a third person.

Damien took another swig of beer. His face was red and his eyes glistened. 'I long ago reached the status of Terry Hatchard, Jeremy Wilkinson and the other men who didn't tire of her before she tired of them. Without the Spillsburys to occupy her, she'll go, which is unfortunate, because I don't think I can live without her. I greatly admire Julie as well as love her, though sadly my resources for dealing with her vagaries seem limited to either an indulgent vacancy – a mechanical nodding dog – or peevish sarcasm, neither of which . . .'

Ben thought it best to ignore Damien's emotionalism by ascribing it to drink, while himself trying to be sober enough to assess the situation and turn it to profit. But he was by nature neither soberly analytic nor politically devious. His method of dealing with a novel situation – especially when he had taken drink – was to throw words at it, which he now did.

'Marriage guidance is not my speciality, but to keep Julie you need to enliven the inducements on offer. The physical and emotional side is your business and I want no embarrassing details. Your money in itself is not sufficient because she's been wed to you long enough to claim a slice if you split up, and from what you say she isn't mercenary. Sparrow Hall is the best you have to offer and what you need, what Julie needs, what Sparrow Hall needs is a new direction. A new theme. Your derelict kibbutz needs redesigning into a multi-media Parnassus. Poets, novelists, sculptors, potters, studios, workshops, seminars, communal events.'

Damien listened a bit sullenly. He was used to Ben's hectoring tone but detected extra bounce conferred by his own abject confession.

'Let me expound the advantages of culture over socialism as a theme for a community. Socialism is bound and flawed by economic stricture whereas culture is allodial. Socialism posits a rigid structure and can only breathe in rarefied air, whereas culture is ubiquitous and adaptable. Culture helps one surround oneself with like-minded people whereas socialism demands that one gets along with those with whom one has nothing in common. Culture invites one to follow instincts and feast emotions whereas socialism consists of acting against one's interests and denying basic feelings.'

Flushed of face and watery-eyed, Damien peered through the rhetoric towards Ben's real agenda and told himself that he was prepared to pay any price in pelf or folly to avoid Julie leaving. He saw Ben's concepts were a long shot but there were no other cards left to play.

'Julie's a culture vulture herself, a sculptress, who likes her films in black and white with subtitles. She deserts you, for Christ's sake, to go on weekend film courses and incidentally get fucked, so why not bring the films to Sparrow Hall and have her fucked there – preferably by you? I admit that your other residents sound as inconducive to a cultural commune as they were to socialism. But whereas at the moment they feel at home, having ousted socialism, and you are stuck with them, when culture and Ben Stott arrive they are going to feel very out of place. You can rely on me for that. In no time at all we shall be able to replace them with a higher life form.'

As he was finishing his last sentence Ben rose and set off for the bar with empty glasses. Returning with full glasses he began his next sentence as soon as he was within earshot.

'We need to act quickly, and not give Julie time to actually bugger off. Best if you don't divulge, in the first instance, that we're interested in moving in. Just tell her you'd like her to meet your old college buddy at last. We'll bring the kids and stay the weekend, sometime when Julie isn't going anywhere. My impeccable behaviour will be a source of innocent amusement for those who know me.'

7

Ben's voice was tetchy as he ushered Sonia, Netta and Kimberley into the back of Damien's Granada. It irritated him that his family were in high spirits: the trip counted as an event to them because they rarely went anywhere together, Dad needing to spend all his time and most of their money at the pub writing deathless verse for posterity. Netta and Kimberley, eight and seven, civil, dreamy lasses with their father's ginger hair and their mother's freckles, discreetly drew each other's attention to roadside phenomena: the yellow gorse, brown heather and cropping sheep, one of which, interestingly, had been struck by a car and lay in the ditch with four hooves pointing into the sky.

Damien remarked that the gentle demeanour of the girls reminded him of his own daughter. This interested Sonia, as did any reference to children, and she questioned Damien during the winding ascent from Castleton to Blakey Ridge, but got little from him other than that Paulette was now an adolescent in Kankakee, Illinois.

Ben knew that Sonia was happy about both the weekend and the Sparrow Hall project, which coincided with her own motives. She had always been impressed by Damien as her husband's only Oxford survival, the representative of an alternative mode of existence. Damien's periodic visits, though sometimes a nuisance for Sonia, were an earnest that she had maybe not, after all, married a drunken liar but the great poet he claimed to be, who would some day be illustrious and justify the years of beer and penury.

Listening contemptuously to their conversation Ben confirmed that his best friend and wife were people he despised. Sonia, a plump, freckled blonde, had been prestigious enough to escort when he first took up with her, but possessed none of the physical qualities that really attracted him – neither an ethereal Botticellian poise nor the suggestion of emotional fathoms evoked for him most vividly by the countenance of Jeanne Moreau in *Jules et Jim*. She had not been the most brilliant of his female students, nor the best in bed. He had married her because she had been available when the issue arose. They were still together because she was a devout Catholic and though he now thought her fat and stupid his morale required a wife and children. He despised Damien, his only friend and audience for his poetry, less guiltily and with greater relish.

As the car wound over the autumn moors Ben tried to shake off his malaise and practise being benign in preparation for meeting Julie. He was often brusquely attentive to Sonia, enquiring without curiosity as to her comfort and spirits, which she tolerated amiably although it did not compensate her much for his neglect. In addition to overdoing this he now occupied himself with the children in a novel fashion, pointing out topographical features to them and quizzing them about their progress at school like an uncle just back from years at sea. But he soon saw that he was baffling his family and betraying an uncharacteristic nervousness to himself and Damien.

He shut up and occupied himself with misgivings. The advantages of the move to Sparrow Hall, if they pulled it off, would be counterbalanced by considerable hassle. He had launched his retirement plan by starring in a series of spectacular, alcohol-enhanced dramas in the classrooms, staffrooms and offices of the school where he worked, then absenting himself entirely and finding a doddering South Bank doctor to sign the necessary sick-notes. If he moved to Thornham he would either have to go to Teesside each week or find as gullible a doctor in Ryedale. And he had other worries, some long-term, some short. He was revolted by togetherness and suspected he would find Sparrow Hall intolerable. He was worried about how to combine a weekend of diplomacy with enough alcohol to suffer it and withstand the hostile scrutiny of Julie.

They threaded down a valley southwards towards the Lake Pickering meltwater and the Vale of York. At Hutton-le-Hole, a smart tourist village, they took the Westmoor fork then followed the signposts through the hamlet of Misperby to Thornham. As they came into Thornham Sparrow Hall was immediately apparent behind the spiked railings that secluded it from the street: an imposing Victorian building in the same grey stone as the church and cottages, topped by a dark grey slate roof with dormers. Neither the south side, with its terrace, french windows and pompous doorway, nor the gardens were visible from this direction. The Hall looked square and stark, unadorned except for stone quoins and dark brown shutters to the triple tiers of sash windows. Ben, amused by the apprehensive faces his wife and daughters turned towards the building, was at once influenced in its favour.

'It looks like a genteel lunatic asylum,' he murmured.

Julie was charming and serene. Her latest adult-education seminar assignation, a lecturer called Stan with crinkly auburn locks that exactly matched his pubic hair, had let her down badly, by means of a contemptible letter saluting her sexual brio but asserting undying devotion to Rita and the kids. It had left her, for the time being, inclined to nurture equanimity by avoiding such encounters. She was also happy with Sparrow Hall, having replaced her absorption in the Spillsburys with pottery. With her usual prompt energy she had obtained several outlets in local shops and markets.

Ben was gobsmacked by her. He had seen no pictures of Julie and nothing that Damien had said, nor any image he had himself formed of a randy woman in her early forties, had prepared him for how attractive he found her. There was something Botticellian in the carriage of her head and her slender grace, whereas the green sulk of her slightly asymmetrical eyes and the troubled set of her lips proclaimed a latent turbulence only surpassed by the most memorable shots of Jeanne Moreau. What was almost as impressive was her failure to show the slightest susceptibility to Ben's carnal allure.

He saw that preconceptions must be abandoned, including his foreboding about the constraints of the visit. Julie came out of the pottery in grubby denims to greet them. Lunch was a picnic in the panelled dining room, of pork pie and bread and cheese washed down, to Ben's delight, with cans of lager from the fridge. Dinner was fish and chips fetched by Damien from Pickering. Her manner made this casual hospitality relaxing rather than remiss – a whiff of the bohemian informalities of student days that was intensified by the intermittent presence of sardonic, perfunctory Tim. Off to Bristol University in a month's time, Tim was consenting to use the pottery studio for his own art work, deluge the whole premises with heavy-metal music and process mushrooms in the kitchen for himself and a couple of school buddies.

The Stotts' interest in residence at Sparrow Hall was supposed to be the hidden purpose of their visit, to be approached with crabwise stealth, but Julie conducted herself from the first like a landlady welcoming new tenants. They were shown over the property and introduced to other residents as if their coming was a foregone conclusion. They were housed for the weekend in the third-floor guest rooms, since the apartment left by the Spillsburys, though cleaned and repaired, had a traumatised look, as if it had spent a year under water housing killer whales. Yet it was more attractive (and cheaper) than the Lazenby house – and Julie announced that it would be completely redecorated if the Stotts took it.

She reserved her greatest surprise for the evening. It was Ben's plan, after charming Julie all afternoon, to slope off to the local with Damien in the evening, as when Damien visited Ben, to drink and write poetry while Sonia and Julie forged a friendship and looked after the girls. But Julie declared that she, too, was coming to the pub. And when the three of them were settled at the corner table in the Apple Tree Julie took an exercise book and biro out of the pocket of her cagoule and beamed at Ben, who saw that she had applied lipstick and eye-shadow for the excursion.

'Tell me the rules.'

Damien was more discountenanced than Ben by this impertinence. He had given Julie various accounts over the years of visits to Ben and the collaborative verse they wrote while drinking too much, but she had not seemed interested. She did not read poetry, apart from Damien's sparse output, which she usually said she could not understand.

Ben, who had never contemplated writing collaborations with anybody but Damien, who was trained to his requirements, passed this diplomatic test with distinction.

'The only rule', he said, 'is to read what has been written before adding to it.'

The others in the Apple Tree, including Elaine Dobson behind the bar and Bob Pocock when he came in at nine thirty, were puzzled by the spectacle of the trio – the owners of Sparrow Hall and their loud-voiced friend – passing a notebook between them in which they scribbled in turn while consuming draught Guinness (both Damien and Julie drank halves) and discussing a range of social and cultural topics when not wrangling (as they did later in the evening) over what one or other of them had written.

Those who were also in the pub on Sunday evening were treated to a repeat performance. Julie was more enterprising with her contributions, having seen nothing in the mandarin word-plays of her companions to evoke her awe. Ben found her offerings correspondingly more annoying than on the previous evening, but made his protests droll rather than offensive. He himself got sufferably drunk, having consumed several pints of Theakston's Old Peculier when both families (including the voracious and insultingly silent Tim) went for Sunday lunch to the Lion Inn on Blakey Moor.

The Hunters, Pococks and Johnsons were all favourably impressed by their new neighbours. While Netta and Kim were only tepidly welcomed by Clive Hunter (now nearly eleven and a misogynist), they were evidently demure and agreeable children from a different planet than the gremlins. Sonia was deemed highly acceptable. Selina soon preferred her to Tommy as a baby-sitter for their six-month-old daughter, Merline, which suited Tommy fine. Sonia also prepared meals at tea-time for the Hunters when Chris was working, and had these favours returned after she had found a job in a bookshop in Pickering.

At first Ben had to travel once a week to Teesside for his sick-note. He used the decrepit Golf, since he had a driving licence though he did not own a car and detested driving. Then he contrived to get his sick-note service transferred to Kirkby. His impudence was abetted by his headmaster and education authority, who were anxious to establish his medical invalidity and replace him as soon as possible.

He rapidly settled into his routine. Every evening he arrived at the Apple Tree at seven o'clock as Elaine was opening the door. He remained there until eleven, usually drinking six pints of beer. Midday was a problem in so far as the Apple Tree was not open at lunch-times during the week: he solved this by walking a mile and a half in all weathers to Westmoor to be served by Selina.

For several months after his arrival at Thornham he was probably as happy as he ever permitted himself to be. He was amused by the sleepy grey village, the pretensions of the Hall and Sonia's twinges of superstitious discomfort that murder had been done recently on the premises. He was working on a vast poem refuting the validity of metaphor. With any luck he had solved his financial problems for ever, with a pension to keep him in beer and fags. Meanwhile, Sonia was making no waves. And to fill the emotional void in his life, that was nonetheless devastating though mostly self-imposed, he had his utterly uncharacteristic love for Julie: as romantic and hypothetical as a schoolboy crush and as provokingly unreciprocated.

It was a sentiment that played delightful havoc with his preconceptions: the invisibility of women over the age of thirty, his lonely pride, perfunctory lust and scoffing misogyny. It gained obsessive power as the reportedly promiscuous Julie not only refrained from revealing her love for him but even demurred from his dreams, masturbatory fancies and congress with Sonia; she sent, if anyone at all, to paraphrase Ezra Pound, only her handmaidens: Selina, Sally Dobson or the long-ago Manchester nymphomaniac.

Once installed in Sparrow Hall Ben had no intention of carrying out his promise to Damien. In his judgement Julie, whatever her propensity for emotional scrapes, was content at the Hall and unlikely to take flight. To Ben's relief Damien never joined him in the Apple Tree (nobody had proposed a resumption of collaborative verse) or otherwise broached the matter. In fact Damien seemed to be avoiding him. Damien was planning a trip to the USA to research his book and his whole comportment – relaxed, courteous, no more abstracted than was permissible in a writer – gave no sense of a lover in despair. In retrospect Ben was inclined to ascribe the Lazenby supplications to impulse and alcohol.

It was Julie herself who started launching projects similar to those that Ben had proposed to Damien. She showed videos of intellectual films on the big TV in the lounge – and Ben actually absented himself from the pub and filled the lounge with Gauloise smoke and beer-cans while he watched *Jules et Jim*. She gave the use of the library to the local-history society for their monthly meetings, attending a couple of meetings herself but finding them less than fascinating. More enterprisingly, she began to hold a weekly pottery and art class, which she advertised in the pub and post office. This soon achieved a regular attendance of half a dozen pensioners.

Ben watched these antics perplexedly. He was baffled as to how he was going to approach this woman with his own prospectus, which included penetrating her serenity, ransacking her self-sufficiency and chaining her next to his drunken muse in the torchlight of his bleak castle. In the afternoons, between his pub stints, he took to calling in at the pottery and engaging her in chat about Crivelli, Thelonious Monk, etcetera; but any attempt he made to introduce personal matters was nonchalantly evaded or ignored. He could find no chink in the façade, no hint of a woman who prowled like a famished panther through residential courses or kept her husband awake half the night with her compulsive spiel.

Then, one night in April, Ben saw his chance. He blushed more furiously than he had done for many years as Julie sat down opposite him in the Apple Tree.

Damien was in America: trying to give authentic texture to a novel that he suspected bore the mortifying taint of an academic exercise, he was driving from Lula in Mississippi to Grafton in Wisconsin on the same route, as far as possible, that his carload of blues singers had taken fifty-six years earlier.

He was also trying to escape from Sparrow Hall – which he disliked more than ever now that Ben was there to witness it – but not to escape from Julie, for he had wanted her to go with him and almost abandoned the project when she refused.

A third purpose for Damien's trip was to arrive in Kankakee, Illinois, on 11 April, the day before Paulette's birthday. As well as sending Christmas and birthday gifts, he had been encouraged by Julie to enclose brief letters to his daughter with the cheques he sent Dora. These had provoked no acknowledgement, and his plan now was to deliver the birthday present in person. The plan failed because he changed his mind before he reached Kankakee. He told himself that Paulette's birthday was no time to submit her to what she might consider an embarrassing and unwelcome visit: it was hard to imagine that at eighteen years of age she was being prevented by her mother from communicating with him.

Damien's absence in America had large implications in the schemes for adulterous congress with Julie that Ben fantasised. It removed one of the parties whose movements and suspicions would need to be taken into account. The other party, Sonia, seemed less of a problem to Ben: he reckoned that she would find it implausible that her husband had carnal ambitions regarding a woman even older than herself. So Damien's trip was seen by Ben as a peremptory opportunity, obliging him to make at least some predatory gesture or be left with yet another unpublished poem, the masturbatory fantasy of a poltroon.

That very day, in the course of his afternoon chat with Julie, Ben had suggested, in a facetious tone that afforded all parties a means of retreat, 'If the loneliness is unbearable this evening, pop up to the Apple Tree and I'll buy you a drink.'

Julie, perched at her wheel, her face closed, her long fingers cradling the writhing clay, gave his remark neither response nor acknowledgement, so that he was not sure she had heard him, which was irritating, since the offhand nature of the proposal made repetition unthinkable. Several minutes later, as he took his leave of her, he returned more resolutely to the topic.

'How about it, then?' His deep voice, with timbre added by years of untipped Gauloises, this time contained no carelessness. 'Shall I see you in the pub tonight?'

Julie shrugged and said, 'Maybe,' without meeting his gaze.

It was how one treats a suggestion that has no appeal but about which one does not feel strongly enough to rule it out.

'I'd very much like to see you,' he said, with a hint of reproof. But she had turned away and he felt that he had sufficiently put at risk the stance he cherished.

He had no hope of her coming to the pub and prepared nothing, though he had rehearsed a number of such scenes since being smitten by her. He now found himself, like a teenager on a first date, acutely aware that the attention of others in the Apple Tree bar – Elaine behind the counter, Kevin playing himself at darts, Ken drinking alone in the corner opposite – was riveted on Julie's arrival and the embarrassment it was causing him. Just as when he was a teenager, the more it seemed crucial to recapture composure, the more he blushed and sweated. He realised that this bar was the last place in the galaxy for an adulterous tryst.

Ben was confident that the overwhelming majority of people were thick. The almost universal stupidity might easily extend to this desirable ex-sculptress who read Kafka and liked her films with subtitles. It was possible that she had misinterpreted him in the pottery – been too obtuse to understand that his proposal, in Damien's absence, must have the implications of a romantic assignation. But he saw that she had washed her hair, which at present was cut in a jagged fringe on her forehead. There was a blue tinge to the lids of her green eyes and lipstick on her long, wry lips. She was looking chic and slender in a burgundy polo-neck and black denims.

He dissipated some of his confusion by going to the bar to buy Julie a glass of Guinness and get his own refilled.

With absolute effrontery she took up his notebook and peered at the poem he was writing in his decorative but illegible hand. 'Am I interrupting anything momentous?'

She lifted his packet of Gauloises from the table then put it down again.

'Ugh, no!' she said, as if he had offered her one. She produced a packet of Camel Filters, and lit one.

'It isn't very private here,' he said loudly, raising a fierce eyebrow and glaring round the bar. Elaine Dobson switched on some music and turned to polishing glasses, Kevin went back to clumping his darts into the board. Ken looked annoyingly amused then averted his gaze. Ben felt better.

'It's all right,' Julie said. 'I'm not planning to say anything very . . . I've this idea about a weekly poetry evening and wondered if you'd help with it. My plan is that it will also be a social get-together and hopefully a bit of a piss-up, so I'll provide booze and trays of nibbles, then if it takes off people can be asked to chip in for expenses. I say I've had an idea, but in fact I've got two ideas for different . . . One is a poetry-reading evening. Everybody bring poems they've written and reads them to everybody else – or they can bring published poems, Shakespeare and stuff. People can then explain, respond, all that jazz.'

She paused to take a drink then peered at Ben, who snarled within. He wanted to ask her why she could not have spoken in the pottery, but had to dress up and meet him in a pub expressly to disappoint him with this crap. But there was hope that the topic was a mere pretext for keeping the tryst. He was determined not to fail any test that Julie might be setting him.

'Ideally, we should all have copies of what's to be read,' he said.

This was rewarded with a nod from Julie. 'I've bought a computer, a magic thing, a typewriter gone mad. The second sort of evening I plan is much more your speciality. It's poetry-writing along the lines that you and Damien did for years – and you, me and Damien did twice, and for some reason never have since. I don't know how it would work with more than three people – if there were ever more than three! I dare say we could circulate more than one poem. In fact, everybody could start off with a piece of paper, on which they wrote a line – then all pass the papers on clockwise or whatever until eventually . . .'

Ben was nauseated. He was about to say that he thought the idea foolish and philistine when it occurred to him that the suggested practice would seem even more intolerably embarrassing to an introvert like Damien. Which must have occurred to Julie as well, which was why she was canvassing Ben instead of her husband. And his mind ran on from this to a more interesting scenario, with himself and Julie drinking and writing together in the intimacy of the library, the only persevering adherents of an unpopular pursuit. If other people showed up he could flex his ego and discourage them. In any case Julie's notion was a gateway to opportunities that he could not refuse.

'That sounds a bit too busy,' he said. 'Poetry needs space. It's probably best if we just circulate one poem, which will leave people time for casual conversation and the important business of drinking.'

He hoped that she would drink a few beers and be lured into more intimate conversation, escorted home with old-fashioned chivalry and kissed in the dark little lane between the main street of Thornham and the Hall back entrance. If the evening went well enough he might never have to go through with the obnoxious farce she was proposing. She would surely lose the urge for such ventures when she had a *grand amour* with a major poet to occupy her.

But Julie drained her glass and sprang to her feet. 'Nearly nine o'clock! Got to get home for my serial.'

He also rose. She had an effortless capacity for dispersing his assumptions. 'Can't you . . . ? Wait a minute, I'll . . .'

'No, you won't. Don't be crass. I'm old enough to walk home on my own and this is Thornham, not Chicago.'

Ben feared that Julie would advertise the poetry evenings to the public. To his surprise she docilely accepted his point, made in the pottery the day after the meeting in the Apple Tree, that the social aspect (and the drinks and nibbles) would go better if the soirées were restricted to residents – though the residents could, of course, invite other people as they wished. Apart from this mitigation everything turned out worse than Ben expected.

Having confidence both in the unpopularity of poetry and the illiteracy of the Hall residents, he was horrified when the first meeting was attended by no less than seven people. Damien was there, fresh from America, drummed up by Julie and kitted out with a couple of poems, saying little but looking urbane and reading his work without obvious embarrassment. And bloody Sonia was there, having parked the kids with Catherine Hunter. Julie had wanted Sonia to attend as part of an insolent campaign to 'encourage her socially and culturally' – and after Sonia had been so stupid as to agree, Ben's only resource, in order to preserve his own motives from any taint, was to welcome his wife's participation. The others present were Chris Hunter, Delia Pocock and Elizabeth Cope, a vicar's wife who attended the painting classes and had become friendly with Delia.

It was awful. Sonia and Delia had not brought poems but Elizabeth Cope had a sheaf of her own work: religious effusions set to hymn tunes. Chris Hunter had brought along a volume of Kipling from which he read 'The Old Trail' and

'Song of the Banjo'. Ben was inhibited from rudeness by his responsibility to Julie, observing how she sought rapport with everyone, found perceptive things to say at all levels and agilely filled conversational vacuums like a facilitator at a group-therapy session. He drank a lot of canned beer, left the library every quarter of an hour to smoke on the landing, watched the fingers clomp round the face of the carriage clock and wished that he was in the Apple Tree. The worst thing that happened, from his point of view, was that everybody claimed to enjoy the meeting; even Sonia and Delia who had read no poems and said little.

The writing evening seven nights later was worse. All the people who had attended the reading meeting turned up, with the addition of Catherine Hunter, 'come for a chat, really'. Clive Hunter was playing Monopoly with the Stott girls in the room along the landing and Sonia left the library from time to time to 'see how they were getting on'. Two poems were circulated while the company tended to divide into two discussion groups – the Frobisher-Stott and the Hunter-Pocock-Cope factions – with Julie forming a link. Damien was less helpful to Julie – and seemed less at ease – than during the reading evening. When it was their turn to write a line some people kept the book for ages, while others just gave a bashful shake of the head and tried to pass it on. Julie worked hard at seeing that the poems circulated and rules were more or less kept. She was clearly looking to Ben to supervise, but he found it difficult to bring himself to read the offerings. Elizabeth Cope, as a born-again Christian as well as a vicar's wife, felt it obligatory that she should mention God in every line she wrote. Chris Hunter always rhymed with the line immediately preceding his own, at whatever cost. Ben left at half past nine and was shocked to hear later from Sonia that everybody had once again declared the evening enjoyable.

The situation was intolerable. The next Thursday he went

first to the Apple Tree, arriving at the poetry reading half an hour late. He then subjected the other poets to abrasive heckling ranging from exclamations like *What shit!* to a long harangue on scansion. The following week he was even more drastic, treating his fellow-collaborators as he used to bully a school class when he was in a foul mood. Everybody was relieved when he left at half past nine to return to the Apple Tree.

His dislike of the poetry evenings abated in ratio with the enthusiasm of the rest of the group. Elizabeth Cope gave up both poetry and painting groups after being 'scoffed at by that drunken boor from Manchester'. Delia and Catherine only lasted a few weeks. Chris was made of more impervious stuff, being as careless of the candour of others as he expected them to be of his, but even he did not always attend. Both Damien and Sonia shunned the writing evenings. On a Thursday evening in early October Ben rolled into the library at ten o'clock and was not surprised to find Julie alone there, taking wine while composing a poem.

Everything now transpired with prompt simplicity. Ben sat next to Julie at the library table, as if to read what she was writing. He observed that her cheeks were flushed with the wine and that she was again wearing that occasional trace of makeup – the blue eyelids and the scarlet lips – that he censured on other women and found sexually arousing on this one. She turned her face towards him at abrupt close range and they kissed instantaneously, calmly and deeply, like committed lovers. His right hand was on her waist, her left on his shoulder, as if they were about to dance. She did not give an intense little sob and thrust her head into his shoulder, as she had done to alarm Damien and others. Ben managed not to say, *Hello, Julie. It's been a bitch of a world without you* – which was what he usually said at that juncture, inserting the appropriate name. They just looked at each other solemnly for several seconds, then kissed again.

'There's the guest room upstairs,' she proposed. Her slightly asymmetrical eyes and discoloured tooth made her seem very human and lovely to Ben Stott as she grinned at him, then added, 'You look a bit taken aback.'

'Surprised, is all,' he retorted, recovering a bit of composure. 'I thought you only wanted me for the poetry.'

'Communal poetry? Don't talk daft.'

'The rules that govern my haiku are semantic rather than formal. The haiku is convenient for models of Hegelian dialectic.'

She shifted her head on his arm and laughed. 'A novel line in pillow talk!'

Naked on top of the duvet, they were able to admire the ivory pallor of their flesh in the curtained daylight. They always pushed the two single beds together so that they could sprawl and smoke and doze but as often as not they lay talking like this, intertwined, till they were ready for sex again.

'Sarcastic bitch! Would you censor my discourse? Already, to sate your finicky whim, I abstain from lunchtime alcohol and verse in order to perch my afternoons on this squeaky plinth making love.'

'Shagging. Three times a week. I appreciate your sacrifice.'

'While Damien peregrinates the Thornham purlieus insulated in the Mississippi mud of his unwritable book and Sonia sells unreadable books to Pickering illiterates.'

'So the coast is clear. I expect it's weird for you having sex sober.'

'I've certainly never had sober sex with Sonia and I wouldn't fancy it.'

'I wonder how she feels about that?'

'Apart from her, the occasional encounters permitted by

160

the exigencies of my service to Bacchus and Apollo have been almost exclusively with barmaids or sixth-form pupils. Misogyny, impatience with arrangements, intellectual arrogance and latterly a reluctance to distress Sonia have truncated these relationships and limited data.'

'You're a pompous Oxbridge pillock. Luckily you have redeeming features. Your prick is miraculously undamaged by all the booze, fags and metaphor.'

'Prior to you all my lovers were morons. And the only woman over thirty in fact or fiction to whom I ever paid serious attention was Shakespeare's Cleopatra, an infantile bimbo.'

'I bet you were expecting something trollopy and exotic and are a bit disappointed.'

'On the contrary, I'm delighted by both of us and our effortless carnal complicity. I'm inspired by the orgasms we orchestrate to fantasise a galaxy where their number might be at least doubled and time be allocated for delicious dawdlings and variant doodlings.'

'Hmm. In what other ways have I surprised you? Extol me a little.'

'You're neither demanding nor neurotic. You've not assailed me with the monologues that Damien complained about. Maybe that's just because we never spend a night together.'

'No, it's because with you there's nothing to confess or resent. We need to keep it like that.'

'Neither do you confront me with the ruthless candour, the urge to be without guilt or apology, that insisted on Damien being aware of and in a sense condoning your adultery.'

'I've come to see that there's nothing the matter with a secret if it's not a guilty one.'

'I must admit your discretion's a relief to me. I've discovered *inter alia* that when I consider Damien and Sonia I'm not the all-licensed poet that I've always proclaimed.'

'Hey, let's not start maundering about relationships and responsibilities. I want this room to be ours. Private. A crap-free zone.'

'You're also an intriguing threat to my prejudices: I find myself cherishing in you the sort of particulars (hatred of Velcro, discoloured tooth) that have always irritated a transcendental eleutherarch like me, since they're the clues that distinguish phenomenal woman from the aristocratic incubi, the ideal Simonetta Vespucci and Jeanne Moreau of my neo-Platonist reveries and doctrines.'

'You can exaggerate my attractions if you like.'

'I've come to suspect that for the first time in my life I'm in love with a real person, a flawed and transient dancer rather than the intricacies of the dance.'

'That's bullshit. You're maundering again.'

'We've done our stint in this dump,' Delia declared.

The Pococks were giving a farewell dinner to the Hunters – the only people in the Hall they had dealings with. Clive had not been invited because the Pococks didn't like children: he had already been fed and was doing his homework in the Hunter suite, after which he had permission to work on the remote-control model aeroplane that he and his father were building. At ten o'clock, if his parents had not returned, he was on his honour to go to bed.

The Pococks had been going to 'see the world' when they came into their money but more prudent notions had prevailed: they had bought a terraced house on Trafalgar Square in Scarborough, backing on to the cricket field, very similar to their old hotel. Rents from the upper floors, together with their pensions and the interest from some reinvestment, would keep them for ever in modest pomp in the ground-floor apartment.

Bob was particularly pleased. He would be able to toddle

across town to the Archives on Valley Road, his favourite pub in the universe, for his evening potion. 'It's been a rum old three years but we'll write it down to experience,' he now said, grinning.

Delia grimaced. 'We certainly shan't be sorry to see the back of Ben Stott.'

Bob replaced his grin with a scowl. 'You haven't got to let that sort of chap get to you. I ignore him. I must say, though, that when I was younger the blighter would have got a punch on the nose.' He brandished his fist, the fist of a trained killer, then spread the fingers and watched them quiver.

Delia's cooking was proficient, if trapped by xenophobia. Her efforts were always rapturously acclaimed by Chris, who did all the Hunter cooking, and who had specially ordered the duckling with orange sauce and roast potatoes that were the centrepiece of the meal. The Pococks had a half-bottle of burgundy and had provided pure grape juice for the teetotal Hunters. They had also opened a little bottle of champagne, just a small glass for everybody, to give the occasion a celebratory feel. Catherine had accepted hers and become subtly flushed and giggly. Chris had refused his and Bob had drunk it.

Thirty years – as well as the childless domesticity of the one and the career of the other – separated Delia and Catherine, but their social and political attitudes were similar and they had *EastEnders*, *Coronation Street* and *The Archers* in common. Bob and Chris despised each other but were prepared to try to be civil for a couple of hours to oblige their wives. Along with Delia's cooking, the offensiveness of Ben Stott was one of the few subjects that found them in any accord.

Chris said, 'I'll tell you one thing for sure. I'm not going to let that Ben Stott have the satisfaction of giving me the push.'

Delia cried indignantly, 'Nobody's *given us the push*! Sparrow Hall has served its purpose in giving us accommodation we could afford until our investments matured. We are leaving according to plan and in our own good time.'

Catherine said, 'That's what we'll do. I'm applying for graded posts all over the country. As soon as I get something suitable we're off.'

Chris repeated, in a louder and more plonking voice, 'I'm not going to let that Ben Stott have the satisfaction of giving me the push.' Then he went on in the same tone, 'I'm not going to kow-tow to his posh degrees neither, nor have the likes of him tell me what's poetry and what's crap.'

Catherine patted his wrist, a half-calming, half-reproving gesture. Though both the poetry evenings and Chris's own poetic efforts had ceased months ago, he still regarded himself, with embattled stubbornness, as a crusader against the pseud and sloppy in poetry. It went with his Methodism and trade-unionism – like his enemy Ben Stott he was perfectly comfortable when in a minority of one – but there was more to it than that and Catherine was troubled by it.

Since their roles had reversed and she had gone back into teaching, Chris had become a DIY fanatic, a brass-band trombonist, a pigeon fancier, a Bible buff, a campanologist, an odd-job man, a numismatist and latterly a poet. He did everything without flair or pleasure but with the grim arrogance of somebody making a statement. It was getting worse as his son grew more critical and less adoring. He was suffering from the lack of validity that afflicts many housewives – and coping less well than they usually do, because he had known the pride and prerogatives of a man.

Catherine said, 'Sonia's lovely, though. I'd like to make a friend of her if it wasn't for Ben.'

This got Chris out of his mental short-circuit. 'A grand lass,' he agreed. 'And the girls are right enough. They deserve a sight better than yon comedian.'

'I don't know about that,' said Delia. 'No woman with any

self-respect would put up with a nasty drunk like him.' She gave Bob a cool look as she said this, not having forgiven him for the unseemly promptitude with which he had annexed Chris's champagne.

'And an adulterer,' said Catherine. 'I'm sorry for her, though. She's got the children to think about.'

Delia snorted. 'If she had any thought for her children she'd get them away from that sot.'

Chris said, 'She's a devout Catholic. She thinks marriage is for ever. I admire folk what stick to their principles.'

Bob lifted his empty glass to his lips, put it down again and rechecked that the bottle was empty.

Delia said, 'He seems to have gone out of his way to be particularly . . . personally unpleasant to us . . . to Chris and Bob and me and . . .'

Her morale was not as high as Bob's. The Spillsburys had drained her pluck, making her unwilling to leave the apartment even to go for walks. In the relief of their departure she had taken to attending Julie's art classes and even given the poetry evenings a try; then Ben Stott's sarcasm had cowed her more than the incoherent menace of the Spillsburys. Age had brought her to pester her wounds and brood on impossible revenge. Hell for her was other people – and she was already worrying about the noisy weight of tenants on the fragile ceilings of the house in Trafalgar Square.

'Of course he has,' said Catherine. 'And it isn't hard to work out why or who's behind it.'

Chris said, 'Cathy's got a theory.'

Catherine frowned. She did not like Chris to call her 'Cathy' in public, because she preferred everybody else to call her 'Catherine'. 'It's not a theory, just common sense. Julie's given up the political rubbish but not the notion of having a little community she can be queen of. Only she's decided she wants her own kind – high-brows . . .'

Bob said, 'You mean Ben is following instructions?'

'She can get some men to do whatever she wants. Look at Damien.'

Bob put his head on one side as if to let the concept move down a groove in his brain. 'Damien's civil enough.'

'Damien's not in on the plot,' said Catherine. 'He's getting the push too.'

'You mean her ladyship and Stott . . . ?'

Catherine said, 'Bob, you're priceless. Everybody knows but you. Even dozy Damien knows.'

Delia said icily, 'What's more, I've told you all about it at least twice.' She rose to remove the plates and bring the syllabubs. 'I've always seen the sort of woman she is.'

'Very suitable for the likes of Ben Stott.' Chris took a sip of his grape juice and smacked his lips loudly, a habit that Catherine had tried for years to cure.

8

CHRISTMAS 1987

Christmas came with heavy snow. Snow ploughs cleared the road through the village, but then more snow fell. It lay churned and brown on the road, thick and white in the verges and gardens and on the roofs of barns and empty holiday cottages. Thornham became a muffled monochrome of black timber, grey stone and dark grey tiles sketched impressionistically on the whiteness, with only here and there a vivid dab of colour provided by a motor-car or the bobble-hat of an intrepid pedestrian.

Nobody left the Hall that Christmas except the Hunters. The Stotts had always spent Christmas with grandparents: 1987 was the turn of Ben's parents, but since Christmas 1985 Ben's mother had died and he had fallen out with his father for ever. The previous year the Frobishers had gone to Susan's, but this year Susan and Paul Drummond, with two-year-old Graham and five-month-old Fiona, were at the Hall by nine in the morning. Tim was home from Bristol University with Ingmar, his new flat-mate, and the Johnsons had this year decided to stay in Thornham. Selina now worked at the Apple Tree, where she was in demand over the Christmas period, though free on Christmas Day. She was glad to miss the family rancour that made London visits gruelling. Christmas Day was therefore a heavily attended event and one of the rare occasions when the claims of the residents to be a community might not seem too far-fetched.

The Pocock suite was now occupied by Nick Townsend and Corinne Cotterell, a couple from Teesside. Nick, an acquaintance of Ben, was an art teacher in his mid-thirties: tall, with straggly blond hair and a prominent Adam's apple. His own art work consisted exclusively of arrangements of treacle tins and wire. Corinne was nineteen, plump, pale and sulky, her hair cropped short and bleached yellow. Until she was seventeen she had been a sober virgin, a headmaster's daughter, toeing the line in school and at home for fear of her father's wrath and mother's grief. Her teenage rebellion had come later than most and the explosion had been more spectacular. Now she and Nick were in flight from Corinne's first lover, Sloopy, a tattooed psychopath with Bullworker muscles and bad teeth who had taken her defection badly – cornering them in Corinne's flat, brandishing kitchen implements, laughing and snivelling and emitting spectacular threats.

Susan bounced into the kitchen. At twenty-two she was a tall, strapping lass who had no problem about accentuating her stature with a white trouser-suit and chunky sweater. She was strong, too: toting Fiona at her breast while swinging Graham easily with her free hand.

'Merry Christmas, everybody. God, what a shambles!'

Actually, things were moving along with tranquil competence. The beef and ham had been cooked on Christmas Eve, the monster turkey heaved and kicked into the oven at dawn. Julie was stretching pieces of streaky bacon and wrapping them round sausages. Damien was crumbling bread for sauce. Sonia was cutting little Vs into the Brussels sprouts.

Julie said mildly, 'We're doing fine.'

'You never cooked a decent meal in your life, Mother. It's a bit late to start trying now.'

'Merry Christmas, everybody.' Paul Drummond, a sturdy fellow whose thick sideboards and thinning pate made him look like a Victorian waiter, appeared grinning from behind his wife and gave his mother-in-law a kiss. He had a carrier-bag full of presents in one hand and a globe of aluminium foil balanced on the palm of the other as a waiter might bear it.

'The pudding,' he announced. Susan had made it in November and it was supposed to be her only contribution, since she had cooked the whole meal for the family the previous year.

'Put it there,' said Julie. 'By the microwave.'

'Mother, you're clueless,' said Susan severely. 'It's not going near any microwave. It needs steaming for three hours. And that oven needs turning down or the bird will be incinerated.'

Julie took her apron off. 'You take over if you like,' she murmured. 'I'll look after Graham.' She bent to hug the infant she adored.

Susan took the apron from her mother. 'Sonia can look after him. You're too soft with him.'

Tim came in with Ingmar, a slender Swedish lad with almost painfully fair hair. He greeted his sister with a nod. She didn't greet him at all, but Paul bellowed, 'By, Tim lad, you've grown! You must be seven foot tall!' – which was exactly what he had said last time he saw Tim.

Tim said, 'Is there any chance of a bit of toast? Breakfast seems ages ago.'

Susan said, 'No way. There are too many drones in this kitchen.'

Tommy slouched in behind Tim and Ingmar. He had been thrashing them at snooker in the old games room upstairs. When he saw Susan his habitually morose expression was transformed into an ecstatic grin. 'Hey, Sue!'

Susan abandoned her officious stance and responded with a smile, her lips curling childishly away from her teeth and gums. It was only when she smiled that she looked at all like Julie.

'Merry Christmas, Tommy,' she said fondly. 'You silly sod.'

*   *   *

A vast Christmas tree from the Drummond copse had been erected a few days earlier in the vestibule and hung with lights and baubles by Julie, Sonia and the Stott girls. Under it a multicoloured mound of wrapped presents was assembled. The girls (Netta was now ten and Kim nine) had also been instrumental in the entire ground floor of the Hall being swathed and spangled with decorations. There were paper chains, bushy streamers, tinsel festoons and folding bells, so that just above head height the air was thronged with a festive galaxy. There was holly, mistletoe, Christmas cards pinned to the panelling – and the parquet tiles and Axminster rug were soon littered with exploded present wrappings, toys, which either Graham Drummond or Merline Johnson had found under the tree or brought from upstairs, and gobs of snow and slush that everybody had trodden in from outdoors.

Conspiring with this spectacle was Christmas-medley music from the hi-fi, which had been lugged from the drawing-room to a more central position. The TV in the lounge was offering a Disney video featuring pastel landscapes and euphoric morons but only adults were watching it – Tim, Ingmar, Paul, Tommy. The children, who furnished the excuse for everybody to indulge themselves and suspend their critical faculties, were playing on the Axminster rug in the entrance hall.

Netta and Kim, squat and frizzy-haired like their mother, found the infants more interesting than the presents they themselves had received. Kim was jogging Fiona on her knee, clapping the baby's hands together and shouting some jingle. Fiona was bouncing happily with shining eyes and a wet, gummy grin. Netta was trying to protect a too-delicate doll's house from the boisterous messing of Merline Johnson. Graham was fascinated with a marble run, clustering as many as he could manage on the top floor of the edifice then letting them zigzag their way down the wooden shutes. It was a purely aesthetic pleasure, since he had not graduated to the notion of racing the marbles against each other. Nor had he the wit to put any sort of arresting device at the end of the run; so the slaloms were punctuated with pauses while he retrieved all the marbles he could reach from under the sofa.

Julie, Sonia and Selina were watching. Selina giggled. 'Look at that dumb kid. Typical bloke.' Serving men drinks had given her a low opinion of the gender.

'Mum! Stop her!' wailed Netta, making a petulant mouth, so that her ten-year-old face reverted to infancy. 'She's wrecking it!'

Merline was trying to garage a yellow truck, the property of Graham, in the fragile sitting room of the doll's house. Sonia leaned over and put a restraining hand on the truck: gingerly, in view of Merline's known combustibility. 'The truck won't fit in the house, love.'

Merline scowled histrionically, pursed her lips and wrenched the truck out of Sonia's grasp. 'Gizzit!' she hissed.

'Hey, angel!' Selina called brightly. 'Come and look at this!'

Merline flashed her eyes, suspecting a ruse. She cherished the truck beneath her arm while she went over to examine the somewhat disappointing marble that Selina was holding.

Julie said, 'I've always wondered if Christmas is good for kids.'

Selina gloried blithely and proudly in Merline, never disciplining her and amusedly indulging her wilfulness. Susan, on the other hand, was a controller and moulder. Graham, four months younger than Merline, was supposed to use a plastic knife and fork, eat everything put before him, keep reasonably clean, obey instructions instantly and say 'please' and 'thank you' hundreds of times a day. Susan now popped out of the kitchen to check that her son was not deteriorating too rapidly from exposure to permissiveness – and overheard her mother's remark.

'Let's face it, Mother, these kids are getting the sort of Christmas your kids never had.'

Julie grimaced. There was no way of stopping Susan making vicious remarks without a full-scale row. She found it best to let them ride and hope they were a conversational habit rather than representative of a real attitude.

In any case Susan had trotted back into the kitchen where other matters needed her supervision. Soon Merline and Graham were playing together (a bit fractiously) on the marble run. Netta was trying to mend the doll's house. Kim was delighting Fiona with a rattle.

Selina watched broodily. 'All play, innit? Mind you, grown-ups are as bad. Tommy with his soccer. The punters in the bar. You lot with your poetry and stuff. It's all messing around, playing games. None of it's real.'

Selina had made an effort to partake in the political commune, but since it had become cultural she had distanced herself, relating to critical outsiders like Susan Drummond and Elaine Dobson. She disliked Ben.

Sonia wasn't sure how she felt about being lumped in with poets. She had taken her daughters to midnight mass and was now weary. 'What's real?' was all she said.

'Bringing up Merline so she knows where she is and doesn't have to take any shit is real.'

Sonia blurted, 'I get so that looking after kids seems no more real than anything else.' It was the sort of thing she sometimes said to the priest in confession.

Selina's scowl was remarkably like her daughter's. 'It's more real than all that religious stuff.'

'Religion is the ultimate cop-out from reality,' Julie interposed. 'Even drunks are sober sometimes.'

Sonia was offended by the sudden double onslaught but before she could retort Kim shouted, 'Fiona's filled her nappy! Pooh!'

Graham, who was going through a phase of emphatic repetition, echoed with relish, 'Pooh!' His thin and peevish features, reminiscent of Susan's when she was a child, took on an expression of malicious jollity, then he rolled onto his back and laughed without constraint, shouting, 'Pooh!' as often as he was able.

Netta had sprung to her feet. 'Let me help change her, Mum, please!'

Ben had picked his way queasily through the greetings and present-swapping to escape from the Hall. He was in the Apple Tree as soon as it opened, only to be subjected to the same seasonal cheer.

His stance towards Christmas was Scrooge-like at the best of times. He had thought not going to his father's would improve things, but formidable alternative irritants had transpired. Ingmar was in the guest room, the trysting place of Ben and Julie. Julie was absorbed in furnishing Christmas for her children and grandchildren.

The Apple Tree was less attractive these days, with insolent Selina behind the bar, food served and children tolerated. Neither was poetry the resource it used to be. He had a notebook with him today to stop people talking to him but he did not usually write much in the Apple Tree. He had become the pub grouch and caustic wit, as well as a star of the quiz team, which gave scope to his penchant for pedantic bombast (*'I know what it says on your card – it says Christopher Marlowe – but in fact Marlowe was paraphrasing Horace'*). He wrote more poetry when he went to the Half Moon in Westmoor, and that was where he wished he was today when Tim, Ingmar, Paul, Corinne, Nick and Tommy breezed into the Apple Tree.

Susan had made Paul lead the expedition in order to 'get people from under the feet of the workers'. The bar was full of men spoiling their appetites for the Christmas dinners their wives were frantically preparing, so the youngsters didn't see Ben for a while, but in any case he was flattering himself if he thought them likely to throng round and pester him. But they came close enough to his corner for their conversation to be within range of his contempt.

'Which beer in Yorkshire is the one I should most savour?'

'Women look better with flesh on them.'

'They do that.'

'It's for head-bangers, morons. The musical content is zero.'

'All my princes turned to toads, so I started looking at toads.'

'Any pro footballer'd have done what Maradona done.'

'They would that.'

'I speak English yet cannot understand these people in my vicinity.'

'She just held it up and stared at it. It were hilarious.'

'I'd join the hunt saboteurs but I can't stand animal-lovers.'

'He blanks out just like that. I don't know what he uses.'

'Pigs can see the wind, you know. Very deep, are pigs.'

Corinne was particularly lively and cheerful – normally she sulked like a kidnapped princess. Nick was a disappointment and so was Sparrow Hall: she had envisaged a hippy commune full of sexual and narcotic licence. But the trite Christmas spirit and an influx of people closer to her own age had transformed her for the day. She was finding both Tim and Tommy tasty and giving considerable effort to ogling one or other of them.

Dinner, finally delivered at twenty to three, was a major undertaking, aimed at feeding seventeen people including the breast-fed Fiona. The monster turkey was reinforced by an aitchbone of beef and a leg of ham. The accoutrements were bacon, sausages, roast potatoes, Brussels sprouts, stuffing and cranberry sauce. The Christmas pudding was swart, sweet, heavy and fruity, served in a bonfire of rum and brandy. All this was washed down with various combinations of sherry, wine, iced water, fizzy pop and Irish coffee. To succour those who fell hungry before or after dinner there were nuts, figs, dates, chocolates, mince pies and Christmas cake almost as soggy and sinful as the pudding, accompanied by Wensleydale cheese and marzipan.

Julie managed to take a time-switch photograph of everybody by balancing the camera on the scullery hatch then scampering back to her own place. The photograph was to bear witness to the six disparate adult couples: hulking Damien and slender Julie; grinning Paul and sombre Susan; skinny Nick and plump Corinne; Tim with his brown curls and Ingmar with his white helmet; Ben in his bomber jacket, Sonia in matronly blue; Tommy hunched over his plate like a tom-cat in an alien yard, Selina waving a long, lissom arm like a dancer.

After a while Paul gasped, leaned back and loosened his trousers. 'By, this is grand! Reminds me of Christmases when I were a kid.'

Tim said, 'Yeah, I wanted to show Ingmar a real English Christmas.'

Susan said, 'If we got any sort of Christmas when we were kids it was Jerry provided it. Mother was too busy doing her own thing.'

'That's bollocks,' said Tim. 'We had some great Christmases and Mum did her share.'

Susan said, 'Tim, you've always talked crap.'

They smiled at each other. Both knew better than to delight the other by losing their temper.

Nick was looking at the red wine in his glass and wondering if it would be transparent when held directly to the light. His long strands of yellow hair, through which his boozy eyes peered doggedly, gave him a superficially youthful look.

Damien said, 'I always envied kids in big families at Christmas.'

Sonia said, 'There were seven of us. My parents were devout Catholics. I've always felt sorry for Ben being an only child.'

Ben snorted. 'I never missed siblings. If there had been any, they'd doubtless have been as stupid as my parents, who were the living disproof of heredity.'

Julie said, 'I'd have given anything to be an only child. There were four of us and we hated each other and wrecked Christmas. I don't know why we were such twats because Mum and Dad stayed together and treated us okay. Dad was soft, an old easiful, while Mum tried to knock us into some sort of order. Us kids all left home as soon as we could to get away from each other.'

'Us too,' said Susan. 'But then, there came a point when we were made to feel distinctly unwelcome.'

Tim said sarcastically, 'We were given bricks to eat and beaten with barbed wire.' Absence had mellowed his attitude to home, but not to his sister.

Ingmar said in perfect, careful English, 'Tim, you have a crumb on your lip.' He leaned forward and carefully, caressingly, removed the item with his finger. Susan looked from Ingmar to Tim to Paul to Julie.

Corinne had been an only child in a house of immaculate Draylon and polished pine. Christmas had been as demure as all other events. She said, 'If Sparrow Hall was always like this! It's great here today.'

Nick said, 'It is that!' When relatively sober his conversation consisted mainly of agreeing tersely and judiciously with what had just been said. This got him a reputation for discreet sagacity.

Corinne ignored him. Now that Sloopy was not binding them together, like a mad father with a shotgun, they liked each other less and less.

Julie quietly asked Tim, 'How's university?'

'I'm quitting.'

She gave a little moan of protest. 'It's only a few months to your finals!'

'I don't want a degree and a career and all that bullshit. I'm going to travel the world, a scummy drifter, and find myself.' He smiled at her shyly and added, 'I thought you'd understand.'

By the end of the meal spirits were raised and tempers mellowed. The children played their part in this. The Stott girls were the sort of people for whom Christmas is customised, enhancing everything with their undiscriminating zest and glee. Graham Drummond and Merline Johnson toddled tirelessly and demandingly among the debris ensuring that nobody's spirit flagged, and baby Fiona was a valuable focus of attention and conversation.

Yet it was the young adults who contributed most. Tim, Ingmar, Paul, Selina, and Susan as soon as she put her mind to it, made a blithe and vivacious bunch, their motley interests finding common ground in levity that delighted the children and won over most of the other adults. Even Tommy, tongue-tied with other residents, blossomed in the presence of Susan and became voluble and droll. In the course of the afternoon almost everybody loosened up, wore silly hats, bellowed cracker mottoes at each other, pushed snow down each other's necks and were rendered helpless with mirth by mild inanities.

While several people dozed off at some point in the day and most grew blurred and emphatic nobody was unpleasantly drunk. After the meal there was a futile attempt at a siesta in the lounge by some while others watched TV or listened to music. Then Tim led a sledging expedition to the sloping field known as the Tofts, east of the village. Plastic feed-sacks stuffed with straw made thrillingly erratic sleds and a monster snowball-fight with everybody against everybody else was incorporated, so that all returned drenched to the Hall and had to change into dry clothes. Then there were games of Monopoly, Risk, Trivial Pursuit, snooker, table tennis, chess – and a couple of concerted attempts at clearing up: jamming all the rubbish into bin-liners and stacking the new, giant Bendix dishwasher in the communal kitchen. All activities were accompanied and bedizened by quips and quiddities, gossip, histories and confidences, witty and/or fervent discussion of books and films, vehicle maintenance, music, football, God, child development, Utopia, maladies of the digestive system . . .

'A normal woman – a woman like Sonia – does not have a mental domain of her own. Her faculties are fixed on finding a suitable mate to impregnate her and feed her brats. There is truth in that much reviled Milton quote – "He for God only, she for God in him" – if one takes it to imply that women will have the whip hand in practical relationships, being focused on utilising men, whereas men must content themselves with suzerainty over the hypothetical and abstract.'

The evening invasion of his refuge had been worse for Ben than lunch-time. All the adults except Sonia had thronged into the pub in paper hats – even Damien, pink and beaming – had drunk beer, laughed, giggled, shouted and sung carols. The locals had joined in and everybody had applauded themselves and each other. Now Tim, Damien, Ingmar, Julie and Selina had gone back to the Hall. Paul, Susan, Tommy and Corinne were having another drink at the bar.

Ben was haranguing Nick, who had flopped down opposite him. They had drunk together on Teesside and were becoming cronies in the Apple Tree. Nick had first been amused by Ben's boasts of iconoclastic teaching (asking latecomers to the lesson if they had enjoyed their wank and ordering sets of *Finnegans Wake* as third-form readers), then impressed both by Ben's articulate erudition and the unsociability that made it flattering to be tolerated by him.

Nick said, 'That's very true, is that.'

'Julie is a good example. In her attempt to adopt a male psyche she surrendered many of her female powers and became vulnerable and unhappy. I like to think I've straightened her out a bit. But don't tell her I said so.'

'Corinne's a bit like that.'

'No. Corinne's stance is mere adolescent perversity. Brutality and neglect are called for, so that she will either adore you or bugger off altogether.'

'That's how I should have treated bloody Barbara.' Barbara was the wife who had divorced him because of his drunkenness, about whom Nick lamented if he was given the chance.

'Be brusque and unreliable. Apologise if you like, but explain nothing. Make sure that you are never soberer than she is, however much it costs you. Never promise anything or ask for anything or lie to spare her feelings. Above all, never mention love. Talk, if you must talk, about intelligent topics like metaphor and prosody. Even in the throes of lust avoid avowals and endearments.'

The kitchen, in which people had made cold-meat sandwiches and opened cans of beer, was a mess again. Green Teeth were playing on the stereo, frenetic and high-pitched but with a persevering bonging bass like a deep-water pulsar. Susan and Paul had left with the children and Sonia had taken Merline and the girls upstairs.

Corinne said, 'Tommy, come and dance. I bet you're a great dancer.'

Tommy looked at Selina.

Corinne said, 'Do you have to ask fucking permission?'

Selina laughed. 'He's crap. Just because he's black doesn't mean he can dance.' She caught Tommy's reproachful eye and relented. 'He was ace at footer, though. Simply the king.'

'I bet he's ace at other things too,' said Corinne.

'Don't count on it!' Selina ruffled Tommy's hair fondly.

He scowled at her. 'Leave it out, Sel.'

Ingmar said to Corinne, 'If you wish to dance I should be pleased to dance with you.' His pallor and silver hair next to Tommy gave the pair of them an allegoric look.

Corinne looked blankly at him.

Tim shouted, 'Bollocks, we don't all have to pair off, do we? Christmas is unisex. Let's all just get up and dance.'

They did so, but once they were dancing they tended to align in pairs: Corinne and Tommy, Tim and Ingmar, Selina and Dean Baggins, who had followed her back from the pub. Long-haired Dean and statuesque Selina made the most picturesque couple. Tim and Ingmar were the best dancers.

Sonia kept her back to Ben when he had climbed into bed. He lay and listened to the music sludging up the stairwell and pestering against the apartment door.

'If they don't pack it in soon I'll go and put my foot through the fucking stereo.' The obscenity and the extra resonance in his deep voice told her that he had drunk more than usual.

'Please don't do that, Benjy.'

'That was one of the most excruciating days I've ever spent.'

She was going to say, *Everybody else enjoyed it*. But instead she said, 'The girls enjoyed it.'

'Christ, did you see the state of Julie? In full granny mode.'

She didn't say anything to this. After a while he said, 'We need to get away from all this. Away from all this fucking prose.'

She wasn't sure who he meant by 'we'. She didn't say anything.

When Nick got into the bedroom Corinne was sprawled on one of the twin beds, propped against the wall with her plump legs splayed. She had found the bottle of wine he had won in a pub raffle and was clutching it by the neck. Her mood had turned as morose as Ben's.

'A bunch of shitheads,' she said.

Nick opened his mouth to say, 'I thought you were enjoying yourself.' But he was aware that he was close to the stage of inebriation when he became unintelligible, though his manners and actions were usually not impaired. He shut his mouth.

Corinne said, 'That conceited black bastard thinks I fancy him. Just because I wanted to dance. And poofters give me the creeps.'

Nick thought, *There's no point talking now when we're both pissed. And no point talking tomorrow when we'll have hangovers.*

He sat down heavily on the unoccupied bed. For some reason he remembered their arrival in July, crossing the cattle grid with Thornham Common to the right and a quarry to the left. The gorse on the common was licked with cement dust that blew across from the quarry. There was a sharp turn at the top of the hill into Thornham village, a wide street of grey stone cottages. When she first saw the hall through the spiked railings Corinne had laughed with delight. 'It's like a film set! It's going to be great here!'

Corinne took a swig of wine and belched. 'But at least some of them are young shitheads. That makes a change in this fucking old folks' home.'

Nick lay down with his back to her and forgot to keep quiet, saying, 'Graw blee spruggle a torp nonty.'

*   *   *

181

Julie had lain in darkness listening to cheery leavetakings and folk plodding upstairs to their various apartments. A couple of persevering revellers were still drinking and chatting but the music had been turned down so low that it was a far-away rumour in the Frobisher suite.

'Poor Ben!' she said, and chuckled. 'Did you see his face in the pub?'

Damien did not respond immediately, so that she thought he was asleep or absorbed in some contemplation of his own. Then he said, 'It wasn't his scene. He isn't sociable.'

'Except on his own terms,' she said disloyally. 'I thought it was all perfect. The whole day. Perfect. The odd glob of bile from Susan, but that's par for the course, and even she came round in the end.'

'The kids make a difference.'

She laughed with delight. 'Fiona's gorgeous. And did you see Graham at the Tofts? It was hilarious!'

'I mean your kids, Susan and Tim.'

'Our kids.' She corrected him automatically, as she had done countless times over the last nine years. 'Yes, but the others too . . . We've got a better crowd in the Hall, these days.'

She was basking in this thought while awaiting sleep when Damien said, 'I saw my father today.'

She switched on the light and turned towards him. He was lying on his back like a crusader's effigy, his head propped up slightly on the pillow, his hands parked one on the other on top of the duvet. Turning his face towards her he chuckled, his eyes glazed by lack of glasses and the blinding light.

'Oh dear, have I frightened you? It wasn't anything, really. Just a trick of memory.'

'What the frigging hell are you talking about, Damien?'

'I saw my father. I was in the lounge by myself when the rest of you were starting dinner. I looked out of the window and there he was, just across the terrace, sitting on the little balustrade and looking away from me, towards the fountain – just the way he used to sit, like a cormorant on a rock out at sea, somebody once said. He was wearing that red and black check lumberjack coat I've inherited but he was bare-headed, even though it was snowing a bit. He hadn't brushed the snow off the balustrade but was perched in it, not bothered. Then the Stott lass, the eldest, came in to tell me I was wanted to carve the turkey. I glanced away from the window for an instant and when I looked back he was gone. Just an hallucination – a trick of the memory.'

Julie switched off the light.

9

'You can see York Minster and Ferry Bridge cooling towers from here on a clear day. This is supposed to be neutral ground, is it? Neither your bloody pub nor my siren grot.'

'I didn't want to drink anything,' Ben mumbled. He was aware, as if by radar, that the Hambleton Arms was sitting hospitably a hundred yards up the road.

'Nor waste a nice grey afternoon shagging when we could be sat smoking in a car park.'

Before them was the vast view across the plain of York: the dwindling fields like an exercise in painterly perspective, blotched and dotted with trees and seamed with roads. To the left, the long spine of the Wolds framed the horizon; to the right the foothills of the Pennines rose to great dim leviathans in the north. In the foreground there were gentle, pelted hills, with Gormire a metal disc under a matt sky.

Ben said more resonantly, 'I didn't want to drink anything because I didn't want you to say, "Ask me again when you're sober."'

'If you've something to say, spit it out.'

He took a drag of his cigarette. His proposal need not wait for her to be in a more propitious mood: it would flatten whatever obstacles it met. But her peevishness was distracting him from his script and even threatening to change it.

'I'm leaving Sparrow Hall and want you to come with me.'

The car windows were wound down since they were both smoking. The sleeves of Julie's sweater were pushed back to leave her slender, freckled forearms bare. Beyond the car park, lambs and ewes were blundering around missing each other and bleating. A skylark dribbled out a cursory phrase, discouraged by the lack of sun.

'To Paris, maybe. Or Trebizond or Heckmondwyke, according to your whim. Where we can be together and concentrate on each other without the enforced company of nincompoops to distract us.'

He had foreseen her look of panic when he broke the amnesty she cherished. Normally they swapped reminiscences, shared jokes and compared opinions but never discussed their relationship or uttered love.

'You're offering me Sonia's functions?'

'I want to spend the nights with you. I want to awake and discover you beside me.'

'Tender domesticity. How drab.'

He was amazed. It was he who had suggested they should not sleep together, out of embarrassment for Damien, Sonia and the children. He assumed that Julie had agreed ruefully but still yearned to share his bed. With the tone of a tetchy pedagogue he said, 'Julie, try to stop looking for reasons to cavil at what I'm saying and focus on the fact that I love you. I daresay I seem an unlikely person to be advocating romantic love . . .'

'That's not romantic love you're talking about.'

'I never met the goddess till I met you. I've written lots of poems about her and lived for years with one of her messengers but had given up hope of the incarnation, the once-in-a-lifetime chance that most people are never lucky enough to get. Is that romantic enough for you?'

She threw her cigarette out of the window and looked at him critically. He had grown a beard, which he was tending narcissistically, keeping his upper lip shaved for a biblical effect. She thought it made him look like a billy-goat.

'Shall I tell you something? I hate it when men talk about love. Love is a spoiled shag. It's a word used by bullies and hypocrites. It means possession and responsibility and commitment – all the bits of sex that are no fun.'

This offended him. 'It satisfies you just to whore around?'

'I don't find satisfactory partners. They're all either slaves or enslavers. You were supposed to be my free man, the peregrine spirit I'd been seeking.'

A plane from the gliding club was tranced over Sutton Bank, balancing its shivering wings on the wind like somebody on a tightrope. Ben watched it morosely. 'All you want's a couple of hours' fucking three or four times a week and a bit of chat about poetry?'

'Apparently it doesn't mean much to you but it fills my life with spice and syrup. And it's fragile.'

A bottle green Lada containing two young couples nosed into the parking space alongside, pop music thumping out of its cassette player. Raising a histrionic eyebrow Ben flung open the door of the Granada: an ugly confrontation with strangers would relieve his feelings. But the Lada reversed immediately, all its occupants arguing and gesturing at each other, and drifted off to the other end of the viewpoint.

He shut the door again and said, 'Nothing need be wrecked. Our only necessary commitment is that we leave that stifling manse together. Whether we perish, are faithful, drink, share household chores or find we sleep better apart are insignificant particulars. I want us to join hands and leap into the blue. If we land among rocks or crocodiles we'll cope as best we can. Haven't you the courage for that?'

She narrowed evil eyes at him, which he had once informed her were 'the secret green eyes of a Neptune ascendant', and curled her lip. 'I want you as a lover, you pillock, not as a fellow-suicide or a cell-mate. What about the courage needed to take each day as it comes and trust each other for tomorrow? If you want us to literally sleep together, let's have the courage to do it at Sparrow Hall, in front of the world, with free consent.' She raised her left hand and made the bird-releasing gesture that accompanied some of her more important statements.

Accustomed to dumbfounding others with rhetorical flourishes, he suspected he was losing one of the few arguments that had ever mattered. He also suspected that he needed for once in his life to say something terse, literal and affectionate. But he said deliberately, 'Don't ask me to act against my nature. I'm not Damien. I won't jump through all your hoops in whatever colours you choose for me.'

'You're just like Damien and all the other would-be despots. You want to smear me with your spoor. You don't want anybody's teethmarks on me except your own.'

The last of his constraint collapsed and he boomed, 'Without daring to invoke the dishonest word "love", I do feel that instead of jeering, you perverse bitch, you might acknowledge that I'm asking more of myself than of you. All other women, fuckable or not, disgust and bore me. For you I've thrown over the mind-set of three decades, pissed on my self-esteem, my scruples, everything.'

'I know how privileged I should feel,' she said drily. 'And grateful, at my age.' He had recently made the mistake of jokily confessing his (strictly carnal) penchant for youthful bimbos.

He shut his mouth on the topic for ever. Then, when all was destroyed, she repented and searched for some mitigating formula. 'We're both hopeless negotiators. Too paranoid. Too cumbered.'

He was whistling jazz, almost silently, through his teeth. She wound up the window and started the engine.

Tommy was on the roadside near the bottom of the common swearing at his wounded bicycle when Corinne chugged up on her Lambretta. Nick had bought it for her second-hand and got Tommy to fix it. She used it to escape from the Hall and Nick – clubbing in Scarborough where she'd got in with a group of acid heads very similar to Sloopy's clique.

It was March. She had been watching Tommy vaguely since Christmas Day, and he had been vaguely aware of it.

'Where you off?' she demanded.

She saw him mouthing an answer but couldn't hear properly because of the safety helmet that Nick had provided along with the Lambretta. She scowled, lifted the visor and asked Tommy to say it again.

'Nowhere. I got a bleeding puncture, innai? And no bleeding puncture kit.'

He grinned at her. Apart from Sue, Corinne was the only person at the Hall he felt easy with. She was like a lot of kids he and Sel had known at school – rich kids with attitudes, who talked and acted harder than the real yobbos.

'What you riding a fucking bike for anyway? You got about five cars in the garage back at the Hall.'

'They're crocks, that's why they're in the bleeding garage. Sel's got the only wheels that go.'

'Hop on. I'll take you wherever you like. Your wildest dreams.'

He acted coy to tease her. 'I don't have a lid. And you're only a learner, you're not allowed passengers.'

'Nobody's bothered about shit like that. Sling your bike in the hedge.'

'It's a good bike.'

'Are you coming, or what?'

He carried the bike off the road and hid it tenderly behind a gorse bush. As he walked back to her he said, 'I wouldn't mind a lift down Kirkby.'

He straddled her pillion. Before she dropped her visor she

turned her face to his and said, 'Grab hold hard and don't be fucking shy. I don't want you falling off.'

He put his hands round her waist and his thighs round her buttocks, so he could feel how plump and warm she was through the cladding. After these preparations for headlong speed the scooter wobbled decorously over the cattle grid and down to the main road.

'Wrong way!' he shouted at the deaf helmet, then prodded her in the back with his index finger, but got no reaction. After a couple of miles she turned off into Bilberton and pulled up at the Fox.

He dismounted. She dragged off the helmet and gasped for air like a surfacing diver. 'Fuck it!' she shouted, and threw the casque to roll along the gutter. She smirked facetiously at Tommy, who smiled back, forgetting to protest. He knew that some white girls were curious about black boys, having heard the myths and rumours.

'Drink stop,' she said, and walked straight into the pub, leaving him to prop up the scooter.

The Fox was a quiet, justly neglected pub. The landlord had a cigarette drooping from his lips as he leaned on the bar in vest and braces, desultorily wiping glasses with a soiled rag and arraying them on the shelf above the bar. Tommy knew the old slob well, having played darts matches there.

Corinne bought them beers, then chattered away about Grunk Funk and Jabber Anthems, two groups who were one of the things she had discovered she had in common with Tommy. Another was soccer. Sloopy had been a rabid Middlesbrough fan.

'Another drink. Your round,' she said soon.

'Nah, I'll buy one when we get to Kirkby coz I'm due to meet Gazza there at half past.'

She amazed him by standing and zipping up her padded jacket. Outside she refused to let him pick up the helmet. 'I'll never wear the cunt again.' By now he had her sussed for a poser who liked to impress.

Instead of doing a U-turn back to the main road she went on up the little valley through Bilberton. He yelled at her about meeting Gazza.

'Gazza can get sucked. We're going to Max's.'

They chugged through the snobby village, all mown verges and painted bridges, till the road became unpaved. They stopped at a tumbledown cottage with the roof lolling over the porch like a drunkard's hat. Corinne bent to fumble behind a bucket of mouldy rainwater and came up with a door-key.

'He'll have fucked off to Pickering market.'

Tommy knew about Pickering market, because that was where Sel had gone, on her afternoon off, with Sue and the kids. He wondered if he was going to get back to the Hall before they did.

Corinne led the way into a disgusting room like the cell of a mad hermit, the floor littered with buckled beer-cans and bean-cans that had been re-employed as ashtrays. She straightened the sleeping-bag on the camp bed that was the only furniture apart from the TV in front of it.

'But he won't mind us using the facilities,' she said, unzipping her padded jacket. He could tell from her voice that her juices were stirring and her pulse thumping, though she was trying to sound nonchalant.

He was aroused too, as he saw how her heavy breasts swagged in her sweater and her thighs bulged her jeans. She was what Sel would call a fat slag.

'Fucking stupid, this is,' she said softly. 'Selina and Nick are out most of the time and we could have the run of the Hall.'

When he was interviewed eleven years later Tommy was ruefully self-analytical about both the scooter trip and its consequences. *'In June I went with her to a pop festival in Dorset where Grunk Funk and Jabber Anthems were gigging.*

We left in a banger I'd more or less made and neither of us ever went back to Sparrow Hall. We lived wild all that summer camping in the woods with other scumbags. Then rain set in and she pissed off on some geezer's pillion. I still don't see how I passed over Sel for that dumb white scrubber. She wasn't as good a fuck or anything that made sense. The truth is I was heading back in a roundabout way to the warehouse parties and the rastas and the dope. All the time I was a cripple drinking weak beer in Yorkshire I could hear the voices of my own people saying y'aaright yeah wickedness man gimme a sarf drink and stuff like that. And I was making my getaway from Sel and the kid and the garage and the responsibility and I did that good because there was no way back to Sel when the scrubber had ditched me.'

But all he said now was, 'It pongs in here.'

'The Stotts are going, will be gone, sooner rather than later, because his father's death means they now have a house in Southport and Sonia wants to get him away from Sparrow Hall and me. Being an unreconstructed Roman Catholic she feels it incumbent on her not merely to stay with her shit of a husband but actually to fight to prevent him setting her free. He'll be glad to go with her, partly because he's pissed off with the set-up here – he likes to be the lonely poet, the last cowboy, the singer to a tone-deaf land – and partly because he's crushed at being turned down by an old bag his own age. He thought I'd leap at his offer to go off with him to Paris where Gauloises are cheap, to partake in the ghastly last chapters of his biography. Ben was luscious, my beery bard, my oasis of poetry and passion in the desert – then he turned into a mirage like the rest of you. Men need the rules that keep them in power though they break those rules whenever it suits them. Ben couldn't stomach free love. He couldn't sustain his respect for me unless I was available only to him. He wanted love polluted with the usual poisons. He'll be better off in Southport, with a wide choice of bourgeois pubs to terrorise and Sonia sitting at home cooking his grub. I don't want to travel the world again and refuse to be responsible for the fulfilment of anybody's dreams. All the same I'm not so sure I wouldn't have been better off as a boozy poet in Paris – after Ben had died or left me, one or the other of which he pretty soon would: a stark old bird with a long woolly scarf and an assortment of cats I forget to feed. Better that maybe than staying with Damien and listening to his emptinesses, increasingly aware of old age creeping around inside me like a caretaker patrolling the floorboards and doomy stairways of Sparrow Hall – or like a saboteur among the corridors and gantries of my industrial complex, closing valves and stopping conduits. I look into the glass and view my wasting skin. I view my wasting heart, too, my troubled heart, a caricature in its own right, speaking metaphorically, of course. I know you don't want to hear any of this, Gavin, but I'd be grateful if you'd be generous for a few minutes and pretend you do. I used to tell Damien, rub his face in my mess, though he never wanted to know. In order not to know, he's now turned weird – not silent, like his father went by all accounts, but empty. There's nobody in there behind the eyes, driving the words. Or if there is it's not Damien. I have to tell somebody, and it shouldn't matter to you any more than I do – the woman who shows up once in a blue moon to pop pills, sniff crack and be shagged. Damien will be glad that Ben is gone because it's been particularly painful to countenance – his being a friend, an old college pal. An extra embarrassment adds to the humiliation of a husband whose wife seeks succour elsewhere. And his chagrin about his own judgement adds to the outrage, because he was secure in the notion that me and Ben were incompatible. I think he reassures himself that I won't leave him altogether while he stays at Sparrow Hall, where I feel

special and irresponsible, like an actress playing a tragic queen
– but it's hard to say, because he's a fake, an even bigger poser
than me. That book he reckoned to be writing fooled me for
years, so that whenever he evaded me with that bland . . . I
used to even apologise for interrupting his sodding creative . . .
But it was a spoof. All the time I thought he was tweaking
plots or concocting dialogue he was in some banal, obsessive
sub-reality such as is inhabited by any humdrum loony. And
it isn't just because of me, not all my fault, because his poems
are the same that he wrote before he met me. Spoofs, like
their begetter. Soft and bright on the outside, glistening and
soggy with self-pity. Dull and hard on the inside, a small
stone core of egotism that doesn't give a shit. Down the
dark road, as his frigging blues singers say, I'll have at least
the consolation that I'm in better shape than hubby. Maybe
all my throes and flourishes will vanish at the menopause.
I have my grandchildren for a few years yet to occupy and
console me and help me dodder down without getting too
aghast. And there's poetry, thanks to Ben. Poetry is a bloody
sight more tractable than art, especially as you get older. It
only needs a second or two and a cheap biro to write what it
takes months to paint or . . . The problem is I'm pissed off with
poetry now, just as I've got pissed off with everything, story
of my life, that didn't beat me to it by getting pissed off with
me. You don't need to look so bored, I'll take one of those
goof-balls in a minute and settle down. What are the orange
ones? You haven't a clue, have you? You just pop stuff inside
you and hold on tight for the trip. Still, I'm not going to start
worrying about you, I've enough frigging responsibilities.'

On most Wednesdays Sonia and Julie baby-sat together while
Selina went to work and Susan to her aerobics class in Kirkby.
Since Tommy had absconded Merline had become difficult to
leave, sometimes kicking up such a fuss that her mother was

herself snivelling as she set off for work, but today Graham and Fiona kept Merline occupied till Selina had made her getaway.

Ben was in his corner with his notebook and a pint by the time she got behind the bar. He was always waiting at the pub door at seven sharp. Selina was supposed to be there at seven but always arrived a quarter of an hour late, out of breath, and saying sorry to Elaine, who pretended it wasn't a problem. Selina and Ben despised each other and did what they could to spoil each other's evenings. He spoke to her with abrasive hauteur, made her change perfectly good pints, counted his change slowly, as if she was a proven thief, and defamed her to Elaine as lazy, stroppy and too thick to pull draught Guinness properly. She played reggae on the hi-fi system – only turning it down slightly if he protested, then turning it back up soon afterwards – and ignored him for as long as possible when he went to the bar for a refill.

Elaine watched TV, did yoga or soaked in a bath rather than serve in the Apple Tree bar on weekday evenings, and in her place Selina would have done the same. At the Half Moon in Westmoor there had been cricket and soccer teams as well as a lot of regulars, a livelier scene altogether. That was where Selina had got the habit of 'putting on the sexy style', like old Mrs Dawkins said barmaids should. A few months back she had still been squeezing into tarty finery to spend long hours in the Apple Tree with two or three topers and a dog, but now she wore a sweater and jeans.

Kevin and Dean played darts for an hour, keeping themselves to themselves, as they did unless Dean was drunk. Otherwise the only folk in the pub from seven o'clock to half nine were Ben Stott and Ken Filbert. When Selina first started work at the Apple Tree Ken had sat quietly under the clock with his buddy Dobbo, but now he perched on a bar stool telling Selina obscene jokes or relating his life history, while Dobbo no longer used the pub. At half nine, half drunk, came Nick Townsend, who had a few beers in Teesside after school then stopped for a couple as he drove over the moors. As usual Ben threw down his biro, as if he was exasperated at being interrupted in his great work, then for the rest of the evening harangued Nick about books, music and the proper way to handle drink and women. At ten o'clock came Lionel Knight, a slime-bag with a smoother front, who tut-tutted at Ken's coarseness, slipped in scummy little items of his own and quizzed Selina about her intimate habits while trying to feed her booze. He was an old customer from Westmoor and used to her filling time as a stooge for his quips, a target for his leer and hopefully, some lucky evening, a bargain-offer tart.

She had the idea that because she was black she got less respect and more randy harassment, which often had a sneer behind it. She had talked about it to Susan recently, on a park bench in Pickering overlooking the kiddies' playground. It had been the first time she had unburdened her grievances to anybody since Tommy's going.

'Blokes who prop bars up expect to treat barmaids like that,' Susan had said, 'and any other woman they fancy who'll let them get away with it.'

'Nowadays I don't pretend to play, and sometimes make it clear I'm not even listening, whereas in the Half Moon I used to smooch along by drooping my eyelids and jutting my tits.'

'But anybody who pushed their luck soon got to know you weren't the sort of girl you were acting.' Susan had held out a packet of caramels so that Selina could take one.

Selina had watched Merline warily following Graham up the daunting steps of the big slide. 'I was a virgin when I first went with Tommy and he's the only bloke I've ever screwed, very near the only bloke I've seriously kissed. I'm not religious, or moral or any of that bullshit, I kept myself for Tommy because I only wanted Tommy, even when he was cheating on me, whether he was a West Ham wonder-boy or a tosser in dreadlocks mooching round bars and pool-rooms. That's why I'm so utterly gutted that he's gone off with that slag, though some of it's just crushed pride. After the warnings my family gave me about that bastard, since I was fourteen, and the scary rows we had, I'd sooner stay here as a comic coon bimbo in white woolly Yorkshire than go back to Finchley and face them. One thing certain is that I'm no Sonia Stott. Tommy can piss off forever, and the rest of them with him, with their lies and poses and smelly grins and silly bollocks.'

This Wednesday she got home just before midnight and found that Sonia had taken over Merline so that Julie could go to bed. Sonia never went to bed until Ben had come back from the pub and eaten cheese sandwiches while being derisive about late-night TV. Selina was grateful that Ben always chose to ignore her – and all that had happened in the pub – when she arrived to collect Merline.

Julie had unplaited and combed Merline's hair, so that it was a fluffy nimbus round her head. The child was fast asleep, taking slow, soft breaths as if sipping oblivion. Selina picked her up carefully, wrapped in her rainbow-coloured blanket, and carried her off.

She thought she'd got away with it this time, but half-way across the dim landing Merline awoke. Pushing herself away from her mother she arched her back and stared around her. It was very quiet in Sparrow Hall.

'Want Tommy,' Merline announced.

She sometimes called her daddy by his name like that, because she'd heard her mother use it so often. When she woke in the night was the only time she asked for him. Selina used to roust him out of bed to see to her.

'You and me both, angel,' said Selina.

She wanted to cry. She saw how she had just contradicted her proud speech to Susan. To shut out the thought of Tommy, she remembered more of that talk a couple of weeks back – sitting in the sun chewing caramels, watching Merline pause to gather her nerve at the top of the steps to the big slide.

'I'd do anything for her to have a happy life, full of fun and choice and love. But the way she calls for her no-good daddy in the middle of the night makes me think she'll be a sucker, like me.'

'Women are pathetic – and men are worse. You're a pathetic bunch at Sparrow Hall.'

'We were better when it was a political shambles, constitutions and motions and all that crap, when the problems weren't all personal. Now it's all like a ghastly soap on telly.'

'Snakes and ladders. Musical chairs.'

'Sly dogs and cheated bitches. Sluts and tossers.'

'Only the Hunters are a normal family so it's no wonder they want little to do with the rest of you.'

'And it's no wonder we couldn't get it together as a community when we can't even make it with those we're supposed to love.'

Damien walked along the riverbank then mounted the riding. He had negotiated the stile and was close to the copse below Long Acre where the daffodils grew when the music came clearer: the barbarous and beautiful throb and peal of a Delta blues guitar. Instead of continuing as usual on the footpath till it met the farm track back to the village he was lured off at a tangent into the wood until he arrived at the source of the music in a glade of birches further along the hillside.

The black musician was sitting in the grass, leaning against a tree, his guitar on his lap, his feet outflung at twenty to four in battered hobo brogans, which had holes in the leather plugged with frayed cardboard. He was practising quietly, watching the fingers of his left hand as he performed a much-used Mississippi guitar pattern of the nineteen twenties and thirties.

Damien first recognised him by his playing, a characteristic snapping of the bass string with his thumb.

As Damien approached the man looked up, under the shapeless soft hat that was low on his forehead. A skinny little ugly fellow, the possessor of a face that was creased and wrinkled like a prune. His blubbery lips, beneath an unsuccessful moustache, were flecked with vitiligo. His eyes were seeping with a sort of rheum as he squinted into the dappled sunlight.

Without ceasing to play he said, conversationally, as though Damien had been with him all along, 'The first I hear play this was Ben Maree. He's dead now. It wants tuning in Spanish. Run that E down.'

Damien said, 'You're Willie Lee Brown. You used to play with Charley Patton.'

This had a dramatic effect. The guitarist drew back his flecked lips and snarled, then raised a wheezy smoker's voice into the autumn woodland, over the bouncing, cascading tune.

'Just a clown, is that jerk. He messes around, y' know, when he plays, talkin' and grinnin' like a coon-show nigger, puttin' his box behind of his head, scratchin' his ass with um, all that stuff. An' he don't play near as good as me.'

Damien was fascinated by the contrast between the husky petulance of the words and the assured, tranquil cadences of the guitar.

Willie went on: 'But Charley goes into town, all the midnight steppers, the pig-meat riders, run to hear um play. All of the other musicians has to move over. He git his breakfast fixed for him every mornin', stole from the white folks' kitchen, that loppy-eared, yaller-skinned, motherfuckin' clown.'

Damien wanted to inspect more closely the phenomenon manifested so incongruously among the Ryedale birches, but suspected that if he moved closer the vision would explode.

There are no photographs of Willie Lee Brown but Son House, who knew him for decades, had furnished some candidly graphic descriptions, which Damien had read. He saw that the Willie he had invented conformed to these accounts – and he was fairly sure that Willie's speech was composed of dialogue from the novel that Damien had striven for so long to write.

'He's welcome to the womens, though, that big-eared, fat-mouth son of a bitch. There's only one things womens is good for, and a lot of um ain't too clever at that neither.' Playing more quietly and lowering his voice he suddenly spoke confidentially and directly to Damien. 'You wanna trash that cheapie, that Julie, man. That cocksucker gonna wreck your life, totin' her jelly, raisin' sand.'

'I beg your pardon?' Damien was shocked.

Willie shrugged. 'If you're cold in hand it ain't none of my red wagon. Just dry long so. There don't seem to be in the world no reasonable sort of half-way average woman. They either sanctified an' holy, an' want a guy to sign the pledge an' cut his nuts off – or they goddam cocksuckin' mistreaters.'

If Damien closed his left eye Willie Brown vanished from the woodland glade but the voice and music remained. Willie had raised his voice again.

'Jus' keep on tellin' yo'self that they ain't worth none of it. Not the cutest lil jelly roll ain't worth none of the bother an' burdenin'. You just gotta keep on tellin' yo'self each time you sets eyes on a piece of pigmeat.'

Damien closed both eyes firmly for several seconds and when he opened them the musician was gone. It was like when one becomes aware that one is dreaming and deliberately elects to wake. The music was gone too – but the voice of a character from an abandoned novel, authoritative, insistent, was still in his ear:

'Them chancers like that Julie, you gotta leather um. Take

a knotted rope to um, if you ain't got a belt with a buckle. Like with a sportin' dog, y' know. You gotta get um to fear you before you can do anythin' with um.'

The day the Stotts left Thornham was bright but cold. It would have been pleasanter to move in spring or summer but Sonia was not prepared to wait.

There was no threat from Julie now – she was Sonia's friend and they told each other everything. But Sonia was desperate to separate Ben from Nick Townsend. Since he had finished with Julie and taken up drinking with Nick, Ben was nasty drunk a lot of the time. So far the nastiness was confined to sarcastic humour but Sonia could see future horrors looming. One bad sign was that he was no longer sorry and attentive the morning after.

He was standing in frosty sunlight and smoking a Gauloise next to the van he had hired. He was scowling. Sonia decided it was just at the thought of the day's driving (across England to Southport then back to deliver the van before seven p.m.). She knew he was happy to be leaving Sparrow Hall and thought it was his own idea.

For one thing, his local pubs were almost no-go areas. In the Half Moon at Westmoor he had taken some old bore (a crony of the landlord) by the throat. And he had had a sabre fight with snooker cues with Dean Baggins in the Apple Tree. What was worse, he was at war with Selina, so he could hardly get her to serve him – and Elaine was on Selina's side. He would be happier in Southport, Sonia told herself, for a while at least. The five years since they last lived there should have buried old debts and grudges – and a few landlords. When he was in his routine the drinking would settle down.

He had been nagging her, when beery but cheerful, about his resolutions. He intended to cut down on drink but as a long-term project rather than an urgent priority. He would be a proud poet again, 'allowing no social distractions to the austere and lonely toil'. He would be much more ruthless about discouraging tedious acolytes like Nick. She would be rewarded with more esteem than recently. He would make a mammoth effort, with her secretarial help, at getting his poems published – or he would punish ungrateful posterity by destroying all his work, and anything new as soon as written. He had never said anything to Sonia about his affair with Julie but spoke of the latter with dismissive spleen ('that philistine chameleon', 'that menopausal mess'). He had evidently resolved that any woman he consented to misuse in future would be young and vacuous.

The van could squeeze all four of them onto the long front seat. Netta and Kim were elated, having fond memories of their grandparents' house and having been promised a lot of fun and friends in Southport. People said they were very like each other – and very like Sonia – but to her they were quite different. Each in her own way reminded Sonia of Ben: Netta, though quiet and civil, was stubborn and set in her ways; Kim had his imagination and some of his bounce.

Ben was not unkind to his daughters but thought them plain and thick and mostly kept out of their way. Watching him being gruffly amiable with them, Sonia thought, *If we'd had sons he'd have been different. He'd have played football with them and wanted them to be great poets.*

Julie had told Sonia that she was crazy to give her life to somebody who could not love her. Sonia accepted that she had been a fool over Ben, and that the folly was not all gone. Nor was it just a question of her duty to God and the family. She would have liked to admire Ben again as she once did when he was the scandal of De La Salle High School and an exotic alternative to the eligible males of Basildon.

Today she was not sharing either the joy of her children or the equanimity of her husband. She had liked the people at

Sparrow Hall and felt liked in turn; had shared comradeship and support with the mothers (Selina, Susan, Catherine, Julie) and, thanks to them, found a job and a bit of independent status. Most of all she had formed a real friendship with Julie. *She is honest, generous, free and brave as I can never hope to be.* Leaving seemed at best like returning to the solitary confinement of the housewife – visited from time to time outside pub opening hours by her lord. At worst she felt launched into threatening weather, with fragile items in her care and a madman at the helm.

Her short-term worry was what Ben would get up to between returning the van to Pickering that evening and arriving back in Southport twenty hours later by train. She was aware that he usually got very drunk if he was away from his family for more than a few hours – and it had also occurred to her, wearily, that he might have refused the expense of a proper removal firm because he had some secret project.

There was nobody to see them off – Julie, Selina and the Hunters had all taken their leave of Sonia and the children elsewhere, none of them wanting to have any dealings with Ben. He climbed behind the driving wheel and was timidly wobbling the gear lever to find neutral when Damien came out of the Hall and ambled across the gravel. Ben could not discover how to wind the window down so had to open the door to talk to him.

'Just off, are you?' Damien leaned on the van and beamed in. They all wondered if he realised they were leaving for good. Ben had avoided him since his affair with Julie.

'Come and see us in Southport,' Ben said. 'We'll write poetry together in the Golden Lion, like old times.'

Sonia knew that this was insincere. Ben had told her he wanted no more of Damien's company and had no intention of ever writing another line of 'collaborative verse'. But she could see that Ben was embarrassed and also that he was sorry how completely things end. Damien was the only friend he had ever kept and the only real fan he had ever had for his poetry.

Damien said, 'Water under the bridge, eh?' The smile on his face had been replaced by a puzzled look, as though he was trying to remember who these people were in the van in his yard. His manners, always so perfect that they were sometimes a nuisance, meant that there was no way that he could bring himself to shut the door or step back from the van.

Ben had to pull the door shut slowly so that Damien had time to realise and get out of the way. The engine started, phew, Ben found first gear, Damien smiled and waved goodbye, framed by the ivied wall of his family home, and they never saw him again.

'Didja read about the guy in Oregon? They're clearing a forest fire and they find this burnt-out guy in diving gear, flippers and snorkel . . .'

'Everybody's heard that story, Mendy honey,' Billie Jean said.

Billie Jean and Mendy had driven up for Tim's birthday. A flash flood down the *arroyo* had taken half the track away, so they had to leave their truck half a mile back. Tim had been their lodger for six months in Las Cruces till he couldn't pay the rent and moved out to the trailers with Pedro.

Big Bo had found the trailers in the desert three years ago when he was biking. They'd been stripped of clues as to their previous owners – Big Bo had heard they'd belonged to 'an old guy who took sick and went back east'. Tim's birthday feast was sited in the cool of the evening on a bald little plateau overlooking the dry bed of the *arroyo*. A low table had been made of wooden pallets, around which the gathering sat or lolled on the earth like Romans to eat pulse stew and drink canned beer. The scene around was of shadowed dunes, with a scrub of grass and thorn – there were spiky yuccas here and there, a few blue asters and yellow Californian poppies.

Normally they listened to Silas Babbit or Urizen Syndrome but the ghetto-blaster batteries were exhausted and the only cable was being used by Reisinger for his guitar. He liked to play as he got stoned but never tunes, just twangly runs and riffs that were spooky for first-time hearers. Reisinger was squat, ugly and specially sour for Tim's birthday. He had been happier when there were just three in the trailers – Big Bo, Cal and himself – getting stoned, riding dirt-track and playing mad guitar in the desert. Then Cal burst his mitral hose and went to die in Las Cruces.

Pedro, a lean, solemn boy, was fixing jimson-weed potion on a little Primus stove that was shielded in a broken tea chest. There were a number of such boxes scattered near the trailers – Tim used them as frames for his monster sculpture in the desert. Fernanda, Pedro's sister, who had been Big Bo's girl, flashed her eyes and teeth at Tim. Her hair was in a long black braid like a Cheyenne squaw. She was making fat spliffs with tobacco and dried mushrooms and lining them up on the lid of a biscuit tin.

Billie Jean, a tanned blonde with a well-mended hare lip, was watching Tim and Fernanda – she liked Tim and was glad if he was straightening out sex-wise. Fat Mendy was gleeful at what he would have to tell the guys at the bottling plant on Monday, but also scared of a bad trip and feeling out of his depth. He said, 'Didja read about the dumb motherfuckers try to restock the Portland coast with lobsters? Air-lift thousands of the bastards from the Atlantic, wire up their claws for the trip and forget to unwire 'em before they dump 'em in the Pacific.'

Tim took a sip of Pedro's potion, with a mouthful of beer. He wasn't anticipating anything spectacular. The most he'd experienced from previous sampling of Bo's herbs was a lurid, bland reverie – as if his memory was being handled by Disney Studios. Big Bo placed a plate of shredded cactus buttons on the table, then opened his great jaws and guffawed, stretching his braces with his thumbs and letting them snap back on to his hairy chest. Reisinger, who loved Big Bo, let out a discordant riff on his guitar.

Billie Jean asked Tim, 'Ain't you gonna open your package?'

Fernanda had given him a necklace of beads on a leather thong, Pedro a pint of whisky that Reisinger was drinking, Big Bo what Tim hoped was a dog turd wrapped in Christmas paper. Billie Jean and Mendy had brought him a travelling chess set but also a parcel from England.

He ripped it open and held a traditional Whitby fisherman's gansey against the New Mexico sky. Reisinger refused it a fanfare.

'Just the job! It gets a bit nippy in the desert at night.' He wondered if he had told his mother that, in the only letter he had written, rather a long time ago.

Sparrow Hall was suddenly very vivid to Tim, a mirage in the evening dunes, as if the jimson-weed was already tinting his memory. The oblong windows of the east façade were visible above the wall of the vegetable garden. Snow clouds loomed above the slate roof, behind the chimneys.

His mother's slim shape was at an upstairs window, like a captive in a tower, holding the curtains aside as she watched him. He had sometimes caught her watching him like that, brooding over him, after he had been particularly rude or disobedient. But what was he up to in the vegetable garden in winter? He didn't remember ever going there during any of his surly teenage seasons at Sparrow Hall.

Big Bo did his guffaw and braces stunt again. The way Tim talked always amused him.

Seeing that Tim was troubled by something, Fernanda

snuggled up to him and admired the gansey. 'Cool. Did your ma knit it?'

'Julie? You're joking.'

'She's artistic, though, you told me.'

'Yeh, but her art's a useless extravagance, like mine.'

'She's like you?'

'Her art is. Maybe she is. Or I'm like her.'

'It must be great to have a parent you can relate to and get along with.'

'I didn't say we get along.'

Billie Jean pointed. 'There's a letter, too.'

Tim snatched up the letter and stuffed it into the pocket of his jeans. He'd read it later, if at all.

That blonde with big tits. Reminds him of . . . ? If she materialises from midnight darkness, boo, or comes clopping up behind on high heels, he's too pissed to benefit. If he was sober enough to cope she'd be out of the question. When he was trying to chat her up he saw that others in the bar were finding him amusing and he knew he was pissed. Nick has developed an awareness when pissed that is not particularly welcome since it cancels a lot of the benefit. Ben, for instance, would in his place either not have noticed the sniggering or beaten somebody up. Brother Jeff, however much he had supped, would not sound pissed.

Awareness is selective, letting Nick make assessments while losing his grasp of geography and history, so he surfaces to find himself on a wide, dark road between cottages; standing becalmed, baffled, swaying slightly like a thick branch when a wind is at the leaves. Nothing can be gathered to assist memory from the humped dwellings, the two or three isolated streetlights or the cloudy moon, hullo moon, a wan blob in a ring of sherry-coloured gloam.

Having been failed by the blonde even as a fantasy, he fills the void with Barbara, little tits, greeting her resentfully. Fuck Barbara. She'll have shut the bedroom door, which on better nights she likes to leave open to listen to the children. She'll also have shut the door to the children's room. His pyjamas will be on the settee downstairs, or even just flung out onto the landing. There's a maudlin blob in the middle of his anger, like the moon up there in its brown zone.

He casts his mind back to the pub, the woozy lights and anthems, the blonde's balloons, the smirking heads, and makes a nasty discovery. Selina is behind the bar, long and lithe, stern and stunning, utterly Selina, scowling at the state of him and refusing to serve him. She's the clue to everything: geography, history, incurable calamity. Because of Selina the pub becomes the Apple Tree. He is standing in the middle of Thornham and westwards, yonder, the glint of a carriage-lamp through rhododendrons is Sparrow Hall. Six years since Barbara threw him out, four since she divorced him, three since he gave up access. The big-tit blonde reminds him of Corinne.

Nick has a purpose now, to get to bed. While his body carries on with that, his mind apportions blame. It's better that Corinne took her petulance elsewhere but all the same it seems bitterly unjust that he should have to sleep alone. Faces of likely culprits float before him. Ben raises an eyebrow. He's got Sonia and Southport and doesn't give a shit. Corinne narrows her eyes and mouths a jeer. Barbara's taut face stares at him, her lips a twisted slit. *I'll not have a drunkard for the father of my kids.* Brother Jeff's sardonic visage swims close to say, *Get it up an' another down, you'll feel better.* A young yob with a shaved skull and the face of a goblin sneers, *Shout a bit louder, sir, they can't hear you at the back.* Margaret Thatcher says something but the sound is turned down. God, complete with billowing beard, flits briefly through the dock, incompetent to stand trial. Nick's own pissed face in a lavatory mirror is followed by mug-shots of his parents, who look guiltier than anybody. They reared him to be weak, then turned against him when little tits threw him out.

Deploring this he gets the key into the lock and discovers it no longer fits. Bafflement transports him again to the door of the maisonette in Eston, lumbering up to plead with Barbara one last time, only to discover that she's changed the locks. Raise a mighty fist and beat on the door, render it to match-wood. No. Stop. Now as then. Barbara's reprisals waste the world. The house becomes a tundra over which she presides spectacularly, a drudge with tangled hair and crooked clothes, washing remorselessly, Hoovering monotonously, draggling a sad, scummy cloth over and over the ornaments and surfaces, slopping the spoiled food listlessly, plop, onto cold plates. Never a word to him. Screaming like a chained bird at the cowed, complicit kids. Hell.

Nick is pissed. Wrong door to wrong den. Go back to the head of the stairs and peer down at the parquet square in the bottom of the well. It gleams like stagnant water.

Sparrow Hall is unpleasant late at night, all dark angles and dizzy effects, like one of those horror films where something is going to leap out of the panelling and sink its fangs into you in a minute. Murder done here not long ago, did you know that? Nick doesn't like returning alone sober when the lights are out and everybody's door is shut. Better be pissed like now, even if you lose your way and finish up on the wrong fucking landing.

Just as he is sinking a-slither along the balustrade everything relevant to his problem assembles so clearly and effortlessly, like a landscape breaking through fog, that it seems amazing that he's been having trouble. It is his key, rather than the lock on the apartment door, that changed when he moved out of the apartment, after big tits left him, into the single room upstairs for a bargain rent.

He is now empowered to go to bed just by climbing another

flight of steps. But when returning from the pub he sometimes likes to switch on the TV and sit in a stupor, waking cold in the small hours. His new room has no TV so he goes back downstairs, has a pee in the downstairs toilet, missing the bowl and sprinkling the linoleum, hullo linoleum, then looks in vain for a beer in the kitchen fridge.

Nick needs a fridge like the one in the film on TV, packed with an anthology of potent and exotic beers: Pabst, Schlitz, Dumbodorfer, Singapore Tiger, intense little Trappist potions. Come to that, he wants a cellarful of women, had without bother or embarrassment, similarly exotic and various: courtesans in farthingales, sirens in bikinis and what-have-you. Fuck shame. Fuck the tuna salad that sulks in the fridge.

Susan yelled, 'Paul, that's thick, even for you! I don't want a nanny! I'm perfectly capable of looking after my own kids!'

She had schooled out her Midlands twang but it sneaked back – she could hear it herself – when she lost her temper.

Paul spiked a dumpling with his fork and used his knife to smear it with gravy and mash before popping it under the moustache he had recently grown to irritate his wife. He was less bouncy than usual, having spent an hour wrestling a ewe out of a cattle grid at the valley head.

Peeved by lack of feedback, she added, 'What's more, it's my business and you've no right to stick your nose in. I don't tell you what to do with the farm or your stinking fox-hunting.'

She drew herself up to her considerable height and pouted and glared at him. He made a dramatic clatter by lobbing his knife onto the table.

'I weren't interfering. I were just making a bloody suggestion. You started badgering me with your bloody problems while I were having my dinner. I should've said I were knackered but I didn't. I heard what you had to say, then I made what

I hoped were a helpful suggestion. So don't bloody shout at me and call me thick!'

'It's you doing all the shouting and swearing. And you're spitting bits of potato over the table.' She was a genius at shifting the goalposts to win points in an argument.

They could have tiffs – even a full-blown row – without resorting to violence or bearing a grudge. They were both sharp-tongued and formidable items not to be messed with lightly. They admired each other for it and kept in trim against each other when there was nobody else to bully.

The table he'd spattered with mash and gravy was part of a gleaming ensemble that was dimly reflected, like the matching pinewood units and Aga cooker, in the luscious polished red tiles of the luxury kitchen. The leaded windows looked out from the back of the farmhouse, away from the corrugated sheds full of hens on racks and pigs on slats, towards the twilit woods, meadows and ploughland that were the more acceptable face of farming to a town girl like Susan.

The farm employed six men. Paul was supposed to be a gentleman farmer but to his wife's annoyance he loved hands-on farming, wallowed in physical labour and was getting more and more like his workers in speech and manner. In her present temper Susan was queasily watching his eating habits and thinking what a bumpkin she'd wed.

He pushed his plate aside and she swooped it up like an eager waitress, replacing it with a plate of rice pudding in which a blob of jam was drowning. A videotape of *The Magic Roundabout* and the whir of a clockwork toy could be heard in the next room where the children were waiting for their baths.

Not able to leave her the last word, he spoke with the plonking sweetness of somebody determined to take the high moral ground. 'It were just a suggestion, okay? You say you don't want to be stuck with the kids all the time. And for some reason you've suddenly decided your mother can't be trusted to help out.'

Both the manner and matter of this so riled her that she spat like a threatened cat before launching her answer.

'There's nothing sudden about it! She's never had the faintest notion how to handle kids. And she's not going to learn at her age, is she? Because she doesn't give a shit and never did.'

Paul was right in a way – she was bothering him about something he considered firmly within her sphere, then resenting his input. Having chosen his stance, he suppressed this gripe, instead saying calmly, 'People who couldn't handle their own kids are often different with their grandchildren. Anybody can see she dotes on them.'

'She ruins them,' she snorted. 'She lets them run wild and do whatever they like. She does it deliberately because she resents me wanting them brought up differently to how I was. Shut your mouth and stop gawping. You look like livestock.'

Paul was staring fixedly at Susan, beginning to wonder if something serious was at issue. It was difficult for him to see her point of view because he couldn't think of his own parents in such intimate terms.

'What's more, half the time she turns up to look after them stinking of drink,' Susan went on. 'And Christ knows what else she's on. A couple of times I've nearly sent her packing. We'd have sacked her without a second thought if she was a nanny or baby-sitter who turned up in that state.'

They were both reflected in the long mirror of the kitchen dresser: Paul still peering up oafishly with pudding on his chin, Susan with arms akimbo, a bit too hulking to be chic in the sheath dress and the pricy new perm that looked like an artisan loaf.

'It baffles me how I ever came to consent to leave my kids in Julie's care – after the way she supervised the awful childhood I'm still trying to survive.'

The Magic Roundabout fell suddenly silent in the next room and there was a wail of anguish. Susan pounced in, gave Graham a telling-off and put the video back on for Fiona. She switched on the light as she re-entered the kitchen to give Paul the full benefit of her scowl.

'It's sickening having a famous slut, communist and junkie for a mother,' she exclaimed. 'She's shamed me all my life but I'm not having her messing up my kids. It's not just I don't want her looking after them. I don't want her around when they get older.'

Her brief absence from the room had given Paul time to decide that he was being brow-beaten and to wind himself up again.

'I understand that! I understood it the first bloody time you told me. That's why I landed myself in the shit by suggesting a way out of the problem. If we employ a nanny – part-time, flexible hours – then it's natural and logical, it follows like night follows day, that we won't need your mother's services.'

'I don't accept we need to spend a fortune on a nanny. All we need's a baby-sitter. That lass of Wainwrights', anybody better than my stinking mother.'

'But if you get a baby-sitter you're left with the problem.' He was talking to her now as if she was an obtuse child. 'The problem of how to break the news to your bloody mother – ease her out without giving offence.'

She shrugged. 'Why should I consider her feelings? She never considered mine. I'm not her carer. I've my husband and children to look after – I'm going to be the sort of wife and mother she never was and the cow isn't going to hinder me.'

'You're going to . . . ?'

'I have. Get it into your thick head, Paul, I'm not asking for advice. I sorted it this afternoon. Told Julie to piss off. We won't be seeing her again.'

*　　*　　*

The crow let out a croak and sailed away over Westerdale. Damien watched it until it was gone from sight, beyond the Rigg on the skyline with its ancient tumuli and flinty causeway. The sky was dark, the clouds racing on a chill wind.

He left the cart-track and took a sheep-path towards the road, which was hidden behind windswept gorse. Stepping through a few half-hearted bilberries he rounded a bluff and came face to face with his uncle.

Desmond was supposed to be a hedge-cutter in this remote spot. He was clad in corduroy trousers tucked into gum boots and a strange, collarless shirt of a texture resembling oatmeal. The effect was deliberately unconvincing, like a yokel in an operetta.

The head seemed superimposed: the out-thrust beard, craggy forehead, glinting malice. Not for the first time Damien was impressed by the meticulousness of the fiend. He remembered how his uncle sometimes played cricket with him: baring his teeth and peering evilly askance, like an Eisenstein villain, while composing his fingers around the ball preparatory to delivering his wayward googly.

When Desmond moved his lips to salute Damien all that emerged at first was a shrill, whining noise like an anxious dog. Desmond looked puzzled, swivelled his head from side to side as if trying to locate the source of the noise, swallowed hard and tried again.

'Top o' the morning, thor!' he then said, in a ridiculous Irish brogue, while pretending to rest upon the long-handled secateurs with which he had previously been pretending to trim the gorse.

'Are you supposed to be a leprechaun?' Damien asked irritably. 'This isn't Ireland, you know.'

'Indeed it is not, thor! It's a pleasure to have dealings with such an astute gentleman!' The fiend was already looking more relaxed and confident, as though the first moments of contact with humans were the most tentative and stress-ful.

Damien said, 'Stop this ridiculous imposture and say what you want.'

'You know what it is, sir, and who sent me.' It pointed at the dark clouds overhead, straight out towards invisible galaxies. It was now speaking in received English pronunciation, with just a hint of something metallic, like radio static.

'I've forgotten all that,' said Damien.

'Not you, sir! The poetry won't let you forget. The strength you knew, the miles you flew aloft in the dun air sublime.'

'I've given up poetry.'

'It was delicious before omnipotence bored you.'

A rabbit moved in scurrying stages across the track, off somewhere. The wind scraped through the gorse.

Damien said, 'I don't want Planet Zog and all that bullshit. I want to stay with Julie in the ordinary world.'

As he blurted this it seemed to him to be the most moving speech he had ever heard. A lump came into his throat and his eyes filled with tears of admiration for the sentiment and pity for the plight. When his vision cleared the fiend had returned to trimming the gorse placidly, concluding each phrase with a snip of the secateurs: 'Yes but the problem is, let's face it sir, you bore the tits off her. Just dry long so, as they sing in the blues.'

A pause followed, several snips of the secateurs.

Damien was again in danger of weeping as he said, 'I want to stay with Julie. I don't want rescuing into madness.' There was petulance in his voice that made him ashamed.

The fiend flung down the secateurs. Its wrath was the wrath of Desmond, the barking voice and flecks of saliva on the beard that had terrified Damien as a child.

'Rescued is an abject, cheating word, because your escape is entirely in your own hands. Try to show more courage and wit. Your wife is profitless even to herself. Shut your eyes and snap your fingers. She will vanish. What has reality ever done for you?'

Collecting itself, it added calmly, 'In any case it is too late to demur. That is proved by the very fact of this conversation.'

A strong stench of shit and corruption was emanating from the fiend.

'The same trick will work with you,' Damien said, 'if I shut my eyes and snap my fingers.' He held out his hand with the thumb and second finger pressed together ready to snap.

The fiend held its ground. It writhed its whiskers like a toothless ruminant. The Irish voice came soft and blithe.

'I'll go for now. But in the long run I'm not as easily dismissed as mere objective phenomena. I'm your personal fiend, sir, and must exist for you as long as you exist for yourself.'

10

BONFIRE PARTY 1989

'I wish I hadn't come and I don't know why I did.'

'It's not much of a do if you don't fancy a lot of racket and folk showing off.'

'There's a very rough element here from Kirkby.'

Everybody was invited by post, and a lot of folk went, considering the reserve towards the Hall and its denizens that was a climatic feature of Thornham. About half of them turned up in fancy dress: it was styled a 'Hallowe'en Bonfire Masquerade' and pitched on the first Saturday after Guy Fawkes Night. As well as villagers and farming families from round about there was a large contingent of gatecrashers from Kirkby, mostly youngsters who had come to the disco in the Apple Tree and took the blame for the damage and nastiness.

A lot of the children went in the Hallowe'en gear they had worn on Mischief Night to go round the village scrounging and extorting – a trick or a treat. The Hall still bore traces of that occasion in demotic aerosol on the outer wall. Tradition ensured that (regardless of treats) it suffered more vandalism than the rest of the village on Mischief Night, if one does not count the house of Miss Garforth, a frail, ancient woman who had been schoolmistress long ago before the school closed and had been the terror of generations of Thornham children. Inherited prejudice meant that on Mischief Night fireworks were invariably thrust through her letter-box, her garden wrecked and her gate carried off to the bottom of the common.

*   *   *

'She shagged like a Welsh rarebit, Max said. Bought her round, an' all.'

'That fat lass?'

'Not that fat. Just meaty.'

'Nice bit o'slack, eh? Anyroad, she fucked off wi' t'nigger.'

'Tommy. The one-legged wizard.'

'The midnight phantom. Who's this Max?'

'Scruff-bag wi' a glass eye, sups in the Fox at Bilberton.'

'Him? He looks about sixty.'

'Had a hard paper round when he were a kid.'

After Susan had banished her, Julie's projects had grown in range and ambition. The old stables were expensively rendered into an art studio, leaving the workshop to Steve Liston, a young potter who had moved into the Stott apartment with his wife (Naomi) and twin toddlers. The Tuesday art classes were revived and a Thursday poetry club was opened to outsiders by an advertisement in the local paper. Julie did the bulk of an abstract mural on the long wall of the dining room, to which art-class members, residents and even casual visitors contributed under her supervision. She persuaded the Listons and Nick Townsend to share a meal in the dining hall each Saturday night, such as had been envisaged at the founding of the community.

The bonfire party was the most elaborate project to date: Julie not only worked hard at it herself but enlisted the goodwill and energy of others. Elaine Dobson, dealt with through Selina, had seen the advantage of the occasion to Apple Tree trade, and a lot of the art class and poetry society were happy to help as well as attend. What was lacking was, literally, manpower. There was a distinct dearth of responsible, sturdy males to police events and prevent excess later in the evening.

It was generally admitted to be a 'grand do', though there was scope for the scoffers and scowlers. The Hall was splendid with Christmas lights. A jazz quartet played in the entrance hall and some of the older revellers jived and waltzed there – the young were dancing to tapes in the pub annexe. The dining hall was stacked with free refreshments – plates of crisps and nuts, pop for the kids and huge bowls of punch that had quite a kick. Those watching the bonfire and firework display were offered slices of parkin, splinters of butter toffee and potatoes roasted in silver paper. Fifty yards down the road the Apple Tree had an extension until midnight (though the refreshment there was not free) so a lot of folk passed to and fro between boozing at the pub and dancing in the Hall.

Those from the village (not in fancy dress) who found it hard to accept wholeheartedly the Hall's hospitality or immerse themselves in the entertainment got pleasure from observing at close range and in fairly revealing circumstances the conduct of the residents of the Hall. The number of residents had dwindled recently, which made it a bit easier for the village to keep tabs on them. A chorus of young drunks and another of aged teetotallers offered rival commentaries.

'What's it all in aid of, anyroad?'

'It won't be to celebrate the Berlin wall going down. Not here at the Kremlin.'

'It's all supposed to be in honour of Damien Frobisher's birthday, according to whatsername at the Post Office who had it off Beryl Ingram who cleans at the Hall.'

'She'll tell you a thing or two, Beryl, about the goings-on.'

'There's a whopping cake somewhere with fifty candles.'

'If there is they've scoffed it themselves. We've not clapped eyes on it.'

'That's their entitlement, isn't it? But they've no right fetching us out if they're going to be tight-fisted with us when they get us here.'

'Have you seen the fancy-dress prizes? I'd be shamed.'

*   *   *

The bonfire was where the big lawn used to be, next to where Julie had marked out a play area – slide, swings, sandpit, pond – for her grandchildren and their buddies. There was not as much wood for the bonfire as there should have been because Kevin Ingram had delivered it a day too soon, so some of it had been stolen by local kids to furnish the November Fifth bonfire on the common. All the same, thanks to petrol and a clear night, it made a lively blaze for half an hour. Ancient George Ingram took it upon himself to tend it, scrambling it together as it sank to red and yellow ashes – at which stage potatoes were provided. Those trying their hands at roasting them were hindered and put at hazard by children who amused themselves – as on Guy Fawkes Night – by leaping the ashes or dashing through them in wellingtons.

The fireworks, supplied and supervised by a professional outfit from York, impressed everybody. They had been set up at the bottom of the garden, against the black background of juniper hedge and night sky. There were crackling serpents, brilliant fountains and rockets galore that exploded into showers of golden rain or dulcet globes. The programme came to a Beethovian climax then culminated with a deafening bang like a galactic full stop.

'He'll tell thoo a thing or two, Max, about the goings-on.'
    'Like what?'
    'Drugs.'
    'Like what?'
    'All sorts. Stuff you snort. Stuff you pop. Stuff you shoot.'
    'Hark at Bazza. The hardened fucking junkie. The hardest drug he's ever had is Tetley's bitter.'
    'And they're up to all sorts of other stuff. Orgies. Y' know.'
    'Don't talk bleeding wet. Orgies? Them swots and wankers?'

Throughout the evening Selina was stalked and pestered

by Lionel Knight, dapper divorcee and veterinarian from Westmoor who was disguised as Al Capone (white suit, black shirt, white tie, fedora). It was the first time she had been seen with any sort of male escort since Tommy's departure so it caused some comment – as did her outfit, a revealing dayglo orange toga and a piled blonde wig purporting to represent Helen of Troy. Lionel did not succeed in monopolising much of her company, since she did a stint behind the bar at the Apple Tree, helped serve punch in the dining hall, presented the fancy-dress prizes in the entrance hall and then relieved Naomi Liston, who was looking after the three Hall children. She was seen vociferously refusing to allow Lionel to go upstairs with her and help her baby-sit, but there were some who claimed he sneaked up discreetly later, an assertion he was never known to deny.

The Listons were relatively new to the village and verdicts on them were still evolving. Naomi was tall with a long braid of flaxen hair; a vegetarian and an environmentalist devoted to organic products. She designed pagan Christmas cards, knitted porridgy garments and played a sort of oriental clavichord when she was not looking after Adam and Emma. Steve, who shared her diet if not her fervour, was a potter who had been lured by the wheel and kiln. A swarthy lad with a slow smile, he favoured a determinedly uncultured stance, declaring himself proud to be an artisan rather than an airy-fairy artist. It was suspected that he was vain and randy – this was confirmed by his appearance at the party in a toreador suit that defined some areas of his figure rather explicitly – but his behaviour on the occasion was disappointing. He danced in the Apple Tree annexe with demons and angels from Kirkby but did not dance with anybody more than once. Then he was witnessed in the pub bar in intimate conversation with a lovely pierrot, Jenny Spraggett from Hutton-le-Hole, but it turned out later that she was his cousin. Most disappointing of all, when his wife, a one-eyed pirate, found him he seemed delighted to see her and spent the rest of the evening in her company.

The Hunters now had as little as possible to do with the activities at the Hall or with the other residents. Once his enemy Ben was gone Chris lost all interest in culture and set to developing the vegetable garden as a commercial proposition. Catherine had become deputy head at her school and given up looking for jobs elsewhere.

'Keep them curtains shut, lad,' Chris commanded grimly. 'And don't let me have to tell you again.'

In a posh, supercilious voice that he had developed to infuriate his father Clive said, 'I happen to be watching the fireworks.'

Catherine put a calming hand on her husband's arm. 'He's maybe upset you won't let him go down,' she said quietly.

'It isn't a patch on the Methodist bonfire we took him to in Pickering. I'm not having a lad of mine mixing with that riff-raff down yonder. If he doesn't like it he can lump it.'

Clive had no wish to go down. He could see some tough characters from Kirkby, as well as local yobs, in the Hall grounds.

He said, not for the first time, 'Dad, you're thick.'

'It's incomers what have wrecked this village with their snooty ideas and their holiday homes but at least most of them are decent folk.'

'This lot at the Hall are a disgrace, hippies and layabouts and all colours of the rainbow.'

'And some very funny ways, according to Beryl.'

'There's the Selina they speak of – the coloured lass dressed like a prostitute.'

'Is that supposed to be art – that mess on the dining-room wall?'

'Who's that young man in the obscene trousers?'

While it is fanciful to suppose that Julie organised the whole event to bring the Drummonds to the Hall, as Gatsby threw parties to lure Daisy Buchanan, it is almost certain that if her daughter and grandchildren had been expected she would have braced herself for the role of sober and decorous hostess. After swallowing her pride again, making the phone call, hearing Susan merely say, 'No chance,' and clomp down the receiver, Julie understood that she was allowed to behave how she liked.

Outdoors, Julie was a Siberian refugee in a huge trench-coat. Indoors she was a houri with cascading curls, a veil of gauze over knickers and bra, bracelets, anklets, and a jewel in her navel. She drank countless paper cups of punch, greeted everybody by the wrong name and smooched shamelessly with a floppy clown while doughtily employing her slim frame as a prop to prevent his total collapse onto the dance floor.

'Did you ever see such a disgusting outfit on a woman of her age and station?'

'It's obscene.'

'It's pathetic.'

'Damien at least is a Frobisher but she's no better than . . . You can tell just to look at her what sort she is, all right.'

'Somebody saw her in Scarborough blind drunk getting into a car with a Pakistani in a turban.'

'Edith got it off her Elaine, who got it off the darkie, that her ladyship there is you-know-whating with that lad with the long straggly hair that's never been seen sober.'

'Nick, his name is, and that's him she's carrying on with this minute, the clown with the big plastic head.'

'She's old enough to be his mother, well, older sister anyroad.'

Damien appeared only briefly and not in fancy dress. He was observed at an upper-floor window watching the bonfire, playing the role of remote, excluded witness that the older villagers remembered him in when he was a child. Then he suddenly appeared next to the flagging pyre, looming clumsily, his spectacles glinting. He had a bin-liner full of papers, which he flung to flare, a handful at a time, watching them avidly as if reading their contents as they were consumed. A few minutes later he was back with an armful of fat paperbacks from the library, which he likewise used as fuel.

Julie, in Siberian mode, watched him. When he had thrown in the last book she went across and put her hand on his arm. 'Go back into the Hall, love, and don't fetch any more.'

He shook off her hand without taking his eyes from the fire. 'By!' he said, like a village lad. 'They go up a treat!'

She took his arm more firmly. 'Come back into the Hall.'

He let her lead him away but looked back wistfully at the erased volumes and the devouring flames. Several minutes later she came back to the festivities without him. He did not reappear.

'That were the Lord o' the fucking Manor. Thoo can see he's off his trolley. He walks downt' village chuntering on to hissen in broad daylight.'

'It's a fucking family tradition. Yer know what went on yonder not ten year back.'

'What's he on about?'

'Yer must know! Even a dozy twat like thoo from Helmsley!'

'Damien's dad went potty and shot his mam – Damien's mother, I mean – and his brother – he shot his own brother – Damien's father did – shot Damien's uncle – and himself . . . shit, I need a drink.'

'They reckon you can still see the bloodstains on the posh carpet. How them cold-blooded posh cunts can live there is a fucking mystery to anybody normal.'

'The brother were having it off with Damien's mother, were what it were all about.'

'That youth Nick wants to watch his fucking step, then, eh? Because Damien's edging over into the land of the daft. And Nick's shagging whatsername, her ladyship.'

There were guests who behaved much worse than the residents, particularly after midnight, when the pub shut and disgorged its revellers up the road in search of the previously despised punch. There was a fight between a caveman and a vampire over the favours of a St Trinian's trull. A very small Hell's Angel (maybe not in fancy dress) produced an enormous pool of custard-like vomit in the vestibule. A Mohican in a tracksuit tried to copulate with a hermetically furred pussy-cat in a standing posture during a slow waltz, bellowing frustrated imprecations. Another copulating couple, surprised naked on the first-floor landing, dashed upstairs and vanished forever before they were identified.

A lot of other bad, even malicious, behaviour went apparently unwitnessed but left its spoor. The fish was smashed from the mermaid's arms in what used to be the fountain. The dustbins were overturned, the bin-liners extracted and disgorged onto the gravel. Indoors, pottery and *objets trouvés* that decorated the ground floor were flung around in derision and there were obscene additions in felt-tip on the dining-room mural. Somebody had urinated against the wall in the scullery. The taps in the downstairs washroom had been left running and somebody, maybe a complete stranger, had written on the mirror in lipstick, *'Julie is a slag.'*

11

Julie was tending the three little grey kittens of an ancient woman who claimed to be sick but who somebody looking a bit like Susan said was a malingerer. The woman was sitting up in bed and asking the whereabouts of a holdall that Julie had a sneaking notion of having seen but could not remember where. A dozen children – Julie could not see her own children or grandchildren among them – were using a cast-iron bath with claw feet, turning dangerous somersaults as they dived into it, and there was a muddy pond under dripping trees where hippos lay. Looking for her glass Julie could only find two-thirds of a broken bottle brimming with wine on which little flecks or stains of garbage rested like mould. Along the rim of an aqueduct above corrugated buildings and iron gantries she was balancing a pan full of cabbage-stalk chunks. *As long as my nerve holds I'll be okay.*

The room was in a tawny gloam, the morning light filtered by shifting curtains. The window was slightly open and children were shouting in the street as they boarded the school bus.

I don't mind waking alone if night is over. I've woken next to various men in my time, one or two of them nasty shocks. But never next to Ben.

Four loud, equidistant knocks on the panel of the bedroom door gave her to understand that a similar but more discreet summons had woken her ten seconds earlier. Since Damien had had a separate bedroom he had evolved a fussy, diplomatic routine over morning coffee.

I wish just once he'd have a woman in bed with him in the morning. I'd serve them egg and bacon and champagne.

Normally there was no need for his discretion because if Nick had stayed the night he was gone by half past eight on his way to Teesside in his rusty Renault Four. This morning the pillow next to Julie was undented and that side of the bed had evidently not been used. She let out a placid cry and Damien bore in the coffee tray. He said good morning, told her that the weather was propitious, kissed her lightly on the cheek, activated the radio on the chest of drawers, opened the curtains and closed the window before exiting.

Julie, in a butch cotton nightshirt with red and white vertical stripes, simultaneously listened to the nine o'clock news and read *One Hundred Years of Solitude* while she drank her coffee. Binky and Braithwaite, her ancient cats who had come into the bedroom with Damien, were patrolling the floor and imploring for breakfast; picking their way through Julie's clothes and the books and fag packets that had tumbled off the mound on top of the pot cupboard by her bed.

She slipped out of bed and looked over the vegetable garden and the roof of the Ingrams' cottage on to the wide village street. The bus was gone and the street empty. Dropping her gaze, Julie felt a hand clutch her throat as she spotted Tim in the vegetable garden. Then she saw that it was not, of course, Tim but Clive Hunter, who had recently grown his hair in defiance of his father. Clive never went on the school bus and his mother never picked up any village children if they were waiting at the bottom of the common.

Julie waded through the furry entreaties of the cats, across the room and the apartment lobby to the bathroom. In the shower she verified, as every morning, that her frame was coping acceptably with the oncreep of age. *My bum's sagged a bit but otherwise . . . I've always reckoned my tits are too small, but it's a comfort that they're keeping their shape, whereas those of lasses I used to envy at school will be flopping round their knees by now.* But she examined her face more ruefully in the candid mirror over the wash-basin. *I'm getting to look like Granny Watkins who we were scared of when I was a kid.* And she remembered how a few days earlier two Thornham urchins had puzzled her by flinging pebbles in her direction then scampering off. *Shit! I'm only forty-six!* There was grey in her hair. She dried it, gathered it into a cursory pony-tail and fastened it with a rubber band.

As soon as she was dressed she trotted upstairs, pursued by the meowing cats, to Nick's room. When the door did not budge she went to the little window in the corner of the landing and craned up on tiptoe to peer into the yard. Nick's car was gone.

He'll still be over the limit, the state he was in last night. He'll lurch into class grey-faced and red-eyed with stale booze on his breath and his morale zero. And he'll go to the pub for a top-up at lunch-time. She frankly wondered how Nick kept his teaching job. He had actually been promoted twice.

She fed the cats, then made a full cooked breakfast of sausage, bacon and tomato for herself and Damien, who was reading the morning papers in the dining room while waiting to be fed.

Damien read out snippets about resistance to the Poll Tax and commented on them mildly. *Don't interrupt him or he'll dry up, drift away.* These days he took long walks in all weathers, otherwise remaining in the Frobisher apartment listening to ancient blues records, or on fine days sitting on the balustrade that edged the terrace, looking towards the defunct fountain and holding a notebook in which he wrote nothing. Presently his constipation might let escape a small, taut poem, but he had given up prose. The bonfire incident, on top of other indications, had worried her enough for her to try to persuade him to seek medical help. When this failed she had taken what seemed the only other acceptable course, which was to reassure herself that the bulk of his behaviour was serene and not threateningly abnormal.

Look at him! Friendly and content. If he doesn't like discussing painful and intimate matters – refuses to trade in the stuff that husbands and wives use to flex their will against each other – I should count myself lucky! She had reciprocated by sparing him the confessions and convictions with which she used to bombard him, especially when they still slept together. *It's me has to lie awake now listening to Nick's gibberish.*

She followed Damien around while he stacked the dishwasher and cleared up the kitchen, telling him about the coming that morning of a landscape gardener from Malton. *He's not listening. His conversational stint is over. He's left the premises, gone to wherever he spends the bulk of his time.* Then she went to the pottery workshop and claimed a clay sculpture that she had put in to fire the previous night. Steve Liston was there, and she talked to him about glazes and firings, but she could tell that he wasn't crediting what she was saying with any importance.

This one can't take me seriously. Partly because I'm a pretentious high-brow artist, partly because I'm a woman. But not a real woman, because I've seen how he looks at Selina . . .

She carried her sculpture round to the studio and put it on a shelf in the storeroom where there were now a couple of dozen similar creatures: mutant toads, or deformed new-born human babies, each about ten inches across, in dark brown clay. She wished that ten years ago she had not destroyed her collection of glass and metal sculptures that had been so comparatively liberated and aspirational. Her artefacts had always been the first casualties of a rebeginning. She could whimsically envisage a retrospective of her work: a series of rooms inhabited by the wildly contrasting tribes of aliens produced in her different epochs.

Whereas all I have are these little orphan sods too ugly to sell.

Her studio was cluttered with the debris of her Tuesday art classes, as well as with Nick's treacle tins and wire, so she was reduced to a corner for her own work. She wedged the clay for a quarter of an hour, periodically pushing a wire through it till she was satisfied there were no air-bubbles. Working it fastidiously, keeping it in one piece, she soon felt the shape coming again: the plangent hump, beseeching, abortive, with stumpy limbs like terrapin flippers gone agley. She was absorbed in this birth, this kneading into being, for what seemed a long time. When she glanced up, out through the window, she saw Damien crossing the Tarmac yard towards the garden alongside a bald geezer in a grey flannel suit. There was a bottle green Range Rover where Nick usually parked.

Shit! The stupid . . . Not only had her catatonic husband ignored her conversation in the kitchen – it had not occurred to him to consult her now that her landscape gardener had shown up. Damien was going to take him round the garden, nod at his pronouncements, maybe even offer him a commission, with that show of friendly coherence that would entirely conceal from the visitor the fact that he was dealing with an empty husk, the cell of an escaped lunatic.

When she caught up with them, still wiping the clay off her hands with the old tea-towel she had snatched up, Damien was saying breezily to the chap, 'I dare say you'll know better than I do what needs doing.'

'Thank you, Damien,' she cut in caustically. 'I'll take over.'

He gave her a bland grin, not remotely offended or even surprised, and mooched off back to the house.

'Mr Collins?'

He was a small, bald, neat man, carrying a clipboard. She

listed her requirements: rockery, lawn, arbour, paths of white pebbles between the flowerbeds.

The Hall's essential to my fragile morale, like Cleopatra's empire, without which, dragged in chains through Rome . . .

The man started to frown as he discovered that not only had she designed it all already – at least, in her head – but that she wanted to see his detailed proposals and estimates on paper before she decided whether to give him the job. He asked her rather stiffly if she wished to keep the children's playground as a feature.

'I do indeed.'

The slide and swings were popular with Merline and the Liston twins, and Julie still intended her grandchildren to play there. After Susan's savage mandate Julie's pride had renounced hope. *Even if she deigns to relent I wouldn't demean myself by accepting the terms of that bitch.* Then she came to see that she was in no position to shout defiance. She loved her grandchildren with a yearning made more urgent by her awareness of the transience of the child, so that their extended absence was devastating. *I'll have to swallow the shit, cringe on my back and bare my belly.* The slide and swings would stay, and the sandpit, which Fiona adored.

After Collins had gone she went back to the sculpture but there was no confidence in her fingers. She did not even dare touch it with her fingertips. She gently wrapped it in a damp cloth then shrouded it in a polythene bag. Going to the apartment she found a biro and a notebook with a draft of a poem and took them to the library. The draft had been written with the aid of a bottle of Beaujolais last night while waiting for Nick to fail to show up. *Drinking while writing alone – writing while drinking alone – that's Ben's influence . . .* She scowled at the poem but couldn't touch it with the biro any more than she had been able to put her fingertips to the clay. *That's daft. This is not clay. With a poem, as with love, the original need not be obliterated.* All the same, she left it as it was, took the notebook back to her bedroom and stashed it in the drawer of the pot cupboard next to her bed.

Descending to the kitchen she prepared a chicken masala ready to bake later in the day. Then she cooked up fish fingers and beans in time for Naomi to get back with the raucous infants from the Bilberton play group. Steve came in streaked with pottery slip just as everybody had started eating. The vegetarian Listons ate fish and eggs, and sometimes chicken if it was free range and organically fed.

Apart from the Hunters the community was co-operating better than it ever had. Lunches were often shared during the week and Saturday dinner had become a relaxed social event.

Julie got on well with Naomi but knew that she would not replace Sonia as a friend and confidante. For one thing, Naomi was significantly younger – more Susan's age – but the real problem was that Naomi was intransigently happy. She could be put out of temper – impatient, indignant – but only in the sense that the healthiest women have periods or athletes get cramp. Happiness informed every stance or movement of her long limbs and shone from her frank gaze. She was at peace with herself, her tastes and doctrines, her calm regime and pagan gods. She knew how to bring up her children, whose conduct so far justified her confidence. She had a secure relationship with her husband based on shared concerns and mutual regard.

Her serenity would be salutary if she was my social worker or therapist but it rules her out as a friend. Friendship has to be reciprocal. Why hasn't Sonia answered my last letter? Why does Tim never write?

There had been over a dozen regulars in the art class at the end of October. Today, at the beginning of April, there were four, including Julie, in the sunlit studio. It was the nadir, so far, of a decline that had bafflingly begun at the Hallowe'en Bonfire Masquerade, Julie's gesture of friendship that seemed to have caused a distinct downturn in relations between the Hall and the locals. *As if I'd done it as a deliberate insult to the whole sodding neighbourhood.* The Local History Society, who had been using the library on Wednesdays for the last four years, had decided they would be cosier visiting each other's houses. The poetry group on Thursday evenings had dwindled to zero. Anybody Julie quizzed gave blank, bland answers, looking shifty.

Julie also perceived that the attitude of those still faithful to the art class had altered for the worse. Betty and Mildred used to fawn on Julie, clamouring for her advice and approval. They now sniffed the air, like a reconnaissance team in hostile territory, watched Julie as if she was a case-study, exchanged complicit glances and whispered together like schoolchildren. If she spoke to them, which was usually to comment on their work, they became provokingly still and silent, their eyes downcast.

I can add these two old sods to Selina, Beryl Ingram and the other narks who handle my public relations. Susan, too, I dare say.

She could vividly see Susan's smug cheeks and sullen lips, the brown eyes burning with the festered grievances of a lifetime. It was an expression that until last August she had not seen for several years. The assault had been all the more devastating because it had come without warning, at a time when Julie had convinced herself that Susan's constant caustic remarks were a habit that had no real significance. She had even had hopes of being forgiven for having been a rotten mother and tolerated, if not exactly prized, as an eccentric who made other grannies seem a bit drab.

It's as though she'd been saving it all, Susan, till she was sure that she had something precious to me that she could smash.

She had a sudden vision of Fiona, an ebullient optimist, cuddling the disgusted Braithwaite and cooing with delight. Graham was more reserved and cerebral in his demeanour. He bossed his grandma around haughtily, but from time to time gave a shy, utterly disarming show of affection. They had now been lost to her for eight months. They had passed her several times in the Land Rover without waving. Once she had spent several precious, painful minutes with them in the Pickering central car park, with Susan in the hairdresser's and Paul trapped and sheepish. Bouncy Fiona had been crushed into utter silence by the event. Graham had asked, 'Why don't you come to see us, Granny? Is it because I'm a bad lad?' Remembering it now she had to swallow, as then, a globe of desolation that had risen into her throat and was threatening to stop her breath.

I love toddlers, and them me. As they get older we grow apart. Story of my life. Of everything. I need them now before it's too late.

Phil Froggatt, the Frobisher solicitor and a brief old flame, had told her that grandparents could claim right of access but in practice it was just upsetting to everybody if the parents were opposed. She had also seen a psychiatrist (at Naomi's suggestion) who had soothed her into not hassling Susan. 'She'll very likely come round in her own time.' All the same Julie had resolved on taking presents round to the farm on Christmas morning, challenging Susan to find the nerve to turn her away. Then she discovered, a couple of days before, that the Drummonds were gone for Christmas and New Year to the other grandparents in Hull.

By then there was no frigging time to post the presents, which would arrive late from daft Granny. If that bitch Susan let them have them at all.

Fortunately Celia Burridge was demanding more than her share of Julie's time and attention. Celia was a recent acquisition to the painting club, having turned up in January, and seemed unaffected by the malaise of the rest. She was a large woman, about seventy years old, who wore flowing purple robes, lots of jewellery and a bandanna. She brought a substantial oil-painting kit with her and canvases a metre square on which, with the aid of a mirror, she produced a series of lurid, manic self-portraits.

Betty and Mildred won't last much longer, then I'll be left just with Celia. Two weirdos together. The Thornham witch and her crony. I wish Tim would write.

When the painting club had gone she locked the studio and went back into the Hall, where she put the masala into the oven to bake.

Selina came into the kitchen and said, 'Hey, that smells good!'

'I'm afraid it's only for two,' Julie said curtly. Selina was out of favour. There was in fact enough for three, since Julie hoped Nick would be back in time.

Selina just shrugged good-naturedly, which made Julie feel a bit ashamed of herself, but all the same she couldn't bring herself to mitigate or explain what she had said. She fetched her book from the bedroom intending to curl up in the big armchair in the lounge until it was time to make the rice and salad.

On her way downstairs she passed Catherine and Clive Hunter coming up. The women greeted each other with the brevity that had become the theme of any meeting.

Cathy and Chris disapprove of me. They also disapprove of everybody else in the Hall and hold me responsible. It's a pity, because I admire them. Chris is straight and incapable of malice, he doesn't smile at your face and gossip behind your

*back like Selina. Cathy's a snob and a philistine but she's loyal
and intelligent. Like me, she has a child who despises her and
a husband who's turning peculiar, losing control.*

Sitting alone in the library at night Julie quite often found
herself eavesdropping on the Hunters through the partition
wall. She could not make out much of what was said but
the tone and cadence of the voices marked the progress of
the dispute. Chris would begin with the measured, dogmatic
emphasis that characterised most of his speech. Clive's still
juvenile voice, dawdling and supercilious, would first interrupt
the homily then transform it. Soon Chris was blustering and
ranting in a paroxysm of impotent outrage, Clive responding
with shrill spleen determined not even to seem to be quelled.
Catherine could be heard trying to intervene, her mild voice
striving against the cudgel of the father and the razor of the
lad. The row seemed to loom on the brink of tears, physical
violence or cardiac arrest. It usually terminated in a crescendo
of simultaneous fury and a slammed door. Sometimes it went
on so remorselessly that Julie fled from the library.

The lounge was half panelled in oak, the upper walls roughly
plastered and mottled white in an effect that resembled *crépi*.
The room had suffered a lot during its occupation by Mary
Spillsbury and her children: there were still scars on the wain-
scot and panelling though the suite had been re-upholstered
and the rug replaced. From where she was sitting in Marjorie's
armchair Julie could see through the french windows, beyond
the balustrade where Quentin used to perch (and Damien did
sometimes nowadays) to the fountain yet to be mended, the
swings and slide and site of the costly bonfire, the juniper
hedge, gorse-covered hills and pale sky.

Julie loved Sparrow Hall. She had difficulty in locating the
source of her affection for what, after all, should have few
claims on her. It was redolent of privilege and snobbery. It
was her husband's gift, a debt she abjured. It had witnessed

the disappointment of her hopes and the crushing of her pretensions. She loved it like a film director might cherish a problematic film – not in its failed entirety but for passages and flourishes: herself and Ben trying tipsily to climb the servant staircase to the third floor; Binky and Braithwaite, stupid with spring, scampering like kittens up and down the carpeted main stairs; Christmas, the presents under the big tree, Damien carving the turkey in the dining room, Selina smiling, Corinne sulking, Graham and Fiona making footprints in the terrace snow; Michael barking vociferously at the end of his tether, which he had shortened to a metre by winding it round the tree.

She could not settle to reading: she was disappointed by Marquez. *Or am I prejudiced by the nauseous blobs of sexism that occasionally escape from his urbane and cultured lips?* A lot of literature was spoiled for Julie like that. *Shakespeare is vicious enough with prejudice and stereotyping to need banning. And what about the chapter on 'Community of Wives' in* The Communist Manifesto? *It's only intended for half the workers of the world, that call to liberty.*

She closed the book and looked out of the window, more moodily than before. Chris Hunter emerged from the gate of the vegetable garden with his arms full of cabbages, which he bore towards the house.

I've never been a serious feminist. Promiscuous females like me and Corinne, trying to behave like men, are not feminists.

I envied Corinne. She had the gall I've always lacked when the chips were down. But she was a kid, she's maybe grown out of . . . Look at me, a granny, still getting pissed and dropping my knickers for the likes of Nick.

Nick took over from Ben, the disciple following the master, one piss-artist succeeding another, when I was swigging wine alone in the library, as I used to do when I waited for Ben. For a wild moment when I heard the heavy footsteps like a wounded ogre moving along the landing I thought it might be Ben come back from Southport to surrender to my terms for ever. But when Nick opened the library door and loomed in like a character in a farce I was able to laugh. I still think, whatever he says, that Ben gave him the notion some boozy night before he left. 'If you're short of a bit, lad . . .' – as a farewell sneer. I was wondering about this even then while Nick moved towards me like somebody wading through cheese, plonked himself next to me, giggled, and without palaver, as if he was in a brothel, put his hand inside my dungarees and started fumbling his fingers into my pants. And I just leaned back and opened my legs, without even asking him if he'd washed his hands lately. The girl who can't say no. Gloria Graham, wasn't it? The rich man's moll. The tender-hearted trollop who gets carved up half-way through the film.

Damien was back from his ramble in time to have a bath before dinner, which he and Julie ate alone in the dining hall.

He laid the table, then seated himself and waited for Julie to serve the food. He sat upright, facing the door with his back to the windows, so that the evening gleamed pink through his ears and lit the light brown floss that meagrely thatched his skull. Julie put the light on. He had grown heavier as he got older: bulky rather than fat, round-shouldered and heavy-handed, with an inept strength that sometimes reminded Julie of Pierre Bezhukov but more often of Lennie Small.

As she brought in the cold puddings, which she liked to put on the table before she produced the hot main course, Julie caught him talking to himself, or not so much talking as mouthing a script, the way some people move their lips when they read. This had become a frequent mannerism of Damien's and troubled Julie, who associated it with geriatrics. Sometimes, if he thought nobody could hear him, he said the words of his reverie out loud. From what she had heard of them, they composed the same comfortable banalities as his ordinary talk.

What he should do is bugger off to Trebizond, dye his hair blue and start again. But somewhere along the way, dealing with Dora, dealing with me, he's lost impetus. It's less hassle for him if nothing matters a shit.

Unlike at breakfast, when Damien both read the paper and used it as a conversational prop, he gave all his attention to the food and his fellow-diner. He spoke of the weather, the walk he had taken and other trivia of his day. He made several complimentary remarks about the food before him, asking Julie for the ingredients and method of preparation in excruciating detail, as if he was planning to cook it himself later in the evening. He also questioned her about her day, getting her to tell him all over again about her plans for the garden and grilling her minutely about the art class.

It was as if he didn't want to leave any space for unwelcome topics. She knew that if she broke his flow with anything personal or controversial he would lift his head so that his spectacles glittered, wipe his chops with his napkin, give her a sheepish yet reproachful grin and either go straight on with his bland crap or shut up entirely. Sometimes she complained directly, lost her temper, hissed obscenities and was on the verge of throwing food at his head. The most she had provoked was: 'Calm down, Julie. Nothing is served by us getting upset.' If she had wept it might have shaken his composure but Julie never wept.

The problem with Damien is his plaintive ghost has survived his demise as a lover. It's what he wanted, what I agreed to, hell for us both.

He had recently developed some weird habits. Julie had served the main course so that the masala and rice each occupied half of the plate, rather than with the chicken in a mound in the middle of the rice. Damien started eating at the side of the plate closest to him and moved methodically and tidily outwards till first the lower hemisphere of the plate was empty, then there was just a segment of food in the Arctic Circle, then the plate was empty, the chicken bones neatly aligned on one of the paper napkins. His method had meant that he had eaten almost all the masala before tackling the rice. The side plate of salad he ignored. The yoghurt and fruit he simply spooned from the side closest to him. At the end of the meal, as at breakfast, he cleared the crockery and cutlery from the table exactly in the order that it had arrived there, stacked the dishwasher and tidied the kitchen, while never faltering, when he came within range of where Julie was hunched over her wine, from the breezy, trifling discourse that he had despotically imposed on the whole occasion.

Did his father used to eat like that, like an autistic child? I need qualified advice about him, but it doesn't come easy to report your husband as a loony behind his back. So I'm passive and gob-smacked, like he used to be in the wolf-hours of insomnia when he was the doctor.

Nick's car was in its usual parking spot under the lamp in the yard. Julie re-entered the house, climbed the stairs and tried the door of Nick's room. She looked in her own room and the library on the first floor, in the kitchen, dining hall and lounge on the ground floor.

When she got back to the car she discovered that it was unlocked and the keys were in the ignition. The bonnet of the car was still warm.

He's done as I asked him, come home instead of staying in Eston until the pubs shut. All the same he'll have been drinking. Then he's gone straight up the road to the Apple Tree, as if he was dying of thirst, without even coming into the house.

Torn between relief and exasperation she actually walked to the gate, out into the lane and onto the street, to where she could see the apple tree on the lit wooden sign. *I might persuade him to come home and have something to eat. What I should do, what Barbara should have done ten years ago, is lug the childish bastard out of the pub by the ear.* The incongruity and futility of this last notion calmed her. She knew she wasn't going to go to the pub. *We've given too much entertainment to those bitches. Selina even turns the music down so she can eavesdrop.*

She retraced her steps into the house, into the dining room for the half-empty bottle of Beaujolais, which she took, along with her glass, upstairs to the library. Then she fetched her notebook and biro from the pot cupboard in her bedroom. Damien was playing spirituals: Blind Willie and Angeline Johnson singing 'Fully Saved Today', his false bass barking like the fiend in *The Exorcist*, her soprano dawdling sublime and nonchalant in the background as if she was peeling potatoes in the kitchen. Julie did not look into the living room but knew that Damien would be sitting motionless with his eyes shut, neither listening to the music nor asleep.

Julie had recently had the library refashioned, because she didn't like the thought of Damien maundering in a museum of childhood horror. The dark oak shelves and panels were gone, along with the gaunt jury of high-back chairs and the vast oblong table they surrounded. Now there were white and orange walls, easy chairs from Habitat. Fauve and Impressionist reproductions had replaced the photographs of ancient Whitby and the sepia tints of Trebizond. A lot of the old Victorian books – sets of Dickens and Thackeray, bound copies of the *Quiver*, *Sunday at Home*, *British Battles on Land and Sea* – had been junked or sold: paperbacks and glossy art books had achieved dominance.

She poured out only half a glass of wine, then set it by

untasted for the moment, because she wanted to restrict herself to the one bottle. What she really fancied was a joint, or a brown pill from the envelope on her pot cupboard, but she had already started drinking alcohol and only mixed her fixes on special occasions.

I'm acting as if I was Nick's bloody mother. I didn't used to worry about how much my men drank or what else they got up to – I let them do the worrying about me. No, that's crap. I was never all that brave and carefree. Greedy and scared of the dark.

She opened the notebook and looked at the poem for a while. She crossed out the word 'resemble' and wrote 'remember' above it. Then she closed the notebook.

I can't write poetry unless my morale is high. Like one of Damien's bloody bluesmen says, if you really got the blues you don't sing about 'em, you just have 'em.

She reread a letter from a Birmingham writer of detective stories (two published) interested in what Julie still thought of as the Pocock apartment, which had been empty for nine months since Nick was eased out. Last summer and autumn Julie had searched hard for congenial tenants. Then, after a couple of late cancellations, she had lost enthusiasm. This man was a widower with three teenage children. She was going to drop the letter into the bin when she relented and put it back in the desk drawer. *I'll give it a last chance when I'm in a better mood.* She had been doing this for nearly a fortnight.

Taking the cover off the Amstrad she started up and inserted a disk.

Dear Tim, I'm typing because you always used to complain about my crap handwriting. I don't want anything to increase your reluctance to read this or reply. That's if it gets forwarded to you, or if you're still at that address in the New Mexico desert you described so vividly sixteen months ago. This is my seventh letter since then, she mewled. In the last five I've implored you for news, if only one of those laconic cards you used to send.

I've not kept copies so might well be saying the same things over and over. My impression is that my letters display a psychological evolution that guards against that though not against being tedious. The first were coolly discursive, trying to be both provoking and entertaining, so you might reply out of genuine interest rather than out of a sense of duty or (even worse) pity. Then I decided I might as well use this one-way correspondence to unload baggage and focus angst. That's how I used to use Damien in the middle of the night. He has his own room now.

If you read this you'll snort at the nerve I've got, expecting you to be a dutiful son and correspondent, daring to express maternal concern (see below) with the record I've got of looking after you very badly if at all. Your mother was always an egotistical bitch, expecting others to fulfil her needs and adjust to her agenda. A hypocrite, hassling you with moral pressure to keep up a dialogue now that she's run short of other friends and relations.

My case, if I have one, rests in you. I can't think your silence is based on the sort of mind-set that has made your sister banish me. Last time I saw you, three Christmases ago (is it as long ago as that?), you'd got over the horror of being my child. You'd emerged from curmudgeonly adolescence strong and free, a rediscovery of the brave, optimistic kid that had seemed long dead. I wasn't proud of you, because I didn't flatter myself that it was any of my doing, but I rejoiced and wanted to get to know you, form an adult, allodial relationship with this shining stranger.

You said then that you were going to 'travel the world and find yourself'. Later, in your letter, the only letter, that otherwise breezy opus, you said you were undergoing 'a bit of a crisis about life and art'. I understand if in the course of such a search, such a crisis, you wish to distance yourself from your history and its representatives. If that's how you feel it would be simple to let me know, and save you bother in the long run.

I recently made an effort to sneak up and find you, or at least find out if you're alive. I wrote to Professor Kenyon, your Bristol hero, and asked if he knew of your whereabouts. He was very kind, putting me onto two or three people who might be contacts. Of these Ingmar, the lad you brought to Sparrow Hall, was the most forthcoming, but didn't know where you were any more than the others did. Your disappearance, so far, is complete, but I've plenty of money to hire detectives to track you down, and will bloody well do that if I don't hear from you soon. My other idea is to come to America myself and start making enquiries at Las Cruces. Eventually, to shun me, you'll have to move home, grow a beard, adopt an alias. You can save me trouble and preserve your privacy with just a few words.

I'd be amazed and distressed if it was your homosexuality that was causing you to want to break ties with your past and me. If you reckon I'm in any way offended or disconcerted by your being gay (I don't know which term you prefer) you have a remarkably obtuse picture of me. Out of all the faults for which you might justifiably shun me you've picked one of the few I don't have. I'll be disappointed, from a selfish point of view, if you don't provide me with grandchildren (to replace the ones that your bitch of a sister has abducted). My only other reaction is worry for you in case homosexuals have an even slighter chance of happiness than heteros. If you are no longer homosexual – or never were – please ignore this daft paragraph.

At least my letters contain none of the usual maternal crap, intimations of obligation based on recollections of your forgotten childhood. You know yourself (and if not there are plenty who will tell you) that I don't have normal maternal feelings. This means that if you are in any sort of trouble I'd be a useful person to contact. I'll not be as distressed as other mothers by the predicament you're in, or have as demanding an agenda of gratitude and obedience in return for what help I give. I don't dwell on the past, hardly at all. And I have money.

If you've received this, opened it, read this far, I'll reward you with the local news headlines, in lighter vein. Your stepfather is now insane. His brain harbours enigmatic aliens. Your mother has been accorded the status of neighbourhood witch, pelted with dung, brickbats, barbed

The ogre's boots were clumping across the landing. Julie thought briefly of Ben as she saved the letter, extracted the disk and switched off the Amstrad.

Nick had learned to open the library door quietly and efficiently, however drunk he was. He came in balanced upright, carrying an opened bottle of red wine and a glass.

'Yasmin gorrocks up for a wan blend,' he announced proudly, then proceeded to fill Julie's glass and his own. He performed both operations with commendable steadiness: a perilous blurt of wine from the bottle in each case but no spillage.

'Is wine a good idea after all that beer?' Julie said impulsively, then grimaced at her own folly.

Nick's pale eyes peered out, mindless and reptilian, from the fronds of yellow hair. He spoke coldly and deliberately, the way practised drunks do when acting sober. 'Binnifer cosharack grun wist weevil slaw. Orshee for plinths is easy fucking niven?'

He's picking a quarrel with me because he knows he's too drunk to shag properly.

She smiled at him. 'You're a good lad for coming home. I'm grateful. What sort of day have you had?'

'Thrommon caddle genghis.' He emptied his wine glass in three methodical sips, like the beer drinker he was. Maybe he was going to pass out before he started vomiting. 'Barbara did petherall fucking once. She did for once more petherall in her binny procting. Butter fucking simkiss wither cray.'

Julie gulped down her wine and refilled her glass.

12

THE SPARROW HALL MASSACRE 1990

Beryl Ingram woke in the night to hear fiends yelping, great wings flapping and bones cracking. Beyond the reassuring lump of her unconscious husband she saw that the bedroom curtains were lit with a flickering brilliance, as if a great host with flashlights and cressets was assembled for mayhem in the cottage garden. She got out of bed, padded round to peer between the curtains and stood gobsmacked.

The cottage was actually inside the grounds of Sparrow Hall. It had once housed gardeners or grooms and the cooks or maids they married, but since 1985 had been let rent free to the Ingrams on condition that Beryl spent two days a week cleaning in the Hall. Julie saw the arrangement as romantically old-fashioned – a sort of barter – whereas from Beryl's point of view it was a reinvention of serfdom. It meant she couldn't get a proper job, and she bitterly resented being bound to the labour, which she did as badly as she dared.

From the bedroom window the east wing of the Hall loomed forty yards away above the vegetable garden wall. Tongues of flame and billows of smoke were issuing from all four storeys of the building, to a soundtrack of flames roaring, glass and plaster cracking and joists collapsing.

Dan Ingram, a security guard, was now sitting up in bed, the alarm on his countenance made more dramatic by the shifting, lurid light.

'What's up?'

'It's the Hall. Come and see. By, it's going like billy-o!'

*   *   *

Not long afterwards the din of the fire-engines, police cars and ambulances had brought out the village to watch the impressive event. The combined Kirkby and Pickering fire services were helpless to quell the blaze, which had taken ferocious hold before it woke Beryl. By frantic heroics both inside and outside the building, with oceans of water and acres of foam, assisted by a favourable wind direction, they had managed to contain it: in the morning, when the fire was gone into hissing cinders, the west side of the building was untouched except by superficial heat damage, and most of the north and south side structures intact. But the east side was gutted, the floors consumed and collapsed to make a gulf behind the black façade, with the metal contents of all four storeys fallen among the ashes in the stone cellar below the dining hall.

The astonishing virulence of the fire could be attributed to the wealth of timber in the Hall – particularly on the east side, with a cellar full of firewood, the oak-panelled dining room on the ground floor and the first-floor Frobisher suite lavishly redone in Norwegian pine. The total destruction wrought by the fire ensured that the actual source remained a conjecture. The oil tank in the west-side cellar was undisturbed: the oil-fired central heating was not usually activated in June. At night individual rooms and apartments were warmed by electric fires and storage heaters if necessary. It was thought that there was also a wood fire in the dining-room fireplace, to add cheer to the Saturday-evening communal dinner. The conflagration was assumed to have begun either in the dining hall or in the wood-store below.

Evidence of five corpses was found amid the ash and debris. At the inquest these remains were fairly confidently identified as Damien and Julie Frobisher, Nick Townsend, Selina Johnson and Steve Liston – the entire population of the Hall that night. The only other residents in June 1990 were far away. The Hunters were visiting relatives in Barnsley. Naomi Liston had taken Adam and Emma to their grandparents in Basingstoke for the weekend. Merline Johnson, the same age as the Liston twins and friendly with them, had gone with the Listons.

It was difficult to determine where each of the victims had been at the time of the disaster and where they had met their deaths. From the location of their meagre remains Julie Frobisher and Nick Townsend were judged to have been either in the dining room itself or in Julie's bedroom on the first floor. Their liaison was well known and Nick regularly slept in Julie's room: his own room on the second floor north-west was in such a state of bachelor squalor as to be almost uninhabitable. Damien Frobisher was thought to have been either in the dining room or the lounge of the first-floor Frobisher suite. Steve Liston and Selina Johnson were allocated to the dining room, or the Frobisher lounge, or the Liston second-floor apartment above the Frobisher suite. All conjecture was further complicated by the possibility that one or more of the victims moved from place to place in terror and agony before being either overcome by fumes or consumed by flames.

The fact that all five residents had died in the fire was at once seen as a suspicious or, at least, curious circumstance. It was as if they had deliberately gathered above the site of the outbreak. Selina Johnson, for instance, had no business on the east side of the building at that time of night. If (as was almost universally assumed) she was sleeping with Steve Liston, it seemed logical that they would have sited that liaison in Selina's room, undamaged on the second floor south-west, rather than risk leaving evidence for Naomi to find. Most suspicious, of course, was the fact that none of the victims had been awoken by the fire until they were trapped.

Speculation throve from the first, both welcomed and fed by

the media, which found Sparrow Hall a savoury item for a while. Early headlines like *THE CURSE STRIKES AGAIN!* and *SECOND BLOODBATH AT HORROR HALL* accompanied an approach heavily influenced by the events of 1982 as well as by the need to be sensational. The easily accessible concept that the victims had been already dead before the fire led to a range of proposed solutions – a passing maniac, a local with a grudge, a panic-stricken burglar – the most popular of which, of course, even at this early stage, centred on Damien Frobisher as the upholder of a family tradition of homicidal lunacy.

No bullets were discovered, nor any damage to the corpses that could not be explained by the fire. The 'remains' presumed to be of Julie Frobisher and Nick Townsend were too inciner-ated to offer anything reliable to forensic examination. Under post-mortem the corpses of Steve Liston, Selina Johnson and Damien Frobisher all revealed quite heavy traces of nitrazepam – a sedative in the benzodiazepine group. It later transpired that Julie Frobisher, an insomniac, had recently been prescribed Mogadon. Since it was assumed that Nick and Julie had taken the drug in the same quantities as the other three, the presence of nitrazepam explained why none of the victims had been awakened by the fire before it trapped them. What still needed explanation was how the fire began – and how the population of Sparrow Hall came to take, simultaneously, such strong doses of a sedative.

This produced a flurry of refocused theorising, the daftest example being an article in the *Sketch* under the title *DEATH PACT AT HALL?*. According to this hypothesis the five residents, having agreed to suicide, submitted to the sedative after piling furniture in the dining hall and soaking the logs in the cellar below with petrol. One of them, before the drug took full effect, lit the pyre. This theory was supported (in the absence of direct evidence and in the face of plausibility) by

selected quotes from Thornham villagers: Elaine Dobson –
'They were a rum lot. Nothing would surprise me'; Elizabeth
Cope – 'The ambience was ugly, Godless, with an imponder-
able sense of sin and pain'; Ken Filbert – 'From what I hear
they were up to drugs, free love and all that carry-on but they
never looked like they were having a right lot of fun'; Arthur
Lumb – 'It's sad what happened but they were a lot of weirdos
and the village is well rid of them.'

Chris and Catherine Hunter, Naomi Liston, Beryl Ingram
and Susan Drummond were all called as witnesses at the
inquest – as was the local GP, Alistair Black. The doctor
testified to Julie's prescription, 'a standard sedative unlikely to
have spectacular consequences', but otherwise knew nothing
remarkable about the mental or physical state of the residents.
The testimonies of the Hunters, Naomi and Susan were likewise bland, but Beryl gave her opinion that at the Hall there
was a 'funny atmosphere' and 'a lot of drinking and stuff'.
She would say little more when pressed for details, but a
few weeks later (after the coroner had declared an 'open
verdict') she was persuaded in an 'exclusive' in the *Sketch*
to be much more categorical: broken syringes, bloodstained
rags, a 'weird, choking smell' in the library and 'books full of
gibberish'. She also gave an opinion of each of the victims. She
said of Julie, 'She gave herself airs, like an actress in a play, but
I was never fooled by it. Men and drugs were her trouble – she
couldn't say no to neither'; of Damien, 'Always the gentleman,
but he was not "all there". He looked right through you';
of Steve Liston, 'You could see he fancied himself. Men are
all the same'; of Selina, 'I never liked her, she seemed vain
and sly'; of Nick, 'I never saw him sober. His room were a
midden.'

After the inquest verdict the police gave up their investigations: it was decided that the chance of any criminal
being at large was negligible, so the mystery did not justify

further police time. The media lost interest soon afterwards – surprisingly quickly, in view of the morbid human-interest ingredients of the events. The Frobisher estate became a matter of uncivil dispute between Damien's first family, represented by Dora Goldman, and his second, represented by Susan Drummond. Once it became clear that a number of factors, including death duties, had severely diminished the prize, the parties avoided further legal bills by reaching a grudging agreement that left everybody feeling swindled.

In early 1991 Pamela Linklater of Baluth Productions, a freelance TV production company, decided that there was a lot more human-interest mileage in the events at Sparrow Hall. Her documentary, *The Sparrow Hall Massacre*, sold to Umbria TV and broadcast in September of that year, was successful enough to be bought by other channels – and a book with the same title was published (Glebe Press, 1992) based largely on material gathered for the programme.

Linklater used interviews with expert witnesses (police, fire, drugs, a psychiatrist) and various villagers including Beryl Ingram, Janet Otterburn and, more exotically, Max Tomkins from Bilberton. Members of the poetry circle, the painting group and the Local History Society were also recruited. Ex-residents who were located and agreed to co-operate were Tommy Johnson, Corinne Cotterell, the Hunters, the Pococks and the Stotts. Ben's consent, given the contempt he had often expressed for the media, or for any sort of audience, was another mystery to add to the Sparrow Hall dossier: his motives presumably included the coltish allure of Pamela Linklater and his recent discovery that he had cancer. A number of people, including Tim Hatchard, Naomi Liston, Susan Drummond and Dora Goldman, would not co-operate with Linklater.

The Sparrow Hall Massacre followed the formula of many

such documentaries. Homicidal and suicidal blues songs by
Big Bill Broonzy, Furry Lewis and Howling Wolf accompanied
the opening and closing credits and were periodically played
behind the actual programme ('. . . if my baby won't behave . . .
put her in her grave . . .'). Damien's obsession with the blues
was referred to a couple of times, but his own favourites were
not deemed acoustically suitable. Most of the information
was provided by talking heads. The interviewees were each
set in a defining environment and introduced on their first
appearance with a subtitle like those little labels that people
wear at conventions: *Elaine Dobson – landlady; Ben Stott –
poet.* Their testimonies were heavily cut and spliced so that
most of them appeared a number of times uttering a brief
soundbite, a telling sentence shorn of its original context.
These fragments were usually arranged so that several would
appear in rapid succession to support a point that Linklater
had just made. She was the principal informant: occasionally
a voice-over, but more usually confronting the camera, her
chin tilted pertly and her cool gaze challenging, in a variety
of locations and poses – at the wheel of a Land Rover, on
a seesaw in a beer-garden, perched on the balustrade in front
of the shuttered, sullen Hall – and in a distracting succession
of costumes ranging from combat camouflage to a very short
skirt and striped leg-warmers. She had the air of a karate bimbo
cop from a TV series full of pistol shots and somersaulting
vehicles. Variety was provided by newsreel footage of the
1982 and 1990 slaughters, sequences of still photographs,
film of Thornham and environs, the Hall and gardens, and
a number of long, creepy tracking-shots through the forlorn
and shrouded interior of the Hall as it was in 1991.

The programme began as if it was investigative – a number
of Aunt Sallys were set up to be triumphantly demolished.
Linklater dealt briskly with some of these (burglars, local
lunatics . . .). She rejected the 'death pact' theory with the

astute observation that the people involved were clearly not co-members of any sort of sect and had no common reason to kill themselves. She went on to conjecture that the sedatives might have been mistaken for stimulants in the course of some orgiastic devilry that gave rise to the conflagration, the suicide verdict being thus replaced by one of accidental death. Her main objections to this were the ferocity of the fire, the potency of the drug and the timing of the disaster when the Hall was relatively empty – particularly when all the children were absent. These, she claimed, if they were not freak coincidences, showed deliberate purpose – and a psychopathic impulse that was paradoxically subject to compunction and prepared to await an opportunity to target and limit its consequences.

Having settled firmly for the probability of foul play, Linklater proposed her own scenario for the evening. On Saturday night, those residents present ate together in the dining room. The wine was heavily spiked by Damien Frobisher – himself, at this time, a teetotaller. When the other four had yawned and stumbled their way to bed, Steve with Selina and Nick with Julie, Damien then prepared the petrol-soaked bonfire in the dining hall and the cellar below, sedating himself a couple of minutes before he struck the match.

Damien, as perceived by Linklater and her witnesses, was the obvious suspect. His own sexual activities had been presumably curtailed by malfunction and his wife was blatantly sleeping with a younger man. He was 'weird', 'withdrawn', 'brooding', 'getting worse all the while'. He was reported as 'wandering about waving his arms and shouting at nobody'. His performance at the bonfire party was shakily but vividly related by George Ingram. 'He were fair capped. Off his chump.' The scenario assumed Damien's deliberate emulation of his father's crime and that the latent murderous lunacy inherited from his father was always bubbling under the mild

façade. Julie was presented as the demanding and betraying
femme fatale who tortured him to madness.

Striking features in the programme were the testimonies of
Celia Burridge, Max Tomkins and Corinne Cotterell. Celia's
remarks were uninteresting – apart from the art classes, she
knew little about the Hall and its residents – but her spectacular appearance, in a room full of ghastly self-portraits and
pub mirrors, exuded such eccentric gravitas that the people
she was talking about seemed weird by association. This
syndrome was even more evident in the case of Max Tomkins,
a cave-eyed junkie living in utter squalor, whose incoherence
seemed eloquent testimony to the Hall being a drugs hell that
cast its evil shadow on the whole neighbourhood. Corinne
was in punk mode: corpse-grey with a purple quiff and black
lips. Thrusting her plump face aggressively into the camera
she spoke with explicit gusto of drug sessions, satanic rituals,
orgies, perversions . . . her utterances interrupted by bleeps as
her more uncompromising demotics were censored.

If other matters had not been occupying his attention by
then, Ben Stott would have been disappointed by his performance on television. He featured only twice, cramped into
a corner of a bar, like a saint in a niche, with his props
of draught Guinness and Gauloises. On his first appearance
Pamela Linklater, in a tight pink kimono, had a swig at her
pint of draught Guinness and said, 'Ben, you knew Damien
longer than anybody – you were with him at Oxford. What
do you reckon?' *Ben Stott – poet* took a thoughtful puff of
his fag and said, 'Damien was fundamentally inarticulate
– blatantly so in his social traffic and also, ultimately, in
his literary efforts. Inarticulate people often feel compelled
to violence.' His second appearance, in the same pose at
the same venue, permitted him an even briefer statement,
presumably in answer to another question. It is not certain
whether he had drunk more or less than when he made his

first speech but he seemed strangely altered – shrunk into h[...] niche of spleen and his features pulled onto his bones as if by a claw within.

'Julie was an ageing cocotte. Beneath her pretensions she was disappointingly trite.'

He was dead before Linklater's book appeared – extracts being serialised in a national newspaper prior to publication. In emotive prose that seemed curiously incongruous to the trendy cool of Linklater the book embellished the argument of the TV programme and largely relied on material gathered for the broadcast.

Damien's biography was expanded and the pattern leading to his lethal act delineated in detail. There was a history of insanity on both sides of his family and his childhood was 'famished and lacerated by a vicious triangle of unloving parents'. His distancing himself from the Hall – civil-service career, Dora, Paulette – were features of his escape from his background into 'normal, stable, bitter-sweet contentment'. Two events ended this process and wrecked his life: the advent of Julie and the death of his parents. After 1982 he was trapped in the Hall ('where tragedy had transformed his childhood demons into monsters') by his compulsion for Julie, who had made it clear that the Hall, which embodied her own projects for personal fulfilment, was what kept her with Damien. She imposed intolerable terms on their relationship, 'flaunting her infidelity like a whore's creed' and filling the Hall with people and practices that offended his 'moral dignity' as well as his increasingly obsessive need for privacy of thought and person. He resisted the 'fatal pressures' by immersing himself in literary activities, and with the company and support of his best friend, Ben Stott, who had moved to the Hall at Damien's request – but Stott left the Hall early in 1989 for family reasons, by which time Damien 'was already starkly contemplating, in the lurid mirror of madness, his own abject failure both at literature and love'. His mental condition then deteriorated rapidly. Linklater concludes:

At some point, when he was brooding on incurable grief, his brain slipped over the rim of the abyss into insanity and he hatched the plot, inspired by his father's example. After that it was a question of waiting for an opportunity when the innocent would not be hurt. The fact that he *did* include Selina Johnson and Steve Liston leads me to suppose that he had noticed their liaison and detested it, aligning it with Julie's conduct, which had goaded him to lunacy. But it is probably wrong to try to apply logical analysis to the workings of a mind that was giving birth to nightmare.

The Sparrow Hall Mystery (Nathan Nicholson, Olmec Press, 2001) mostly consisted of a regurgitation of known facts enhanced by fresh contention, using material from earlier items as well as interviews with Sonia Stott, Naomi Liston, the Hunters and Pococks, Tim Hatchard, Tommy Johnson and a host of local residents and relatives of the dead. Corinne Cotterell was by this time a member of the Church of Kether, for whom the past does not exist, and Nicholson had searched in vain for Max Tomkins.

Providing a ground plan of each storey of the Hall, Nicholson gave a history of the Hall before the first 'massacre' and a detailed account of the community in the eighties. He then reviewed and evaluated all previously proposed solutions to the mystery of the second 'massacre' and offered a couple of his own. After accepting Pamela Linklater's verdicts on the invalidity of several solutions (the death pact, the accident, the outside killer), Nicholson argued that her main thesis, although neat, was built on a lazily trite interpretation of Damien Frobisher's character:

The testimonies in Linklater are both dishonestly selective and evidently wise after the event. Most witnesses describe Frobisher in 1989 and 1990 as civil, urbane and relaxed. This is quite unlike any account of his father. Frobisher had a lifelong history of non-violence and non-assertiveness – being passively led by others in his lifestyle and opinions. He had given up sex with Julie – not out of physical disability but out of apathy of the libido – long before she had resource to Townsend. His reaction to Julie's earlier betrayals, and to all problems and pressures, was a simple and adequate refuge in mental abstraction. It is implausible that this bland retreat could mask an impulse that was to drug an entire dinner party and instigate an inferno.

In short, Nicholson asserted that Damien was quite simply the wrong sort of person to either envisage or carry out such a plan:

If it were not for his father – a clinical case of severe withdrawal – nobody would have suggested it. And even if Frobisher had been capable of the deed his father's example would not have led him to the 1990 Sparrow Hall shambles. Like Quentin he would have used a gun to target his victims selectively, including himself.

Nicholson went on to raise technical objections to Damien's guilt:

He knew nothing about drugs. How did he know about the effects of Julie's prescription, or what dose to give? How did he introduce the Mogadon tablets into the wine? His whole plan – and the whole of Linklater's thesis – depends on his being able to do so confidently. The notion of him pounding them up and introducing them to the 'breathing' bottle (or bottles) undetected must have seemed implausible even to a maniac.

Comparing Damien Frobisher and Nick Townsend, Nicholson suggested that the latter was in greater mental disrepair and the more likely perpetrator of the crime:

All witnesses agree that Townsend's conduct revealed a nadir of the spirit that was the culmination of over a decade of worsening alcoholism.

He went on to reflect that Townsend, since he was sharing Julie's bedroom, had easy access to her medicines, and that the vehicle for the drug might have been soup or coffee rather than wine. But this was mere teasing conjecture. Nicholson shot down the kite he was flying with a volley of counter-argument:

Unhappiness is not psychosis. Those who knew Townsend are unanimous that he was not violent. Even if his unhappiness was suicidal there is no discernible motive for the inclusion of the other four people in his *auto da fé*. His emotions were still trapped by his broken marriage in Teesside. His attitude to those in the Hall – including his concubine – seems to have been cursory and superficial.

At this point Nicholson assumed a sleuth-like pose of systematic rigour. By contemplating the features of the crime without preconceptions one could go beyond Linklater's dismissive diagnosis of lunacy and arrive at a more meaningful profile: the criminal (i) was possessed by a callous egotism that regarded other human beings as disposable, (ii) suffered from a 'cogent psychosis' that could translate into organised and decisive action, (iii) had a 'power compulsion', seeking to manipulate the destiny of self and others at whatever cost, (iv) had 'an arsonist's craving for the spectacular and nihilistic'.

Nicholson concluded that of the possible suspects only Julie Frobisher at all resembled the profile – but that in her case there was a significant correlation. He cited Dr Charles Epstein, 'an eminent psychiatrist', who 'on the available evidence' diagnosed Julie as a 'self-sublimating bi-polar depressive' and a potential threat to herself and others. He also claimed that many who knew Julie, once the theory was put to them, were quick to accept the feasibility of her guilt. He quoted Catherine Hunter: 'Julie rather than Damien? That makes much more sense to me!'; Delia Pocock: 'She was a drama queen looking for a disaster'; Terry Hatchard: 'If she got worse as she got older I can believe anything of her'; and Tommy Johnson: 'She was a screwball, man! Scary green eyes.'

Naomi Liston, while not critical of Julie, actually supported the theory with a couple of pieces of evidence, albeit insubstantial ones: 'When I was salvaging property of ours from the Hall I found two poetry notebooks, Damien's and Julie's, tucked one on top of the other next to the Amstrad in the library. Hers were recent rough drafts but his were fair copies from years ago, handwritten and dated – he never used the computer. I've wondered since if the books were put there, out of likely range, by somebody who had a pretty clear presentiment of the fire. That would have to be Julie, wouldn't it? Another detail that nags me is the survival of Julie's geriatric cats, Binky and Braithwaite, who always slept in the Frobisher suite at night. It's hard to accept their escape if they were shut as usual in the rooms that were entirely destroyed. It's more likely that the moggies were put out for the night by somebody in the know. Julie loved cats, whereas Damien never even saw them.'

Julie's motives for the crime were as emphatically presented by Nicholson as Damien's had been by Linklater. She had a history of emotional disasters including her marriage to Damien. All her Sparrow Hall schemes had likewise failed – both her dream of a socialist community and the cultural projects that had tried to take its place. Her failure as a parent had eventually borne fruit in the alienation of both her children and the loss of access to her beloved grand-children. She was increasingly dependent on alcohol and other substances and had become locally a figure of ridicule and opprobrium, a pariah with a crazy husband and a drunken lover.

Her mangled psyche insisted that she did not merely kill herself but made a gesture – a spectacular exit. It seems likely that in her psychotic gloom she became obsessed by the 1982 event. It is also feasible that she perceived her husband and lover as being at least as unhappy as she was. Her inclusion of them in her fate was probably an act of crazed compassion as much as of spleen.

Nicholson proceeded to outline his scenario for the fatal evening:

Julie Frobisher's guilt resolves the problem of the victims being heavily drugged without their knowledge. A much more likely scenario is that she openly issued the tablets to the others – lying about their purpose and effect. She had a long but unspectacular history of drug usage. Since moving into Sparrow Hall she had supplied herself from some contact in either York or Malton about whom she was unusually discreet. She also took sleeping tablets and anti-depressants, which she obtained on prescription. From 1986 to 1988 she sometimes circulated cannabis joints on Thursday poetry evenings. In 1989 the poetry group was opened to non-residents and she judged it more discreet to offer her treats to residents on Saturday evenings after dinner.

It would have been simple for Julie Frobisher to persuade the others to take her tablets. Her husband always fell in with her wishes so long as she focused on him. Townsend was attracted by all intoxicants. Liston was weighing up Johnson and wanting to misbehave – like a boy out of school – in his wife's absence. He was maybe glad of a bit of Dutch courage. And Johnson was truanting from work – disembarrassed of her daughter – remembering what it was to be a young woman looking for fun.

Nicholson now looked in some detail at the subplot of Steve Liston and Selina Johnson, a fruitful human-interest conundrum that Linklater had unaccountably neglected. His account suffered from the reticence of Naomi Liston, but he had no trouble finding other witnesses to the leer of Steve and the flaunt of Selina. He concluded:

It seems implausible that the pair would conduct an assignation at the Hall under the eyes of other occupants. But we should not overlook the possibility of a flirtation impulsively consummated under the influence of narcotics. The presence of Liston and Johnson was an unpleasant surprise for Julie Frobisher. Johnson had cried off work with a migraine. Normally she would have been at the Apple Tree (a late-night drinking spot on Saturdays) on overtime rates until long after midnight – Merline sleeping with the Liston children. Steve Liston should have gone with Naomi and the children to Basingstoke – he only changed his mind about going, according to Naomi's inquest testimony, at the very last minute. Thus Julie Frobisher had expected to be alone in the Hall until the small hours with the husband and lover she was resolved to include in her fate. She decided to go ahead – assuming that a liaison between Liston and Johnson would take them to Johnson's apartment at a relatively safe distance from the fire. Once she was embarked it was headlong impulse rather than reason that guided her.

Nicholson's final suggestion was that, in the light of forensic advances over the last few years, exhumation and further examination of the Sparrow Hall remains might be in order. He then concluded with a paragraph of gloomy rhetoric:

I make no apology for revisiting the perplexities of Sparrow Hall. I have not done so because I am attracted by the morbid and sensational. Nor do I think it important that justice is done to one ghost at the expense of another. But I am fascinated by the symbolic nature of the events. With its corrupt and privileged history, its tangle of conflicting purposes and destinies, its defining acts of barbaric despair, Sparrow Hall seems to me to be both a microcosm of the twentieth century and a dark monument to all human endeavour.

The text of *The Sparrow Hall Mystery* was brief (133 pages) for £12.99, but this was partly compensated by the choice array of photographs. The Hall was seen in the sepia twenties as the background to croquet players in plus-fours and top hats; in 1982 as the weed-caressed, mellow scene of the shambles; in 1990 as a black shell. Similarly, Damien's career was abruptly pictured: a harmless, flannelled lad with a cricket ball in his paw; a bridegroom clamped into morning dress, squiring his shyly laughing bride; a mole and hippopotamus, portly and spectacled, accosting the Christmas turkey with a brandished carver and beatific flush.

The pictures of Julie seemed more tendentious. A pale child in white avoided eye-contact on a park bench in a suburb where it was surely going to rain. A slim brown girl in bikini and sunglasses lay supine on a towel next to a heavily pelted thug whose bulging trunks ogled the camera. A passport photo of a drunken psychopath (1982, cropped hair and facetious ear-rings) was also entered as evidence, unfairly. Everybody has had at least one passport photo like that.

The Liston suite was gutted but there were Steve's pots, a couple of shelves of books in the library and items of furniture and other belongings stored in a third-floor room that had escaped the blaze. Naomi's father set off in the van with the bulk of it: he would wait for her in Pickering where they would have lunch. She had to lock the kitchen door, then the back gate, then return both keys to Janet Otterburn, who – to the disgust of Beryl Ingram – had been appointed concierge.

Naomi had wanted a couple of minutes alone in the Hall. A month after the disaster she still had the impression of being torn awake into a world whose laws were strange and terrible. She hoped that here at the scene she might feel or remember something to suggest how to come to terms with what had been done to her. Now she was not sure that it had been a good idea. The building was oppressive in its stricken, blackened state, bandaged with nailed planks and stanched with acres of dirty polythene. It was a stark fact, inscrutable to logic or philosophy. There was only despair here, or a perverse refusal to despair.

She was not allowed either to succumb to heartbreak or brace her thoughts into defiance: her attention was commandeered by Binky and Braithwaite – the ginger mog and black kitten who had greeted Damien Frobisher in Brosely twelve years earlier. Binky was now over twenty, threadbare and arthritic. Braithwaite had been neutered late in life when Julie decided he was taking too much punishment from rivals: he was fat, lame, and deaf in one tattered ear. Neither of them was equipped to go feral and they were hanging around the Hall in a hapless state. Janet had fed them a couple of times but was of farming stock that held that cats should pay their way by controlling mice or perish. Beryl Ingram did not like cats at all and Naomi could think of nobody else to ask. She herself was indifferent to cats and her parents even more so. She also knew that it made cats unhappy to be shifted to strange territory. But there was no help for it.

She searched through the draped and sullen rooms of the

undamaged part of the house. In the scullery she located some cat biscuits and in the cellar found two wooden wine-boxes, knocking out their plywood partitions and lining them with towels out of an airing-cupboard. When she had fed the cats she put them into the boxes, securing the hinged lids by passing sisal through convenient holes. There were also finger-holes in the sides of the boxes for the cats to breathe and peer out. Braithwaite yowled and tickled her fingers with his nose as she carried him out to the car, but Binky lay phlegmatic.

As she was positioning the second box on the back seat a husky voice close behind her said, 'Is there something costly in the boxes?'

Startled, Naomi leaped round banging her head on the door frame, and discovered a teenage girl behind her. She was tall and slim, clad in a faded denim suit and a black T-shirt with white lettering. Her lank peroxide hair, through which her ears peeped, showed dark roots along the crown of her head. She revealed a startling number of perfect yellow teeth as she laughed.

'Made you jump, did I? What's in the boxes?' Her accent sounded vaguely Irish.

'Cats.'

'I'm not fond of cats. I like dogs.' She extended her right arm in a formal and elegant gesture such as a conjuror's assistant might employ at the end of a trick. This led Naomi's eyes to two huge hounds that were snuffling and pissing round the garages: a shaggy grey wolfhound and something that looked like a cross between a Great Dane and a Rottweiler.

'Big dogs,' Naomi said feebly.

The girl laughed again. 'All sorts of dogs. You haven't a fag, have you?'

This last was said without a lot of hope. Naomi didn't answer. Her horrified gaze was now aimed at the gate where a pit bull terrier and a little sheep-dog with its tail between its legs were making their entry. They were accompanied by a man who looked at first sight like the girl's twin, with peroxide hair only slightly shorter than hers and a frayed and faded denim suit.

'That's Loz,' the girl said. 'Is the whole place shut up?'

'It is. There was an accident.'

'I know there was. I seen it on the telly.'

Loz came up and said, in a growl that was a bass version of the girl's voice, 'I'm looking for scrap.' As he spoke his eyes flickered over the house and outhouses, the boarded doors and windows. He was dark-complexioned and Naomi could see now that he was considerably older than the girl.

Naomi said, 'I'm afraid I can't help you. I'm just leaving.'

The girl said, 'I used to live here once when I was a kid. The dog I had lived yonder down the garden.'

Naomi said, 'You must be Theresa Spillsbury.'

'Tessa White. I was never no Spillsbury. I don't remember you.'

'I wasn't here then. Julie – Mrs Frobisher told me about you.'

Tessa looked towards the house and narrowed her pale, blue-lidded eyes. 'They were all fucking snobs but her. She was worth the lot of them. She was good to me, got my teeth fixed, taught me to draw and make pots and all sorts. I cried when I heard she was dead.'

Loz said, 'Can I have a look round for scrap?'

Naomi closed the back door of her car at last and opened the driver's door. 'No, it isn't possible. I'm going to lock the gate. You'll have to leave.'

She was intimidated by them – their dogs and their gruff voices, their wild poise that reminded her of prairie savages. She was in an alien world, afraid of its denizens. Then she felt guilty about the stance she had taken and tried to think of something sympathetic to say to the girl. But Tessa had turned on her heel and was heading for the gate, walking straight-backed and square-shouldered with the even, silent stride that had enabled her to creep up on Naomi. All four dogs at once left off their investigations and went after her, crowding and fawning round her like the leopards of a warrior queen.

Before this defection Loz had intended to wheedle or bully a bit of scrap as the price of their departure. He gazed after Tessa querulously, then turned to Naomi with a rueful grin. 'You haven't a fag, have you?'

Epilogue

Tim slammed the book shut and lobbed it disgustedly onto the bedside table. Then he sat bolt upright, staring into the distance, his crew-cut bristling with wrath. Paulette paused from brushing her hair to look at him through the dressing-table mirror and laugh. 'You look like a broody chicken.'

'Susan was right for once. I should never have given an interview to that shit.'

Susan had posted them the book, which had arrived just before they set off for England. Paulette had examined it in the aeroplane and up the A1 in the hired Mégane. Last night they had just had time and energy enough for dinner – and cajoling Joey to sleep – but this morning she had pointed out the bits she thought Tim ought to read. He had set to it reluctantly, although claiming that nothing he read would bother him now.

Paulette said, 'Even as journalism it's crap. It'd never have passed at *Platypus* when I was there.'

'The cats got away! Big fucking deal! Really suspicious and significant! Have you seen a cat shift when it's terrified?'

Paulette set to brushing her hair again with slow, thorough strokes as one might brush a horse's mane or tail. Her hair was her major vanity. It was soft and brown like Dora's but Paulette wore it long, so that it fell from a centre parting to cascade onto her shoulders.

'I guess quite a few folk have been misquoted, or quoted out of line.' She turned her head to look over her shoulder towards the small bedroom that used to be Clive Hunter's room and called out, 'Joey, honey, time to rise and shine!'

'The idea of my mum as a mass murderer . . .'

'At least he clears my dad! And at least you don't come from a line of psychos, the way it looked like I did. That kind of stuff can sap confidence.'

'The lies about the drug have enough truth in them to be vicious. Julie was always dishing out stuff to people. It wouldn't be the doctor's prescription – she'd get it from Gavin Meadows in Malton, my godfather and a real head-banger. Where he got it God knows, and he wouldn't know himself what it was supposed to be. Julie was the sort of risk-taker who might pass it round – for the hell of it – with a swig of Armagnac or something after dinner. That doesn't mean she was trying to knock everybody out and have a bonfire.'

Paulette put down her brush and leaned her chin on her hand. They had talked quite a lot in the past about the calamity, but *The Sparrow Hall Mystery* was making them both revisit their ideas.

'He doesn't even respect his own hypotheses,' she said. 'His profile of Julie makes her incapable of the crime he's dreamed up. "Callous egotism" does not lead to suicide. And if she'd been the kind of head-case he figures – taking spectacular revenge on herself and everything and everybody – she wouldn't have let her tracks get covered so that my poor old dad, who had form as a psycho, was framed. She'd have made sure everybody knew her mind, like she always did . . . like those long, creepy letters you used to get . . . At least she'd have taken the trouble to scribble a note. They reckon she took time out to save the cats – and even the poetry notebooks. Then Nicholson has the nerve to say that "headlong impulse rather than reason guided her" – just the kind of cop-out he beefs about in Linklater.'

Tim managed a smile. 'That's good, pet. You should have

been a lawyer or a private eye.' Then his face became solemn again and he said, 'Mum wasn't a quitter. She was used to picking herself up and going on.'

Paulette said, 'Anybody who wasn't trying to make a buck out of hype and drama would come to the snappy, bleak conclusion that the fire was an accident caused by some gismo that didn't get deactivated when everybody was stoned. People weren't in their usual rooms because they'd dropped off in the dining hall or the Frobisher apartment . . .'

She watched Tim fondly through the mirror as he heaved himself out of bed, long and bony with hairy legs and a pelt on his belly. He got into his shorts, jeans and T-shirt without going for a shower or even washing. He was a slob, as he claimed befitted a sculptor. Whereas Paulette had showered and anointed herself before sitting in her fleecy jogging suit the colour of campanulas to brush her hair. She was a media consultant and affected professional chic. But while she had inherited her mother's looks she hoped she didn't have Dora's need to impose her code on passing planets. She thought of herself as more like her father, complaisant and adaptable to a fault. She loved Tim the way he was. On the other hand, there was no harm in trying to smooth a couple of his superficial edges, if it could be done tactfully. She'd maybe ask him to shower after breakfast, when it would seem less nagging and incongruous.

She said, 'Those jerks Linklater and Nicholson are not just trading in hype and drama, though. They're giving folk what they want to believe. We want things neat, we like to see the pattern – as if we were meaningful, part of a purpose.'

She had to admit that this whole trip was down to her benign control. It would never have occurred to him to come visiting roots and relatives. Their wedding had been attended from Tim's side by only half a dozen male buddies, one of whom, Byron, had been a best man whose effeminate mannerisms had amused and disgusted some of Paulette's coarser uncles. And over the years it bothered her that Tim had lost all his relatives apart from a sister he disliked and a father he disowned – she couldn't believe that he was really content, as he claimed, in this orphan state. She remembered how as a lonely, only English child she had loved her holidays among her multitude of American cousins – and how delighted she had been at ten years of age when Dora had taken her permanently to Milwaukee.

She said, 'That's why everybody hates accidents. Whenever there's a disaster we listen eagerly to the shitheads who're looking for somebody to finger. They need to prove human error rather than admit there's a bleep in the system – or no system at all. It's for social control, because citizens won't toe the line unless they feel responsible and liable. But it also goes along with all the rest of the whopping lies – God, free will, the soul – that we need to shield us from the seriously bad news that nobody's to blame, nobody's at the wheel.'

Tim, looking out of the window, nodded slowly as if at awesome profundities. She grimaced at her own pretentiousness, then turned and called loudly towards the bedroom, 'Joey, did you hear?'

She rose and walked over to join Tim at the window, just as Julie had joined Damien in the sitting room about twenty years earlier. The view was actually better from this apartment than from the ground floor. The terrace, with its ancient balustrade more or less invisibly restored, was thronged with wrought-iron chairs and tables, and red and white Stella Artois sunshades, which blocked the view of the rest of the garden from the french windows of the lounge bar. Whereas from the first floor one could look over and beyond, at the fish pond (full of massive carp) with its abstract sculpture spouting a slim column that spattered back onto the surface of the water. Beyond that gleamed the painted metals of the kiddies' play area. Further still there were the dulcet greens and garish plastics of the crazy-golf course.

'I lived here for five years but never really felt part of it,' Tim said. 'I feel more entitled to be here now I'm paying for the privilege.'

He had gone along cheerfully enough with this trip to England – the first for over ten years, since his mother's funeral – but he had had definite ideas about the agenda. He wanted to go to Bristol to see the charismatic Professor Kenyon, with whom he was in touch via email. He wanted to find Jeremy Wilkinson, who had been his father for eight years, and beat him at last at chess. He was prepared to drop in on his real father, to satisfy Paulette's curiosity, and to look up various Frobisher relatives of Paulette's. He was even prepared to spend a few hours with his sister – to Dora's disgust Paulette had renewed contact with Susan, who seemed oddly meek now that she had no mother to abjure and two appalling teenagers. All the same, Tim would on no account stay with the Drummonds. He had proposed the Blakey Lion, but when he searched the Internet he came upon Thornham Hall Hotel – and they couldn't resist revising their itinerary to make a three-night booking.

'I feel part of it,' she said. 'Or I can kid myself I do.'

The door of Clive Hunter's bedroom swung open and Joey came out, in whom the blood of Damien and Julie was conjoined. He was six, thin, dark-haired and clad in blue and white pyjamas. He came slowly, his head bowed over a Game Boy, which was emitting discreet, twittery music, until he was brought to a halt by bumping against the edge of the bed. Then he toppled slowly forward and keeled onto his side on the bed without ever taking his hands or eyes from the machine.

Paulette paused in order to give Tim a chance to deal with Joey, as she sometimes did, without a lot of success. Tim was quite unlike his sister in that he was entirely accepting of the child's vagaries and indifferent to manners and presentation.

Paulette said, 'Joey, go get washed.'

Joey said, 'Daddy, I've transposed the psychodragon and I reckon the moonswallower's gonna evolve. It will be the first time ever.'

Tim said, 'Wow. Isn't that something?'

Paulette said, less gently, 'You, Joey, take that gadget back into your bedroom.'

After a pause long enough to balance on the brink of insubordination Joey slowly rolled onto his back, raised his legs and bent his knees, then slid perilously off the bed into a standing position, all the while keeping his concentration fixed on the little screen. He exited exactly as he had entered kicking the bedroom door shut behind him.

Tim laughed. 'Little pillock.'

Paulette turned back to the window. She would go into the small bedroom in a minute and sort out Joey – ease him off his Game Boy, threaten to confiscate it if he cut up rough – and get him washed and dressed. But just for now she wanted to carry on looking at the garden: they had arrived late last night, in the dark, and it had been invisible. The pleasure it was giving her to see it again seemed a bit indecent – here where her grandfather slew three people, including himself, and where her father was suspected of having gone two better. But it was hard for her to have any quarrel with Sparrow Hall. She was picturing it as it had been eleven years earlier when it had brought herself and Tim together, a technically incestuous Romeo and Juliet, to the horror of their legally embattled relatives.

For the obsequies and legal business her mother had shipped over not only Paulette ('the true heiress') but Dora's second husband, Harvey, a company solicitor who floundered a bit among English inheritance proceedings.

The Drummonds' farm was the site of an awful reception

after the interments. The Frobisher clan – now diminished to fat Hilary, her deaf husband and cackling mother – were being wooed by the two incompatible factions headed by Susan and Dora. Lawyers in the wings were preparing to launch a complex of bequests and codicils. Then Tim Hatchard proposed to his stepsister, Paulette Goldman, that they borrow one of the Drummond Land Rovers and go to have a look at Sparrow Hall.

She had expressed curiosity without seriously considering what she was saying. Twenty-three-year-old Tim and twenty-two-year-old Paulette had held several self-conscious, trifling, insincere conversations. When they had not been close enough to speak they had watched each other covertly, competing as to who could avert their eyes more rapidly if their gazes happened to meet.

The damaged side of the Hall had been swathed in plastic and tarpaulin. It wasn't possible to get into the building because all the doors and windows – even of the outbuildings – had been boarded up to keep out squatters and other interlopers. The gates were chained shut but they went round via the back lane, between the barbed wire and through a gap in the yew hedge. The fountain pond was dry and filling with autumn leaves. The metal swings were still solid enough and Tim and Paulette sat in them, drifting slowly to and fro, passing and occasionally bumping gently against each other as they talked.

They swapped memories of Sparrow Hall. She remembered visiting the Hall at least a dozen times during her childhood – it had always been portentously presented to her by her mother as a treat and a privilege that must be earned by a special display of decorum. It had impressed her as an austere, echoing place with rugs that slid on floors of tiles or polished wood. There had been spooky but enticing cellars, cupboards and attics that she would have liked to explore if she had

J.B. ASPINALL

had a companion. She had not liked her uncle Desmond's
hard hands and smelly beard. Her grandmother had been a
constraining but unthreatening presence, offering the same
compliments (*My, how she's grown!*) and asking the same
rhetorical questions (*Do you work hard at school? Are you
a good girl for your mummy?*). She couldn't remember much
about her grandfather.

Tim's memories of his youth were a contrast to the heavy
history and aspect of the building. He and several other local
boys had solemnly made a giant snowman, which they had
then destroyed in a violent affray of snow and testosterone
while Michael throttled himself with his tether and bayed to
join in. His first substantial sexual experience had been on the
mossy veranda of the old summer house with the fabled Sarah
Atkinson, when he had borne her home on his motorbike,
chickened out of taking her into the Hall and led her down
the garden to look at the moon. In the tangled arbour he
had sniffed glue and gobbled mushrooms with blurred and
queasy pals.

Soon their mood sobered to suit the mourning in which
they were clad. They talked about the funeral and Paulette
said, 'They say my dad . . . Damien . . . everybody reckons he
did it. What do you think?'

Tim shrugged. 'Does it matter? How does it make it better
or worse?'

'It doesn't for those that died, I guess. But it's worse for
me if . . . Mom's been vindictive and I've been weak. I should
have gone against her and found my dad and claimed him and
saved him.'

'Saved him for what? Everybody dies in the end.'

'That's defeatist crap.'

He stopped swinging, putting his feet on the floor. 'Don't
blame yourself, is all I meant to say. There's no point.' He
stared down at his feet for a while, then lifted his head to

look her straight in the face. 'I didn't answer my mother's letters. They were long, embarrassing, weird . . . She pestered and begged me to reply but I wouldn't. I couldn't. I'd give plenty to change that. But it's easy to say so now and proves nothing.'

After a while Paulette said gently, 'Listen to us both. It's ourselves we're sore about, not the dead.'

'Fair enough, too.' Tim recovered his sturdy, cynical tone and smiled. 'Let's look after the bloody living. For a start, let's get ourselves to the Apple Tree.' He heaved himself upright by pulling on the chains of the swing. 'The locals will greet me like a long-lost son. *Now, Tim*, they'll say. They aren't gushing hereabouts. We'll have egg and chips, washed down with a couple of pints of Theakston's warm, weak bitter.'

'I've eaten plenty,' said Paulette. She was entertained by his lanky frame in the suit he had borrowed from some Drummond who was not quite his size. She was deliciously impressed by his fine eyes and tangle of brown curls.

'Susan's bloody baked meats and anchovies, too true! We'll just get pissed, then. The only thing is, it'll have to be your treat because I haven't any money.'

She laughed. 'Me neither. Not a cent.'

'That buggers *that* scheme, then.'

He held out his hand with a mannerly chauvinism that was obviously uncharacteristic – and she took the hand to help herself out of the swing, though it was actually easier to stand unaided. She reckoned his gallantry was a ruse to make contact, preliminary to a kiss. She was very happy to go along with that but disinclined to be provoking, though normally she was not very inhibited or discreet. They were both behaving unusually on a special occasion: standing sheepishly with their fingers interlocked like shy kids put together at a party. The formal, sombre clothes they were wearing conspired with the forsaken Hall and garden to justify their

quaint constraint, as if they were characters in a period play
– the coda of a melodrama or the opening sequence of a
romance.

J.B. ASPINALL

Gringo Soup

You couldn't tell which would be the wise-crackers, the grumblers, the claustrophobics, the cheer-leaders, the thugs, the pressure-cases, the wannabes, the enigmas. All you could be sure of was that they would be a bit worse than the last group. They always were . . .

As tour leader Lisa anticipates supervising the new arrivals on a trip round Mexico, she is finding it hard to summon up any degree of professional good will. But then her passengers aren't exactly ecstatic either – and not only with the performance of their 'rep'. As we discover in the course of witnessing each day from a different perspective, those on the trip are less than happy both with their travelling companions and, in most cases, with the cards life has dealt them.

In this darkly hilarious and utterly original debut, set against the vibrant backdrop of Mexico, John Aspinall explores with remarkable insight the complexity and pathos of human interaction. In doing so he poignantly reminds us that our perceptions of people are an unreliable guide to the frailties and idiosyncrasies concealed by their behaviour.

'A darkly funny look at package holiday hell that makes for perfect summer reading' *Mirror*

'Immensely vivacious . . . very, very funny indeed'
Pete Davies, *Open Book*, BBC Radio 4

'Deadpan delivery ensures that this novel really hits the mark . . . Entertaining, informative and occasionally laugh-out-loud funny, this is an ambitious, well-written novel that equates the disappointments of tourism with the crashing disarray of life itself.' *Marie Claire*

Darkly comic . . . a brisk,
entertaining tale.' *Daily Mail*

SCEPTRE